PAINTED MELODIES

LOST CREEK, TEXAS HILL COUNTRY
BOOK TWO

ALEXA ASTON

OLIVER-HEBER BOOKS

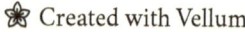 Created with Vellum

PROLOGUE

DALLAS—OCTOBER

Dax Tennyson left his office a little before six and drove home, hoping to find his wife there. Shailene was a realtor and worked odd hours, sometimes showing homes in the evening and oftentimes on weekends. Sometimes he felt they were becoming more like roommates who shared a few things in passing as one went in the door and the other went out it. He hoped tonight would be different.

Because he really was ready for them to have a baby.

They had been married six years, and he was eager to start a family now. Actually, Dax had been ready to have children from the moment they got married, but Shailene had said she wanted to become more established in her career. He had agreed to put it off and kept quiet for five years. Last year, he'd brought up the subject for the first time, and Shailene had seemed surprised. She had agreed, though, to go off her birth control pills and see what happened.

Nothing had. At least, not yet.

With both their careers in full swing, though, finding time to be together—much less be intimate—was getting in the way of accomplishing that goal. Dax hoped not only would his wife become pregnant soon but that it might spark a deeper closeness between them. He longed for the early years when they discussed their plans for the future.

He had given up a lot of his dreams when he married. Before he'd tied the knot, he'd had steady employment with his accounting job and played the market on the side, making quite a bundle. Weekends, he'd served as a DJ for weddings and other events, which generated a terrific income. He'd been dabbling in songwriting for years and had thought about chucking the day job in order to pursue a career in music— until Shailene came along. She was very conservative in her outlook, and the thought of her fiancé giving up his lucrative career in business to try and earn a living as a musician had horrified her. She'd threatened to break off their engagement if he pursued those dreams.

Instead, he'd put them on hold. At least, that's what he told himself. That someday, he would make enough money to break out of the eight-to-five rut and follow his heart back to music. Dax had put his DJ-ing equipment into storage and shelved his songwriting. He couldn't even remember the last time he'd picked up his guitar. He focused on work and had moved up the corporate ladder swiftly, now managing an accounting group of over thirty employees.

His instincts for the market had also paid off, and he was at a point where he could actually quit work if he wanted and pick up music again. Dax had even thought about being the stay-at-home dad to allow Shailene to keep working since she loved what she did so much. It would be a blessing to be able to remain home and raise their kids, writing music on the side, and hopefully performing some on weekends.

But first, they needed to get pregnant. Once that happened, he'd talk things over with Shailene and make new plans for their future, ones that included their growing family and his desire to follow his passion.

He arrived home, parking in the driveway of their Park Cities house, an exclusive area in the heart of Dallas and close to where he'd attended college at SMU. Dax had DJ'd many fraternity and sorority parties during his college years, as well as events throughout the Park Cities. They'd purchased this home three years ago, a pocket listing Shailene had, and he knew today, after the work he'd put into it, that they could sell it for double what they'd paid for it.

Selling their home was something he wanted to broach with his wife. While he liked the house, he wanted more room for their family, even if that meant leaving the Park Cities. His gut told him Shailene wouldn't go for that, though. She liked the fancy address, plus most of her showings were in this area, which made it easy for her to come home in-between clients.

Dax entered the house, calling, "I'm home," but he sensed it was empty. He'd wanted to get a dog, but Shailene was allergic to pet dander. Maybe he could look into dogs that were hypoallergenic. He'd always wanted a pet growing up, but his mom said they were too poor to have one. Since she worked three jobs and they still barely had food to put on the table, he'd known not to press the issue. But he wanted his kids to have a pet and bond with it.

Checking his phone, he saw he had no texts from his wife, which disappointed him. It was his birthday, and a part of him had wanted her to make a fuss over him because of it. Presents for birthdays or Christmas had been unheard of in his household, but now that he had money, he wanted to celebrate some, be it with a gift or an evening at a nice restaurant. He decided to text her and see if she wanted to meet him somewhere.

> Just got home. Can you meet me for dinner?

Dax waited, knowing if she were with a client that she wouldn't reply immediately. After a few minutes, he grabbed a beer from the fridge and went upstairs, getting out of his work clothes and throwing on a T-shirt and faded jeans. He returned to the den, flipping on the TV, holding his beer up to the screen.

"Happy birthday to me," he toasted, unhappiness rolling through him.

He was thirty-two and hoped he would've done more with his life by now. Yes, he made a terrific salary and had a beautiful wife and nice house, but he felt so empty inside. Maybe this would be the year of change for him. He would quit his job. They could buy a bigger house with some land. It was time to start writing music again. And hopefully, Shailene would finally become pregnant. After a year of trying with no results, he'd insisted they both get checked out two weeks ago. Their physicians gave them each a clean bill of health. Her OB/Gyn had even told Shailene not to stress about it. That the more they relaxed, the easier it would be to become pregnant.

Of course, they'd actually have to make love for that to happen.

Standing up, he went to take his empty can into the kitchen and make himself a sandwich since he hadn't heard back from his wife. He tripped over one of her shoes and stumbled, falling on his hands and knees. A fingernail caught against a wood plank and tore, and Dax cursed loudly. Pushing to his feet, he had sore knees, aching palms, and a bleeding finger. He rinsed the beer can in the kitchen and placed it in the recycling bin and headed up to their bathroom to doctor his finger.

Under the strong light, he saw how jagged the wound was. Dax washed it thoroughly with soap and needed an emery board to smooth out the nail since clippers wouldn't do the job. He knew Shailene had to have one, so he went to her side of the bathroom and opened a drawer, digging through lipsticks and other assorted makeup, not finding one. He opened a second drawer and struck out and moved to the third one.

"Bingo!" he said, finding the emery board and sanding down his nail, which hurt like hell.

As he started to place the emery board back in the drawer, he paused. His gut tightened as he dropped the nail file.

And picked up a familiar-looking, plastic package.

Surely, this was an old birth control pack, one Shailene hadn't bothered to throw away. Yet his senses were on high alert as he popped open the pack. Today was the twelfth.

The pill pack was missing twelve pills.

It felt as if a heavyweight boxer had slammed a fist into Dax's gut.

Why had Shailene lied?

Digging around the drawer, he found two more pill packs, both full. She'd always gotten them in groups of three from their mail order insurance company. Which meant she'd recently started this pill pack. All the while, she was bemoaning how they couldn't get pregnant. Everything that came out of her mouth was a lie.

Dax took all three packs with him, closing the drawer, not knowing if or when he was going to confront her. If the pills were missing and she went to take one tomorrow morning, that would clue her in that he had discovered her secret. Should he wait until then to say something? Or should he confront her and accuse her of holding out on him the moment she got home?

His finger was throbbing madly now, as was his head, where he knew a monster headache was building. He put a little antibiotic ointment on the nail and then wrapped a bandage around it, still not quite being able to come to grips with the situation.

Going back downstairs, he placed the three pill packs on the center of the kitchen table and sat, disbelief pouring through him. Then he heard the garage door going up and knew Shailene was home. He steeled himself for the fight that would play out in mere seconds.

She entered the kitchen, looking chic in her smart, designer suit and sky-high stilettos. She spent a small fortune on her wardrobe, telling Dax she had to dress as well as her clients in order to be successful and gain their trust.

"I got your text," Shailene said, setting down her tote on the kitchen counter, along with a large brown sack.. "I thought I'd just pick up something for dinner. It's Chinese."

She turned and started to say something else to him, their gazes meeting. He stared hard at her, anger building inside him.

"What's wrong with…" Her voice trailed off—because her eyes had caught sight of what sat on the table in front of him. Then anger sparked in her eyes. "You had no right going through my things," she spat out.

Dax crossed his arms. "You had no right to lie to me, Shailene. Yet you have. Over and over again. You said you wanted a baby as much as I did. We even had our doctors run a mess of tests, trying to see if either of us had something wrong with us. And all along, you're calmly ordering and taking a birth control pill each morning, preventing the very thing you know we want. Or should I, what *I* want? Because apparently, we are on a different page from one another. Maybe even a different book. I want a family. You obviously don't. And you were coward enough to take these behind my back."

"I'm not a coward," she said quickly, crossing her own arms defensively. "I just wasn't ready to be a mom." She huffed. "Frankly, I don't know if I ever want to be one, Dax."

He shot to his feet. "Why didn't you tell me? We could have talked about this."

"Because you wouldn't have listened to what I wanted," she snapped. "We always have to do whatever you want."

"What?" he said. "Are you kidding me? I'm the one who gave up DJ-ing for you. You told me I'd never make a decent living in music, so I put away my dreams of writing and performing. I've toed the line these last six years of marriage, trying to fit into the corporate world and dying a little more each day when I went to work. And you're never home, Shailene. We don't do anything together anymore. You're always out showing houses and attending open houses and corporate parties. I can't remember the last time we went to a movie or concert together. Couples need to do things together. Spend time together."

He paused. "Make love together. Or else their marriage won't survive."

"This marriage is already dead," she said succinctly, another blow to him.

"No," he protested. "No. We can keep trying. See a marriage counselor. We can—"

"I don't want to see anyone, Dax. I got tired of you a long time ago," Shailene admitted. "I don't want to have your baby. I don't want to stay married to you. I've… I've found someone else."

All the air seemed to go out of the room. He grew dizzy and collapsed into the chair again.

"You don't love me anymore?" he asked dully, suddenly realizing he felt so empty because the love he'd had for her had withered and died a long time ago. That he'd been holding on to her out of habit.

"I don't know if I ever did," she said, biting her lip. "I've been seeing someone else. For a while now."

He shook his head. Just when he thought this day couldn't get any worse, it did.

"Who?" he demanded, but a part of him felt as if he didn't really care enough to know.

Her face flamed. "Alex," she spit out.

Dax went cold inside. "Alex. *My* best friend Alex? The one you always complain about."

She shrugged. "It just… happened."

No wonder Alex had seemed so distant lately. Because he was banging his best friend's wife.

Scooping up the birth control pill packs, he shoved them at Shailene. "Then I guess you'll need to keep taking these. Alex has said repeatedly that he never wants kids."

He turned to go. Where, he didn't know. Just that he had to escape.

"So, that's it?" she demanded.

"What do you want me to say, Shailene? You've lied to me repeatedly. You're sleeping with my closest friend. This bomb has gone nuclear. There's no coming back from it. I certainly don't want to stay married to you. I'll file for divorce online. A guy at work did it last year, so I'm familiar with the steps he took because he talked about it so much. If you don't contest it, it's pretty smooth sailing. We file. Wait sixty days. Get a court date for a hearing and then appear before a judge."

Stubbornness filled her face. "I want my half of things," she said. "You owe me, Dax."

It appalled him that she was thinking about money at a moment like this. "I'll give you this house outright, plus half of what's in our savings and checking accounts."

Shailene had no idea how much money Dax had accumulated through his stock trades. He had several accounts solely in his name. She knew he played the market, but he never really talked about his losses or profits. Giving her the house was more than fair. He supposed in his gut he had known Shailene wasn't in the marriage for the long-haul, and that was why he'd set up a few accounts she didn't know about. Dax felt no guilt at this moment about doing so.

"I'll take it," she said abruptly. "You can leave now."

Dax shook his head. "No," he said firmly. "I'll stay in the guestroom, but I won't leave this house until the day the divorce decree is issued. Then I'll move out. You can keep all the furnishings. I'll want to start over."

She pursed her lips in thought. Lips he used to want to kiss. Once, he'd thought her so beautiful. He realized now her outward shell held beauty, but her heart was dark inside.

"Then I'll come and go as I please," she told him. "Don't

ask where I am and don't expect me to be home every night."

She grabbed the Chinese takeout and her purse and left without a word.

He placed his elbows on the table, dropping his head into his hands. He felt totally wrung out, physically and emotionally, though no tears came. Inside, he felt dead.

Raking his fingers through his hair, he sighed loudly. He had a chance to have a new life, pursuing the things he wanted to do. He definitely would never get married again because his trust had been so badly damaged, he couldn't imagine ever letting any woman get close again.

Dax went to the fridge and removed another beer. He made himself a PB&J and sat at the table.

"Happy Birthday to me," he said, knowing he'd never celebrate another birthday again.

1

BALI—FEBRUARY

I vy Hart stretched lazily, gazing out at the changing colors of the sea on Kuta Beach.

Paradise...

It was a place she had never thought she would visit, much less under these circumstances. She glanced to the lounge chair next to her, seeing Harper also gazed out across the water. The sun was just touching the horizon, and soon they would be witnessing the last, spectacular sunset of this trip.

Reaching out, she took her sister's hand. "It's beautiful here. Thank you for asking me to come with you. I hope being here has helped heal your soul some, Harper."

"It helped. A little." Harper squeezed Ivy's hand and released it.

They continued to watch the sun make its descent, the sky streaked with a rainbow of colors, from oranges to pinks to purples. Artist that she was, Ivy had taken many shots of these sunsets with her cell phone over the past ten days. Tonight, though, she merely committed the beauty of the sunset to memory.

She wasn't supposed to be here. This was Harper's honeymoon. Only without her groom. The night before the wedding, Harper learned she wouldn't be marrying Atherton Armistead—because he was sleeping with Harper's roommate and best friend. The little weasel hadn't even been man enough to face his fiancée and break things off with her in person. Instead, Ath had sent Trey Wilson, his best friend, to tell Harper she wouldn't be marrying Ath.

Trey had been as gentle as possible in relating everything to Harper, but the biggest blow had been that the wedding would still take place the next night, with Cynthia Fox stepping in as the bride. Ath's betrayal was horrific enough, but to learn that her groom's wedding with another bride would occur almost broke Harper. Thankfully, Ivy had been there to step in and pick up the shattered pieces. Trey, who had firmly announced he was on Team Harper and had cut all ties with Ath, gave her the airline tickets and told Harper Ath wanted her to go ahead and take the honeymoon. Bewildered, she'd turned to Ivy, who had agreed to accompany her sister to Bali. The only kink had been Ivy's job.

A job she no longer had.

She had worked for a Houston art gallery ever since she'd graduated from Trinity University in San Antonio with a bachelor's degree in art. Ivy was a painter, but she had needed to find a job to make her way in the world.

The art gallery had seemed a natural fit at the time. She thought she would work there by day and paint by night. Little did she know she would put in between ninety and one hundred hours a week, performing the job of art gallery director and auctioneer, without the title or pay. Lawson Everhart, her boss and head of the gallery, was the laziest person Ivy had ever met. She did his job and hers, with no thanks.

Ivy had been the one to manage the gallery's staff. She had trained them in on how to handle artwork to prevent damage to paintings and sculptures being placed on display, as well as instructing them on how to set up exhibitions. She met regularly with clients who collected art, advising them on future purchases and enabling them to sell pieces in their collections. She had also met with artists, reviewing their pieces and determining which ones would be selected for upcoming exhibitions at the gallery. The shows themselves had all been hers to design, as well as the marketing used to promote upcoming shows and events. All financial aspects had been left up to her, including accounting, budgeting, and the all-important fundraising.

After she had found the artists and put the shows together, organizing every aspect from style to theme, Lawson would swoop in as if he had planned the entire exhibition, taking credit for everything from finding a particular artist to the kind of hors d'oeuvres and wines served. He claimed responsibility for tracking down unusual pieces of art collectors wished to purchase and crowed about the prices he received for the ones they sold.

Lawson Everhart was an ass.

When Ivy had called, wanting to take some of her accumulated vacation time to go to Bali with Harper, her boss had refused, even though she had over fifty vacation days coming to her. When she saw Everhart wasn't going to budge, she did the unthinkable.

She quit.

No two-week notice. No apologies. And uttering those two, simple words had freed her.

Lawson had screamed at her over the phone, but Ivy stood firm. Her sister needed her. She wasn't going to abandon Harper at the lowest moment of her life. She blocked Lawson's number and that of the gallery. Of course, once she returned to Houston, she would touch base with the twins, Arlo and Paloma. They had worked at the gallery for over a decade, and they had become close friends of hers.

She wouldn't stay in Houston, though. Ivy hadn't told Harper yet, but she had called their parents a couple of nights ago. Not only had she wanted to assure them that Harper was doing as well as could be expected, but Ivy told them she wanted to come home to Lost Creek, the small town in the Texas Hill Country where she and Harper had been brought up. Their parents owned a winery there, and Ivy knew the tasting room manager would be retiring soon. She'd pitched the idea of taking on that position. It would be a terrific fit for her, because of her excellent sense of smell and knowledge of the wines Lost Creek Vineyards produced.

It would also finally give her time to pursue her art. Never again would she put painting on a back burner as she had for the last several years. She was determined to use her voice through her artwork. Thankfully, her parents agreed she would be a natural to head up the tasting room. Once she and Harper's flight landed in Houston, she would pack a few things and head for the Hill Country. She only had about six weeks left on her apartment's lease, and that would give her plenty of time to figure out what to save, sell, or donate. Ivy looked forward to starting a new chapter in her life, in a place she had always thought was in her blood. Being back in the Hill Country would definitely inspire her art.

The sun finally disappeared, and Harper turned to her. "Thank you for coming with me to Bali. If I would have come by myself, I'm afraid I might have remained in a dark place. Having you here with me, Ivy, made all the difference. Yes, I could have swum and snorkeled and surfed on my own. Taken the Balinese cooking class and e-biked on my own.

"But you've also let me talk everything to death, too. Thank you for being my sounding board. My rock. I love you so much."

Harper embraced her, and they clung to one another a moment, their love for each other an unbreakable bond, despite the fact they weren't blood sisters.

Harper pulled away. "You even quit your job to come

be with me. I know I was a wreck after Trey broke the news to me, but I'm starting to feel guilty."

"Don't," cautioned Ivy. "I needed something to force me to act. To quit. While I loved what I did at the gallery, I was sick of Lawson claiming credit for everything I accomplished. Plus, I haven't really painted since college. I'm determined to return to it."

"It's always been such a big part of your life. You should pick it back up and devote as much time to your art as you can," her sister encouraged.

"I will. If anything, I will be more vocal in whatever I do now," she promised. "I won't accept compromise like a meek lamb anymore. I am going to be a lion." She grinned. "Or a lioness, I suppose."

Harper laughed. "I will cheer you on as you roar. Maybe I'll even get my own roar back."

A server appeared, bearing the drinks they had ordered. They thanked him and lifted them from the tray, holding them high.

"To us—and whatever we decide to do next," Ivy said, clinking her glass against Harper's and then taking a sip of the tropical drink, laced with the perfect amount of rum.

"I actually have an idea of what my next venture will involve," her sister shared.

"What?" she asked. "I'm excited that you are thinking ahead."

"I've drowned my sorrows for the last ten days. Atherton Armistead isn't worth any more of my time. Neither is Cynthia. She can have him. Good riddance to them both." Harper took a sip. "The biggest thing I realized is that I'm going to need to leave Austin."

"Oh, Harper, you love Austin. And working for Sandra Bellows."

"I'll admit Austin holds a very special place in my heart. After all, I spent the last decade there, first as a college student and then working in the city. But think about it, Ivy. With Ath's dad being the lieutenant governor —and Army probably going to run for governor during the next election—the Armistead influence is everywhere. All the movers and shakers in Austin that I deal with as I plan events either know the Armisteads well or are acquaintances of them. How can I plan weddings, engagement and birthday parties, bar mitzvahs, and corporate events and escape that Armistead circle of influence?"

She nodded in agreement. "You can't. Everywhere you go, you'd be planning business or social or political events that included people who would know what happened to you. Worse, they might try to pump you for information or gossip about what happened."

"Exactly," Harper said. "The Armisteads own that town. I can't change that. But I can change my situation." She took a deep breath. "What I'm thinking about is going home to Lost Creek."

"What?"

Harper smiled. "I know. I always wanted to leave our small town for the big city. Yes, I could land a job in Dallas or Houston or San Antonio. Sandra would easily write me any recommendation I needed. She knows people everywhere, and she could probably help me land a new job right away. I don't want a big city, though. I realize I miss where we grew up. The Hill Country is calling to me, Ivy. I need the peace and serenity it offers."

"What are you thinking of doing there?" she asked.

"I'm going to talk with Mom and Dad about building an event center at the winery," Harper explained. "More and more brides are abandoning traditional church weddings and looking for something unique. What would be a better place than Lost Creek Winery as the setting for their wedding? The event center could be on the property. I could use wines from the vineyards. Have a couple of the places in town cater the receptions."

"Blackwood BBQ would be perfect," Ivy suggested.

"I agree. Barbeque would be my go-to in that kind of setting. Besides an event center, I could also offer outdoor space for wedding ceremonies. While I think weddings would be my biggest bookings, I could plan and execute all the same kinds of events I've been putting on for the last several years. Think about it. Lost Creek is only forty-five minutes or so from San Antonio. I know I could pull in business from there. It could also help out the town. Destination weddings are growing, and this would be one where you didn't need a passport to attend. There are already so many B&Bs around Lost Creek, as well as a few small hotels and a couple of chain ones. Guests coming in could benefit the restaurants and other businesses along Main Street and the town square."

Ivy smiled. "I think you've hit on a perfect idea for you, Harper. It would be a great career move, to helm your own business."

"I just need to talk things over with Mom and Dad. Convince them."

"Hey, you've already persuaded me it's a great idea. It would also be a nice way to showcase the family wines. I'm sure if guests aren't familiar with any of Lost Creek Vineyards wines, they would be by the time they leave the event they attend. You know the winery has the land. That won't be a problem. What about financing? Will you ask Mom and Dad to go halves with you?"

"No," Harper said, determination on her face. "I'll pay to rent the land from them, but I want to build the event center on my own. The big thing will be finding a bank who'll loan me the money. I've made a healthy income the past few years, and I've socked away a lot, but I don't have enough for everything needed."

"Maybe Mom and Dad could loan you the money. I know they put a lot back into the business, but they've had several good years in a row now, especially with the blends Dad has created in recent years."

"That's a thought," Harper mused. "I need to think more about it, but just talking it out with you now makes me know this is what I'm meant to be doing. I'm going to follow my heart—all the way home."

"Since I don't have a job, I believe I'm going to go home, as well," she admitted, not ready to tell Harper yet about her new manager position at the tasting room. Only ten days ago, her sister had been shattered, thinking her life was over, betrayed by two people she had trusted implicitly.

Now, Harper was so excited about her new venture,

ideas spilling from her, and Ivy didn't want to take away from this moment. They would have plenty of time to discuss her own move, especially since they would both be living in Lost Creek once again. This time tomorrow, they would be on a plane, returning to Texas, to start the next chapter in their lives. Ivy hoped it would be both professionally and personally satisfying.

Raising her glass, she said, "To the Hart girls—and our futures."

"To the Hart girls," Harper echoed, touching her glass to Ivy's.

2

HOUSTON—MARCH

Ivy finished packing her car, satisfied that in this second time, she'd combed through her things and was only taking the absolute essentials to Lost Creek. She had left Houston a month ago with two suitcases and a few art supplies and driven to her childhood home, where her parents had welcomed her with open arms. She had even moved into her old bedroom as she had taken over management of the tasting room, where she had met employees Sarah and Melanie, two sisters who worked various shifts. They were in their mid-forties, their kids out of the house and in college, and they had both decided to work part time since they had more free time on their hands. Ivy liked them quite a bit and had found the women knowledgeable about wines, especially those produced at Lost Creek Winery.

Now, she was renting a house in town, a few blocks off the square, with Harper and Braden Clark, the tall, rangy Californian with sky-blue eyes who was the vine-yard's new viticulturist. Braden was a quiet man, thoughtful and deliberate, and the best cook she knew. He had agreed to cook for the trio, while Ivy and Harper would handle the housekeeping. Braden was becoming a good friend to her, but Ivy sensed the sparks smoldering between him and Harper. Hopefully, with her in Houston this weekend, the pair might have enough time alone to figure out they were attracted to one another—and act upon it.

She walked to the leasing office and dropped her keys in the slot, having spoken to the manager yesterday. Her lease would end in four days. Obviously, she would not be renewing it. Over the weekend, Ivy had hauled several sacks of clothes to the local Salvation Army, as well as donating what little furniture and kitchenware she had to one of her neighbors who had recently graduated from college and was starting from scratch. What she brought home with her this time included several art books, as well as her winter clothes, coats, and boots. These items would certainly fill up her closet and the chest of drawers in the rental.

Because Braden had agreed to move in with them, Ivy hadn't been able to use the third bedroom as her art studio. She decided she would look for some space in town this next week, determined to return to painting. The tasting room was running smoothly now, and she had contributed her ideas to the new tasting room which would be built at the same time the event center was constructed. Harper had hired Trey Watson to design both, and the two sisters had met with Trey, explaining what they wanted.

After seeing Trey's finished plans, Ivy was glad Harper had hired him as their architect. At first, she had been wary of Trey working so closely with them, but he made it clear that he had parted ways with Atherton Armistead. Trey had incorporated not only their ideas into both spaces, but he had used many natural elements from the Hill Country to bring a unique perspective to both buildings. The current tasting room, which shared space with her parents' offices, would become Harper's headquarters for Weddings with Hart, her event planning business.

The new tasting room would be almost three times as large as the current one. Along with the typical tasting bar, it offered seated spaces for wine tastings, as well as a couple of areas for visitors to sit and enjoy any extra glasses of wine purchased after their tasting. She was working with The Cheese Connoisseur now, and they had created tasting plates that were an additional cost to the wine tastings, but the plates added a nice element to the experience. So far, they had proven to be a successful addition. In the new space, they would have ample room to refrigerate these pre-made plates, as well as carry additional cheeses and fruits. Ivy already stopped by the new construction of the building every day and was eager to keep her eye on the progress being made.

Harper also had Trey add a large patio to the tasting room being built. It would be covered and have seating for those who wanted to stop by and buy a bottle of wine and sit outside, enjoying the weather and some wine. An outdoor bar would be available for buying wine by the glass or bottle, along with soft drinks and Cecily Hart's famous lemonade for children and non-drinkers. In addition, picnic tables would be scattered throughout the area adjacent to the tasting room. Harper's intention was to eventually have local bands play on Friday and Saturday nights, encouraging people to bring picnic baskets. Of course, baskets would also be available for purchase at the tasting room.

Ivy had been the one to push for the addition of a gift shop. She had gotten online and viewed other wineries and what they offered and was determined to get Lost Creek Vineyards merchandise into the hands of people who visited the winery. Her suggestion of wearing shirts with the Lost Creek Vineyards label had been enthusiastically accepted, as well. Some of the merchandise would be displayed at the tasting bar, and she would direct those who wanted to purchase it to head to the adjacent gift shop. Trey had thought her idea of locating the restrooms at the rear of the gift shop brilliant, with people having to pass by all the goodies to reach the restrooms.

Already, she had stocked some of the items at the current tasting bar, simply to get a feel for what moved and didn't. On display were ball caps, T-shirts, and golf shirts, as well as few bar items such as corkscrews and wineglasses with the Lost Creek Vineyards brand etched into them. Her father, who would soon turn over wine-making duties to Braden once the current crop of grapes was harvested in a few months, would then concentrate all his efforts on sales and marketing. In the past, he had managed both. Bill Hart already had Ivy working on some new labels for the upcoming blends and updating the current logos for the reds and whites the winery produced.

She liked this design work, wanting to freshen the family's brand and make it more appealing to customers. Ivy was also working on designing Harper's website and would be overhauling the winery's website, too. While she liked using her artistic talents in these endeavors, she was determined to get back to painting. Returning home to Lost Creek and taking the job as tasting room manager would give her time to paint, especially now that the work on the new tasting room had begun. She had free time on her hands, and she was itching to dip her brushes into paint and begin to create. Painting filled her soul. After years of neglecting it because of the hours she put in at the art gallery, Ivy was ready to listen to her heart and follow her true calling.

Since she hadn't had the time to spend her salary on things most people in their twenties did, other than on some nice outfits to wear as she hosted events at the gallery, she easily had enough in savings to be able to rent a place in which to paint. Of course, she would also be out and about in the Hill Country sketching, and she knew she would do some of her painting outdoors, especially since the weather was warming up. Even so, she wanted a studio where she could work, as well as store her supplies and finished canvases. Her goal was to find a spot by the end of this coming week.

She reached the restaurant where she was meeting

Arlo and Paloma for brunch, then she would drive back to Lost Creek. While she was looking forward to seeing her friends, she knew they would want to gossip about work.

That was the last thing Ivy wanted to hear about.

Still, they had been good friends for several years, and Arlo and Paloma had supported her in so many ways at the art gallery. If they needed to gripe, she would offer a sympathetic ear.

Entering the restaurant, she stopped at the hostess stand and gave her name.

"Ah, yes, your party has already arrived. Follow me," said the hostess, leading Ivy to a prime spot. On the way, she passed several buffet tables, eyeing the chicken and waffles and Eggs Benedict.

Arlo shot to his feet the moment he spied her. "Ivy!" he cried, wrapping his arms about her and kissing her on both cheeks.

Paloma was waiting for the moment her brother released Ivy, and she did the same, their Italian heritage showing in their exuberant greeting.

"Have a seat, *mio dolce amico*," enthused Paloma, and Ivy knew from her years being in their company that Paloma had called her *my sweet friend*.

Arlo held out a chair for her, and they took their seats as a server appeared.

"A mimosa? Or a Bellini?" he asked.

"A Bellini," she agreed to, thinking those would be scarce in Lost Creek, where neither the Lone Star Diner or Country Hearth served alcohol, and Hill Country Hangout, the sports bar, served mostly beer. She also knew to limit herself to one drink since she would be driving to Lost Creek after brunch ended.

Arlo took her hand as the server left and kissed it several times. "It is so good to see you, Ivy. We have been miserable without you."

"Worse than miserable," Paloma agreed. "Lawson was a bear before you left, but at least he wasn't around very much. He would merely swoop in and make an appearance every now and then. Now, he is in our hair all the time. He's actually having to *work*! That is not a very Lawson thing to do."

"No," Arlo agreed. "He has the knowledge, but he hates having to be there. Paloma and I keep to ourselves. We do only what we were hired to do and no more."

"You used to help me with all kinds of things," Ivy protested. "Even if it didn't appear in your job description."

Arlo sniffed. "That is because it was you, Ivy. I refuse to lift a finger to help Lawson Everhart look better. He needs to be a true director and *manage* things."

"The first exhibition held after you left was decent," Paloma told her. "After all, you had already planned every detail as you always did. But the artist?" She shook her head. "You remember how temperamental he was."

Ivy laughed. "I will never forget how hard he was to work with. I called him Mr. Nasty. Here we were, giving him his big break, and he was being impossible."

"Shall we say how bad it got that night, with you not there to keep him in line?" Paloma continued. "I can tell you that Lawson had no idea how to handle him. Of course, Lawson had to hang all the pieces himself. He was trying to prove to everyone how essential he is. And Mr. Nasty hated, absolutely hated, the design of the show."

"But I had already drawn up the entire placement," she said. "Every single piece. We had agreed—after *much* discussion—on the look of the show."

Arlo laughed. "Lawson said your plans for the exhibition were trash." He laughed harder. "Little did he know how you had coaxed your way to every piece's place. And when Lawson tried to change things and Mr. Nasty saw that, fireworks erupted. It got ugly, Ivy. Worse than ugly."

Her Bellini arrived, and she took a sip, grateful she was no longer under Lawson Everhart's thumb.

"The fighting continued right up until we opened the gallery's doors. You had invited some key art critics. While they may have liked the art being displayed, they couldn't help but observe the tension and arguing that went on all night between Lawson and Mr. Nasty."

"Did the work sell?"

"Not as well as if you had been there, steering people to certain pieces, and suggesting they buy it. Lawson has none of your ease with clients. He is too pushy. Too obvious," Paloma noted. "And then Lawson had to plan an entire showing himself after that. Oh, you could see he was missing you then. He had no idea what to do. How much food and drink to order. Which clients to invite. Which critics to cozy up to."

"It was a disaster," Arlo confirmed. "The gallery is already losing clients. Several have asked where you went. I told them you were no longer with any gallery. That you would be painting your own pieces. You are doing that, aren't' you, Ivy? I ask because clients are curious about what you will produce. I know several you could sell to."

She had shared with her friends how she longed to paint again, and they had encouraged her to do so.

"I'm going to rent studio space this week," she confirmed. "Let's go hit the buffet, and then I'll tell you about what I've been up to."

The remainder of brunch, she shared the designs for the new tasting room and how it would complement Harper's event center. Ivy walked the pair through what her day was like and encouraged them to come for a weekend and do a tasting with her.

"You have always had a good nose and taste buds," Arlo told her. "You definitely know your wines. I suppose you enjoy sharing that with others who stop in."

"It is nice to expose people to different wines. The average person has no idea how to really taste wine. How they need to use their other senses, beyond taste. I teach them to observe the color. I go into how to smell a wine and pick up the different scents within it. Then we do the actual tasting and talk about the various flavors in the wines we sample. I hope by the time they leave, they have a greater appreciation of wine itself and that they've found some new ones to their liking."

"How is Harper doing?" Paloma asked. "She is lucky to have you living so close to her again."

Ivy had shared with her friends how Harper's engagement had been broken and that she accompanied her sister to Bali.

"I'll admit that it was rough those first few days. But Harper is the most resilient person I know. She felt she had to leave Austin because of Ath's family being so prominently connected to many of the clients her event planning company serviced. She is definitely excited about running her own business, though, and the plans for the event center at the winery are simply spectacular. You'll have to come to the grand opening once it's finished."

"We would love to do that," Arlo told her. "It will depend upon if we are still here."

"What?" she asked, surprised. "Are you leaving?"

Paloma nodded solemnly. "We cannot work for Lawson. He is impossible to be around. He yells all the time. He demands things which no boss should ask of an employee. Both Arlo and I have put out resumés. We hope to hear something soon."

Ivy was afraid the gallery would fold if they left. Then again, Lawson had brought all of this upon himself.

"Tell me where you've applied," she encouraged.

"Where haven't we?" Arlo said, laughing heartily. "Dallas. Los Angeles. Chicago. New York. Atlanta. Denver."

"We aren't going to be picky," Paloma insisted. "And we know we may not find a place to work together. But for our health and sanity, we simply can no longer be in Houston under Lawson."

She held up her glass, having saved the last sip of her Bellini. "Then here's to a successful search. I hope you both find a position in a place which will appreciate you and your talents."

"*Salute,*" her friends echoed.

Arlo insisted upon getting the bill, and Ivy kissed both of them goodbye. "Keep me posted," she told them. "And if you need me to write any references for you, I'm happy to do so."

"Thank you," Paloma said, hugging her tightly. "We cannot let Lawson know what we are doing, or he will fire us on the spot. And truthfully, he has no idea what either of us do at the gallery." She smiled mischievously. "And if he thinks work is hard now, wait until we are no longer there to bail him out."

She bid them goodbye and went to her car. As she pulled out of the parking lot, Ivy was thankful she had quit her job. She had known she was under a lot of stress, but it had taken getting away from the gallery before she truly relaxed. She was sleeping better, and her skin glowed once more. Every day when she awoke, she had no knot in her belly and no worries. Her former place of employment was in her past.

And she was eager to see what the future held.

3

LOST CREEK—MAY

Dax rose, not needing an alarm. He'd always been able to tell himself what time he wanted to get up the next morning—and it just happened. He dressed quickly for his daily run and was out the door a little before four in the morning.

He made his way around the square and turned onto Main Street, running down the middle of the road because no one was out driving this time of day. Except for the cops, of course. A patrol car had stopped him during the first time he ran in Lost Creek, unfamiliar with him and wanting to protect the citizens in town. Since he hadn't been carrying any ID on him, he'd been politely asked to step into the vehicle for an escort home. On the way, Dax told them his name and how he'd purchased two spaces on the square, where he'd be opening a coffeehouse in the near future.

That had done the trick. Both cops already knew his

name and that he'd bought—not rented—the two stores. It was his first introduction to a small town and how everyone knew everyone's business. The cops had even gone inside the space with him, first to check his ID, but second, to offer their opinions. Dax had planned to do most of the work himself since he was handy. The cops had walked him through the permits he would need, and one of them, Scott Bartlett, had offered to lend a helping hand. Bartlett had recently divorced and told Dax he needed to keep busy to keep from going insane.

Dax put his new friend to work, and Scott had suggested several ideas which Dax ran with. Scott had worked several days a week after his police shift, doing everything from knocking down walls to sanding floors to painting. Dax had insisted on paying Scott, and the policeman hadn't protested, eventually revealing to Dax how the divorce had wiped him out financially. Once Java Junction opened, Scott had asked if he could stay on as a barista on weekends. He picked up how to make various coffees quickly, and Dax had made Scott weekend manager. It freed him up so that he didn't have to be at the coffeehouse seven days a week. Conveniently, he lived upstairs, so he could always pop down for a stroll through the place to see how things were running.

The coffeehouse had been open since mid-March. Two months later, it was beginning to thrive. He usually was home by five from his run and after showering and shaving, downstairs by five-thirty, getting things set up for the day. Java Junction opened at six weekdays and seven on weekends. He stayed busy until ten on weekday mornings, first from the going to work rush, followed by the moms who either put their kids on the bus or dropped them off at school crowd. They stayed about an hour. The third group, which came anywhere between seven and eight, were the old-timers, the retirees who liked to meet every morning and sip coffee and gossip. They left by ten, and things slowed considerably, when he only had a skeleton staff in place.

It gave him from ten until four on his own. Yes, he kept the books and placed the necessary orders, but most of those six hours were for him. Dax continued his day trading, which usually took a couple of hours, and still proved quite successfully. He'd done so well that he'd been able to put down cash for the coffeehouse once he'd decided to settle in Lost Creek.

The town had called out to his soul. He'd never visited the Hill Country before. Hell, he'd never really visited anywhere because of growing up poor in Dallas, having no memory of the dad who left before Dax turned two. With his mom juggling three part-time jobs, Dax had begun contributing to putting food on the table by the time he was ten. He delivered newspapers. Retrieved lost golf balls and later caddied. Mowed lawns and delivered pizzas. He saved up enough money to buy equipment to begin DJ-ing and had done that during high school and throughout college. After his marriage to Shailene, he'd kept his nose to the grindstone and hadn't been much of anywhere. Shailene had taken a few girls' trips with her friends—and probably Alex—but Dax had never strayed far from his roots.

He'd decided he wanted to stay in Texas after his marriage ended, but he wanted out of the hustle and bustle of Dallas. Houston traffic was even worse, and he'd eliminated that city after visiting it. Dax then simply read about different places online, and the pictures of the Hill Country appealed to him more than anywhere else. He'd driven down, going through towns such as Bandera and Boerne as he weaved through the region.

When he'd hit Lost Creek, it had immediately seemed like home. The town only had about twenty thousand residents. It had enough conveniences, while still laying the claim to small-town charm. The surrounding landscape in every direction was spectacular. It also had a river running nearby, which emptied into Lost Creek Lake. He determined to take advantage of the both the river and lake, thinking it would be fun to take up fishing or boating.

In the meantime, he ran, enjoying the peace and serenity of these early mornings when it seemed as if he were the only resident awake in Lost Creek. The time in such solitude was also spent thinking about songs. Dax had bought a secondhand guitar years ago and taught himself to play. He had a decent voice, and he enjoyed writing songs. He'd pulled out all the ones he'd written before his marriage, tinkering with some while discarding others. Ever since he'd arrived in Lost Creek, he'd also begun writing new ones. When the time was right, he would debut some of these original songs at the coffeehouse.

But he wasn't ready just yet.

He finished the loop he was running, one of several routes he'd established, and approached the town square again. This time, though, he saw something he'd missed when he headed away from the square. A mural. Well, the beginnings of a mural. It had been started on the brick next to the hardware store. He wasn't quite sure what the artist wanted it to be yet, but it was a terrific idea, welcoming residents and visitors alike to the town square. Lost Creek was deep in wine country and drew its fair share of people passing through who wanted to sample wines, do a little antiquing, and just get away from city life for a brief respite. The area was filled with B&Bs, and the square had a variety of cool shops, selling clothing, knick-knacks, and cheese and sausages, as well as housing a sports bar, a diner, bakery, and a restaurant.

He quit running in place and continued back to where Java Junction stood. He stopped two doors down and popped inside, greeting Ethel, the owner of The Bake House.

"Morning, Dax. What'll it be?"

"A sausage roll, Ethel." As she took it out and placed it in the microwave to heat it slightly, he added, "I think we should do some business together. People stop in here for your donuts and Danish, and then they walk down to Java Junction for a hit of caffeine. It would be nice if they only had to make the one stop. What if I ordered a set amount of breakfast items from you each day and had them delivered to the coffeehouse? To make sure you get credit, I'd put up a sign that let people know the goodies were from The Bake House. What do you say?"

"I'll think about it," she said, removing his sausage roll and slipping it into a paper wrapper. "Stop by when we close today, and we'll talk."

"You're on. Thanks," he said, holding up his roll in farewell.

Dax exited The Bake House and returned to Java Junction, downing an obscene amount of water as he ate his sausage roll and readied himself for the day. Being the boss—and liking a casual atmosphere—he dressed in a T-shirt and shorts and went downstairs. Jeanine Jones, his morning barista, was already there, prepping for opening the doors.

"You're early today," he said.

"Couldn't sleep. Thought I'd come in and make myself useful."

Jeanine was a widow, and her last kid had gone off to college several months ago. She was an excellent worker and knew practically everyone who came in the door by name.

"I'm thinking of carrying a small selection of food in the mornings," he shared, telling her about his conversation with Ethel.

Jeanine shrugged. "I don't see why Ethel wouldn't go for it. She'd have a guaranteed sale each morning, plus she'd get credit for the baked goods and wouldn't have to wait on as many people at The Bake House. And it would be more convenient for customers, too. I think she'll give you the green light."

Their morning rush started, both working quickly and efficiently. Dax was beginning to know the regulars by name, as well as little things about them. It made him feel a part of the town. He spied Sam Farrow, the owner and operator of Bluebonnet Montessori Academy. His wife Dianne also worked at the academy, while their daughter Finley was a teacher at one of the local elementary schools.

"Morning, Sam. Usual lattes for you and Dianne?"

"You read my mind."

"How's Charlie doing?" he asked.

"That dog will be the death of me," Sam said. "He got out last night and wound up chasing Jean Bradley's cat up a tree. She called the fire department to get Spooky down."

After hearing too many stories about Charlie's bad behavior, Dax had decided that he didn't want a dog. Nor did he want a wife. Dogs seemed to be too much trouble. As for another wife?

That was never going to happen. Been there, done that.

He chatted with Sam as he readied the lattes, watching the door open as Ethel Frederick came in, two bakery boxes in hand. She set them on the counter and opened them.

"No charge. Offer them up and see if they move this morning." Ethel turned around and left.

Sam's eyes wandered to the boxes. "Mind if I grab a donut or two?"

He shrugged. "You heard the lady. They're for the taking."

Setting the lattes in a small carton since Sam had his

hands full now with a donut, he handed it to Sam, who had lifted a chocolate glazed donut from the box.

"Let me grab you a napkin," Dax offered, getting a stack and setting it between the two boxes.

Sam took the carton with one hand and brought the donut in his other hand to his mouth, claiming a bite. "I'll take the napkin, but I think I'll eat the donut on the way to the car. Too messy to eat it inside it."

He made a mental note, thinking other customers might feel the same. While those who stayed at the coffee-house to consume their coffee probably would enjoy a donut, he decided to order some of Ethel's sliced banana bread and sausage rolls, thinking those would travel better with commuters.

When the morning rush ended, Dax left things in Jeanine's capable hands and made himself an Americano before strolling out the door and down to the mural. He hoped the artist would be at work.

No one was there.

He returned to his apartment and did some trading, eating lunch as he did, and tinkered with a song he was working on, changing chords here and there as he focused on the melody. Sometimes, the melody came before the lyrics. Other times, the lyrics drove the music. Either way, he was happy with the progress he'd made.

Looking at his phone, he saw it was a little after three. Dax went to The Bake House, tapping on the door so Ethel would let him in. They spoke briefly, and she agreed to provide items for him to serve seven days a week. He ordered a couple of boxes of three things, telling her he wanted to see what moved and how quickly it did. They would touch base again before the weekend and discuss how those two days might be a little different since more customers stayed longer at the coffeehouse than on a weekday.

Leaving the bakery, he decided to walk down to the mural again. No one was there, but he was surprised that it had been added to since he'd seen it a few hours earlier. Curiosity burned within him, and he decided to enter the hardware store and see if Mayor Charles Bennett could give him some information about the artist who was painting on the brick wall. They had become friendly because of all the many times Dax had stopped into the hardware store, needing this or that as he worked on the interior of the coffeehouse.

He hung back while the mayor finished up waiting on a customer and then moved closer.

"Afternoon, Dax. What can I get you?"

"A little information," he replied. "I saw the mural going up outside. Who's the artist?"

"Ivy Hart."

He was familiar with the name, even though he had yet to meet any of the Harts. "Hart as in the Harts from Lost Creek Vineyards?"

Charles nodded. "The daughter. She's been working in Houston at some fancy-schmancy art gallery. Ivy's always been a painter at heart, though. Heard she didn't have the time to do much of it working at her gallery all kinds of crazy hours, so she's come home. Working as the tasting room manager at the winery these days. Did you know they're building a new one? And an event center?"

He had heard because the town was full of gossip about it.

"Yes, a few people have mentioned it to me."

"Ivy's sister is the one who'll manage the events. She planned things like weddings and parties and corporate events in Austin." Charles shook his head. "A shame what happened to her."

Bennett let the words dangle in the air. Dax knew enough to ask a follow-up question. That's how it worked in a small town.

"What happened to her?"

"Poor Harper was getting married in Austin. To the lieutenant governor's son, no less. Boy broke it off—and broke Harper's heart. She couldn't stay in Austin. I mean, everywhere she turned, she would've run into Armistead people."

Dax didn't like Armistead's politics. If the son was anything like his father, Harper Hart had gotten off lucky not being chained to him.

"True," he agreed. "So, both the Hart sisters are back in town." He paused. "I'm not sure what the mural will be. I wondered about who was hired to paint it."

"I gave Ivy free rein," Charles told him. "She's that good. And being on the end of the square, it'll really draw an eye to my place. You know, you should think about having Ivy do one for you since you're also on an end of the square. I can put you in touch with her if you'd like."

"That's okay," he said. "I think I'll watch the progress

on your mural and give it some thought. Maybe touch base with her if I see her painting and go from there."

Dax returned to the coffeehouse, keeping busy until closing at eight that night. He ate a light supper and watched a little TV before going to bed.

The next morning, he completed his run, once more passing the mural-in-progress, wondering about Ivy Hart. He paused, taking in what he saw, seeing the artwork starting to take shape, liking the idea of having a mural on the side of his own brick building.

He got caught up in the morning rush and then spent a few hours trading and talking with suppliers. Before he reported back downstairs, Dax decided to stroll down to the mural again, hoping to catch the artist in action.

This time, Ivy was there, high on a ladder, brush in hand as she contemplated the wall.

"Hey!" he called up, causing her to look down.

"Hi," she said, her voice low and quiet.

She descended the ladder and as she reached the bottom, he said, "I'm sorry. I didn't mean to make you climb down."

Frowning, she looked from him to the wall. "I was headed down anyway. I needed to get the big picture perspective again." She fell silent, her gaze moving up as she contemplated the wall.

Dax started to introduce himself but didn't want to interrupt her focus. Instead, he studied her. Ivy was about five-five, with brunette hair and remarkable hazel eyes. As they peered at all parts of the mural, they changed colors, drawing him in, as did her hourglass figure. He told himself he had no interest in her or any woman, in general.

Then a brilliant smile lit up her face. "I have it. I know where I'm going now."

That smile did him in.

Dax had never seen such a genuine, beautiful smile, one that not only turned up the corners of her mouth but reached her eyes and filled her face with joy.

It knocked the breath from him.

She turned, offering her hand. "I'm Ivy. Ivy Hart."

"Dax Tennyson," he managed to get out, surprised he could even recall his own name.

Maybe he had written off women too soon.

Pointing across the square, he said, "I own Java Junction. Stop in when you finish working, and I'll get you something on the house."

Her smile faded. Her face grew serious. She gazed at him a long moment.

"Maybe I will," she told him. "For now, I need to get back to work."

Ivy mounted the ladder again, dipping her brush into a jar of paint resting on top of the ladder. He realized she was completely engrossed now and had no idea he remained behind.

So much for making a good impression on her.

Still, Dax had hope that she would come by the coffeehouse.

Because he was interested in knowing all he could about Ivy Hart.

4

Ivy climbed down the ladder to survey what she had accomplished today. She moved the ladder out of the way so her view would be unobstructed.

She liked what she saw.

It had taken a lot for her to approach Charles Bennett about painting a mural on the gigantic brick wall on one side of his store. She was very reserved by nature and not one to tout her abilities. Still, her goal was to get back into her art and begin producing.

The idea for the mural had come to her when she had seen a sign in the window of the hardware store, offering a room for rent on the second level. Immediately, she had known since the store was located on the end of the row of buildings, it would get excellent natural light. She had gone inside and spoken to Lost Creek's mayor about renting the space as her art studio. They had quickly settled on a price, and Ivy had moved what few paint supplies she had into the second floor area.

Mayor Bennett had been renting it as an apartment, but no one had occupied it for over a year now. The only piece of furniture in it was an old plaid couch, which had seen better days, and a small fridge. She wouldn't use the couch often, but it was nice to have it to sit on as she sketched or to take a brief break from her painting. The kitchenette came with a sink large enough to wash out her brushes. She had brought a microwave that she'd used at work, as well as a tea kettle. She'd hit a garage sale and picked up a large table and two folding chairs and then driven into San Antonio on her day off and picked up a plethora of art supplies, from wooden H-frame studio easels and canvases to a good daylight lamp. She'd also replaced most of her paints and bought a new brush set, ready to start a new chapter in her painting life.

When she could, she drove around the area, allowing the landscape of the Texas Hill Country to inspire her. She sketched what she saw, as well as photographed it with her cell phone, and then painted those images on her canvas. While her preference was to use oil paints, she had also purchased an acrylic set, as well as some watercolors. Ivy was experimenting now, mixing the different paints on a canvas and trying to find her rhythm. Or at least she had been until she'd taken on the mural. Between it and her shifts at the tasting room, she'd put her painting on hold until the mural was completed.

This time, though, she knew she would come back to it. Sooner, rather than later.

Pleased at today's efforts, she carted all her supplies and ladder up the outside staircase at the rear of the building, making several trips. She cleaned her brushes, including the paint roller she'd been using, and opened the miniscule fridge, where she had stored bottled waters, and downed one as she leaned against the sink.

And thought of Dax.

She couldn't recall his last name because she'd been too caught up in what she was about to paint, but she could easily picture him now that she had time to do so. He was six feet in height, with dark brown hair and eyes the color of melted chocolate. His body was long and lean, and he moved with an innate grace. She pegged him for a runner based on his frame and the comfort he displayed in his own body.

It had been years since Ivy had been involved with a man, all the way back to college. The long hours she put in at the gallery had left her with little time for a personal life, much less time to date. Besides, she'd sworn off men after a horrible experience. She'd fallen in love for the very first time—and had been gutted by the man she loved. The experience had soured her on relationships, and she'd spent the rest of her time in college focusing on her coursework.

But Dak Whatever His Last Name Was intrigued her. A lot.

She decided to take him up on his offer of a free coffee. Going into the small bathroom, Ivy washed her hands and face, patting it dry. She left her hair in its high ponytail, not wanting him to think she made any effort when seeing him again, but she did wish she had a bit of perfume to dab on.

"Ivy Hart, you're getting ahead of yourself," she said to her image in the mirror.

Dax Unknown Last Name might have a girlfriend. He might even be married. She only knew he hadn't been in town long. No sense in getting her hopes up. Not that she had any hopes where a man was concerned.

Looking at herself in the mirror, Ivy told herself, "This is *your* time. Concentrate on your art. That's what's important."

She locked up, going back down the stairs, happy that she had access to the studio without having to go through the hardware store. Walking across the square diagonally, she came to Java Junction. From what she recalled, the place had been two different stores at one time. Dax must have knocked down the wall between them and made one large space for his coffeehouse.

Entering, she perused the place, seeing groupings of tables and chairs, with several sofas and love seats scattered throughout the room. It had a trendy vibe, yet it also felt very comfortable. Soft, instrumental music played in the background. She could see Java Junction growing to be a place for people to meet up and enjoy a beverage, no matter what their age.

Turning her attention to where drinks were ordered, she saw Dax behind the counter, along with someone she recognized.

Ivy moved to where the two men worked, lining up behind two women. They received their drinks from Dax, who smiled at her.

"Glad you decided to stop by," he said.

She grinned. "If I'd have known Mr. Shackleford was working here, I would've been here my first day back."

The barista heard his name and turned, beaming at her. "Ivy Hart! Best clarinet player I ever taught." He came from behind the counter and wrapped her in a bear hug. "How are you?"

"I'm great, Mr. Shackleford. It's so nice seeing you."

"You've been in Houston, right?" he asked.

"Yes. Working at an art gallery. I'm back in Lost Creek now, acting as the tasting room manager for my parents."

"I hope you're still painting. You know I have that painting of Lost Creek River hanging over my fireplace. The one you gave me when you graduated."

His words warmed her heart. "I'm glad you've enjoyed it all these years. So, you're a barista now?"

"I retired two years ago. Got my thirty years in and decided to let someone younger take on the band program." He chuckled. "Then I got bored. Did a little traveling, but a teacher's pension doesn't allow for a lot of that." He turned, indicating Dax. "Then Dax came to town and opened Java Junction. I decided to apply for a part-time shift. Work three to eight weekdays. Make a little money. Get to talk to a lot of people. Sip some free coffee. It's exactly what I needed."

Dax spoke up. "Sean is a hard worker, and he knows everyone who comes in. I tell him he's my secret weapon.

That folks stop by Java Junction for a coffee, but they leave with the latest gossip." He paused. "What can I get you, Ivy?"

"I've never been much of a coffee drinker if I'm being honest. And it's pretty warm out, so maybe something else?"

"Well, I do offer a variety of teas and sparkling waters. What would you say to a cold brew coffee?"

She chuckled. "I'd say I have no idea what that is."

"It's a smooth, mellow coffee. I brew it cold in a French press. If you're not a coffee fan, you won't want it black, but I can put ice and milk in it."

"It's delicious," Mr. Shackleford encouraged. "Go for it, Ivy."

She nodded. "I'll try it."

"Go have a seat, and I'll have it for you in a couple of minutes."

Ivy wandered about the coffeehouse for a minute, taking it in, and then sat at a café table in the corner. She'd always been an observer, and she looked about, seeing who was present and thinking about their stories.

She was lost in her daydream, and it surprised her when Dax said, "Here you go. Mind if I join you?"

Glancing up, she saw he held two large glasses. "Of course."

He placed both on the table and took the other chair opposite her.

"I won't get my feelings hurt if you don't like it. Remember, though, coffee is an acquired taste."

"Wine is the same way," she replied, lifting the glass and sipping the drink. "Hmm. It's actually pretty good."

"I heard you say you work at the tasting room. That's at Lost Creek Winery?"

She nodded. "My parents opened the winery with a friend of theirs about twenty-five years ago. I grew up hearing all about the grapevines and harvests and what wines were being produced. I inherited my dad's great nose and taste buds. Those help when teaching people about wines."

Dax laughed. "I've been a beer drinker most of my life. Not a big one, but wine always seemed more for the snobs. No disrespect intended, but I can't ever recall having a glass before."

"I get that. College was all about keg parties. I would nurse a beer all night and wind up pouring more than half of it out, wishing it would've been a smooth Cabernet or a crisp Chardonnay."

"Maybe I can teach you about coffee and learn a little about wines from you," he said.

She couldn't tell if he was flirting with her or not. That's how far out of the game she was. But she hoped that was what he was doing.

"You could always stop by the tasting room and let me walk you through some wines," she suggested, not thinking he would do so.

"What do you do at a tasting?" he asked, and Ivy saw curiosity on his face.

"We have different tastings to choose from. Some strictly are for whites, while others only spotlight reds.

Then there's a mixed one, where you get to sample both kinds."

He grew thoughtful. "I think I'd want to try some of each."

"Most people who try wine for the first time prefer white. It's lighter. Fresher. Reds are mostly darker fruits. They're richer. Smokier. More mature. Of course, Lost Creek Vineyards makes both, but we've been having a lot of success with our blends the past few years."

"Clue me in. Is a blend mixing red and white together?" he asked.

"Blending allows winemakers to mix different varieties of wines together to make a complex wine. Usually, we're talking about red wines, though. The winemaker looks for wines which have different qualities and then plays with the ratio to use in order to make the best wine from several."

"Okay, I'm picturing a mad scientist pouring from test tubes."

Ivy laughed. "Actually, a lot of consideration goes into blending. You look at the climate and soil type of each wine, along with the dates the grapes were picked. You must consider the age of the wines you wish to blend, as well as the time it spent in its oak barrels. Even the type of oak the wines sat in is factor. So, it's not a scattered process at all. It's part scientific and part artistic. After considering all those components, you marry the elements, based on the flavor profile you're trying to create."

Dax shook his head. "And I thought making different kinds of coffees seemed hard."

"It takes years of training before a person becomes a viticulturist, the person who's in charge of the vineyard. He monitors the grapes and decides when it's time to harvest them. The winemaker—or enologist—is the person who works closely with the viticulturist, but the winemaker is the one who babies the grapes. Presses them. Stores them in barrels. Samples them continually. And that's the person who creates each wine's flavor profile, including the blends, mixing various combinations together until he hits upon the right combination."

Dax whistled low. "That sounds awfully complicated. But I've actually done some of that with coffees. Tinkered with blending flavors. When I hit on a great one, I feature it as the coffee of the month."

He paused, studying her, causing Ivy's cheeks to heat. She was known for being easily embarrassed, with the least bit of scrutiny causing her face to flame.

"I think I'd like to have a lesson in wine tasting. Maybe I could come to appreciate wine."

She swallowed. "You're welcome to stop by the tasting room whenever you'd like."

His gaze burned into her. "Do you, as the manager, conduct tastings yourself?"

Now, she was growing warm all over under his scrutiny. "Yes, I do."

"Good. I'd like to take advantage of your great nose and taste buds and learn about wines. When can I stop by?"

Her heart began racing. "I'm working noon to six tomorrow."

Dax nodded. "Then it's a date. Look for me tomorrow afternoon, Ivy."

5

Dax felt like a part of him which had been dead had sprung to life during his conversation with Ivy. He couldn't say why. Yes, she was a very attractive woman, but he'd always been drawn to larger-than-life females, ones with big personalities.

That was not Ivy Hart.

She was a bit reserved, but she had opened up to him, especially when she began talking about her family's vineyards. He figured she did well one-on-one with others and would make strong connections with those who came in to do wine tastings at the winery. He was looking forward to sharing time with her today, as well as learning something about wine. Dax had always had a deep curiosity about everything around him, probably because books had opened the world to him. Now that he lived in Texas wine country, he might as well begin to familiarize himself with what the region had to offer. Lost Creek

Vineyards had a stellar reputation in the area, and he turned to the Internet to learn more about the brand.

His search informed him of the many awards the winery had won in national and international competitions, beating out wines from important regions such as Bordeaux and the Napa Valley. He turned to the Lost Creek Vineyards website, reading the story of how Bill Hart and Jerry Hiller had started the winery, nursing the first vines during the early years before creating the Lost Creek Vineyards label. Hiller had been killed in a car wreck not long after that, and Cecily Hart, Bill's wife, had stepped in to manage the business side, while her husband developed the wines and did all the sales and marketing.

Dax clicked through the website's tab of employees, reading about Ivy and others who worked there. He studied her picture, wondering what it was that appealed to him about her. Maybe it was because she was low-key and unassuming. Shailene's personality had been big and bold. She took over any room she entered. Ivy would never do that, yet Dax believed people would be drawn to her as much as they would a colorful personality such as Shailene.

He mentally smacked himself for even thinking about his ex-wife and also told himself he wasn't interested in forming any kind of relationship with a woman, now or in the future. Ivy Hart, though in her late twenties, seemed the kind of woman who would want to settle down.

That was the last thing Dax wanted.

His focus was on making Java Junction profitable, as well as writing music. He was almost at a point where he was ready to perform on a weekend night, playing his guitar and singing his own compositions. On top of that, he was itching to pull together a band. He'd never been in one, but a part of him was eager to perform not just on his own, but with others. How he'd go about it was another thing on his agenda, so getting hung up on Ivy was something he needed to shove aside.

Still, he would keep the date at the tasting room with her today. No, not a date. He never should have referred to it as that. Surely, she knew what he'd meant.

He went downstairs to Java Junction at four in the afternoon as he usually did. Sean Shackleford was already there.

"Hey, Sean," he said, putting on an apron. "Busy yet?"

"Not yet," the barista told him.

"Do you think you could handle things for a couple of hours on your own?"

"If I could handle a large group of hormonal teenagers, I think I can manage a few coffee orders," Sean said drily.

Dax laughed. "I don't doubt you could. I'm going to head over to Lost Creek Winery and sample a few wines in a bit."

The barista smiled. "Ivy convinced you? That girl can do anything. She may appear on the quiet side, but she's got a core of steely determination. She was my top salesperson in band candy sales her four years in high school. And she was my drum major her junior and senior year. When Ivy stepped up, the kids knew to cut the chatter and focus."

"Really? I guess she didn't seem to be a leader to me yesterday."

Sean gave him a knowing glance. "You've got your bold, brassy leaders—and then there are the Ivy Harts of the world. They lead by example and intention. Ivy's solid gold."

He'd never heard Sean praise someone so much. "You said you still have a painting that she did for you?"

"Yes, she painted it as a thank you gift for our years together. Frankly, Ivy taught me more than I taught her. I was the one always thanking her for things. She's got talent. I just hope now she's home, she'll begin to use it again. I really think she could go places."

Dax was curious and wanted to see her work now. And he already knew he wanted to see more of her, despite what he'd told himself. Maybe they could be friends.

Even better, friends with benefits.

He greeted a customer, whipping up a long macchiato for her, and then circulated around the coffeehouse, checking on the handful of customers present, chatting with them just enough to let them know they were welcome without invading their privacy, a fine line he'd learned to dance along.

When it was a quarter till five, he removed his apron and bid Sean goodbye, going to his truck and driving the ten minutes out to Lost Creek Winery. Dax hoped by showing up around five—with only an hour to go before closing on a weekday—he might find Ivy without any other tasters in sight.

He was right.

She was at a long bar, polishing a glass when he entered. Glancing up, she gave him a warm smile.

"You made it."

Dax approached her. "Yeah. Left things in Sean's hands."

"Mr. Shackleford is the most capable guy I know. You're lucky to have him working for you." She set down the glass and folded the rag, placing it out of sight. "Ready for your tasting?"

"As ready as a neophyte gets. What do you recommend we do?"

"Normally, I'd have a rookie new to wines stick to the whites menu. I think you could handle tasting a few bold reds, though."

He shrugged. "What do you suggest?"

She handed him a laminated card. "This mixed flight is the tasting I'd recommend. Read through it and see what you think."

Glancing at it, he saw the tasting would include three white wines and three red ones. Looking up, he nodded. "Sounds good. It'll give me a chance to try both red and white and see which I prefer."

She took the card he gave her and said, "The first thing you need to know is that a wine tasting isn't just about flavor. While taste is a sense that obviously dominates in wine drinking, it's important to use other senses to enjoy the full experience."

Dax knew with certainty that all his senses were on high alert being around Ivy.

"Let's talk about glasses first, though," she said easily, her voice drawing him in.

She pulled several different wineglasses from various shelves and placed them on the bar in front of him.

"Most people don't really care what type of glass they pour their wine into, but I want to teach you the reasoning behind the different shapes."

He grinned. "So I, too, can become a wine snob?"

Ivy frowned. "No. So you'll understand better."

Feeling like a chastised schoolboy, he decided to keep future smart remarks to himself.

"Stemless glasses have become the rage in recent years. I understand their aesthetic appeal, but you need to know glasses with a stem help your wine stay at its optimum serving temperature."

She indicated the wineglasses to his left. "Most white wines possess beautiful notes which are fruity and floral. Those aromas are best captured in a Riesling glass such as this. The stem has a small, tapered bowl and allows the wine's aroma to be directed to your nose, while keeping it chilled at the same time. You never want to drink a white which hasn't been chilled," she cautioned.

He lifted the glass by the stem and studied it. "This is for all whites?" he asked, his curiosity piqued.

"A Riesling glass is pretty much your go-to wineglass for whites and even rosés." She picked up another wineglass. "When drinking a full-bodied white or a rich, buttery Chardonnay, though, you need to use a glass with a wider bowl."

She handed the second glass to him. "Compare the difference."

Dax did, nodded thoughtfully to himself.

"The wider bowl also helps aerate a wine, making it perfect for capturing the more delicate aromas."

He laughed. "You're starting to complicate things, Ivy."

She smiled in return, a smile that made his heart turn over. "I'm sorry. I usually know my audience better. I only go into a lot of detail if I sense that a client wants it."

His gaze met hers. "I actually do like what you're telling me. I'm one of those people who believes in life-long learning. Keep explaining, Professor. I'm all ears."

"Then let's talk reds. Here's a Cabernet glass." She held it up for his inspection. "I would drink a Cabernet Sauvignon, a Malbec, or a Syrah or Merlot from this. This glass is ideal for a medium to full-bodied red wine." Ivy ran her finger along it. "See how it tapers slightly. That gives you the maximum effect as you smell your red wine."

Reaching for a different one, she raised it so both glasses were side-by-side. "This would be for a Pinot Noir or burgundy. See how it has a wider bowl?"

"Yes. To capture the subtle aromas better that those wines give off."

Her smile widened. "You really are a quick student, Dax. But let's get down to the tasting, shall we?"

"I am a bit parched, Professor," he teased, seeing a dimple appear in her cheek as she smiled.

"Okay, I've got to go back into teaching mode to do this tasting justice. But you'll appreciate what I share with you," she promised.

What he wanted to share with her was a kiss.

"No wine tasting can be understood—and appreciated—without the Five S's. Want to guess what any of those are?"

Dax thought moment. "Sip has to be one. Maybe savor?"

"You're definitely on the right track," she praised. "The first S is see. Really look at your wine with a critical eye."

She took a moment to pour a white wine into a glass and handed it to him.

"Is it clear or opaque? Is the hue light or dark—or somewhere in the middle? Do you see any sediment?"

Holding it up, he studied the wine. He'd never thought to truly inspect a beverage. Sure, he made his coffees with a professional's eye, but this was different.

"Next, you swirl. Gently. You don't want to slam it around the glass, just as you wouldn't awaken someone by screaming in his ear. You shake a sleeping person awake gently. Use that same soft touch with a wine to awaken the aromas."

He did as she asked, delicately swirling the liquid. "I know what's next. Sniff. Because you've mentioned using various senses."

"Very good. Yes, the third S is sniff. But not a quick sniff. Really dip your nose deeply into your glass after you've swirled. Inhale. Hold a moment. You're looking for what we call the notes in the wine. Fruity. Floral. Even herbal."

"I'm getting fruit. And… oak."

"Good," she declared, nodding encouragingly at him.

"Lost Creek wines are aged in oak, and the wood can have its own separate notes. They might be of vanilla or coconut. Even a spice."

Dax swirled and sniffed, giving her his opinion.

"You're spot on. You may have a heightened sense of smell because of the coffees you work with. Go for a sip now. A small one. You want to coat your tongue with the flavor. Do *not* swish it harshly like a mouthwash," she warned.

He did as she instructed and she added, "The second sip is when the notes really begin to burst in your mouth. The flavors will be more obvious."

"You're right," he said after his second taste. "It's light. Clean. This sounds crazy, but I can almost taste and smell grass. "

"Excellent. You're sampling a Sauvignon Blanc. I should've mentioned that at the start. It's light-bodied and has green scents within in."

Dax sipped again. "I know this sounds crazy. Maybe... jalapeño?"

Ivy smiled broadly. "You have an excellent palate. Most people can't figure out that taste. Being in Texas, the jalapeño was something Dad wanted to include in this particular year's wine profile."

"I've got one more S to go."

"You were right on the money before. Savor is the final S. Take a bigger drink. Slowly move it in your mouth before you swallow. See how long the taste lingers on your palate. That's called the finish," she explained.

Excitement filled him. "I've never taken this kind of

time to appreciate any food or drink. Not even the coffees I serve, and believe me, I've spent my fair share of time experimenting with just the right flavors to serve. You've taught me an entire new way to look at my own product."

"I'm glad to hear that. Would you like to continue? I always take customers from the lightest to the most full-bodied wines. Also, we're tasting the youngest to oldest wines, as well as white to red. You get more out of a tasting if you follow those simple rules. But first, eat a cracker."

She handed him one, explaining that it would help clear his palate. She also gave him a glass of water, telling Dax he needed a clean palate to move on with his tasting.

They moved through two more whites and then on to the reds. Ivy taught him how to hold a white napkin up and place the glass filled with red wine next to it in order to see the color better. She taught him about the tannins and acidity and the difference between French and American oak barrels. Dax drank up everything she said.

Just as he was drinking her in.

He was attracted to her physically, but he also was drawn to her intellect and expertise regarding wines. Growing up poor, he'd known education was his ticket out of poverty. Fortunately, he liked learning—especially from Ivy. She made things clear and simple. It also didn't hurt that the wines were incredibly tasty.

They finished with the last wine, and Dax knew he wasn't ready to leave Ivy's company yet.

"Have I made you a convert?" she asked. "I know you said you were a beer drinker, but hopefully, you can see yourself ordering and enjoying a glass of wine in the future."

"Actually, I've grown in appreciating beers since I moved to Lost Creek, thanks to the craft beers available in the area. I used to just grab whatever was available, but I've learned there's a real difference in beers. Wine is now the same way. I don't think I'd ever pick up a glass and take a drink without giving it some thought."

He pushed his empty glass toward her. "You explained things really well, Ivy. I not only understand wine now, I think I could really come to enjoy it, especially the reds. I'd like to learn more about the winemaking process. I respect what I do with coffees, and I think it would be interesting to learn more about how wines come to be."

"I'm sure Braden would be happy to give you a tour of the winery and walk you through the various stages," she told him. "By the way, your tasting is on the house."

"No, you spent a lot of time with me." He glanced up at the price chart for tastings. "And this was way more expensive than the coffee I gave to you."

She shrugged. "No one else came in. I wouldn't have been busy as it is. Usually, that last hour before closing this time of year, people are sparse. Once school is out and people are traveling the state more, I'll have more tasters coming in and staying until closing time."

"I still feel as if I owe you," Dax said. "How about I take you to dinner now?"

His own words surprised him. While he'd become more spontaneous since leaving accounting and his divorce, offering to take Ivy to dinner hadn't been on his mind.

Until he'd blurted out the invitation.

"I don't know," she said, the confidence of the past hour together suddenly gone.

"Do you have anywhere to be after you close the tasting room?"

Ivy worried her bottom lip, sending a surge of desire rushing through him. "No."

"Then let me help you close the place up. We can go to Country Hearth. Or Blackwood BBQ. What do you say?"

She was quiet a moment, and Dax prayed she would agree to accompany him.

"Blackwood BBQ," she finally said. "I can never get enough barbeque."

"Then tell me what to do."

"You can start by turning the open sign to the closed side."

He went to the door and opened it, flipping the sign, and then closing it again. Now that they were truly alone, he yearned to kiss her. But his gut told him Ivy Hart was not a woman to be rushed. It also told him he would patiently wait until she was ready.

And then he expected it to be the best kiss of his life.

6

Ivy watched Dax flip the sign on the door and said, "You can go now. I have a routine as far as closing goes. It'll take me about twenty minutes, cleaning up a few things and getting the place ready to open tomorrow. Can I meet you for dinner?"

"Sure," he said easily. "It will give me time to swing by and check in with Sean at Java Junction."

She giggled, something which never came out of her, causing her cheeks to heat. "Sorry. He will always be Mr. Shackleford to me. Sean sounds like some sexy spy—not a high school band director."

Dax leaned against the serving bar. "Oh, are you into sexy spies?" he asked suggestively. "Because I can't tell you if I'm one or not. Or else I'd have to kill you."

Her face now flamed, as his voice sent shivers along her spine. "Oh, wildly attracted to them," she flirted back, hoping the teasing covered her wild attraction to this man.

He shrugged. "Sorry. I'm just an humble coffeehouse owner in the Hill Country of Texas. Now if I worked for one of your family's wine competitors, I might have been charged with getting all the secrets out of you as to how you make your wines."

She laughed, trying to cover how nervous she was, being around such a hot guy. Somehow, it had been different during the wine tasting. She was on familiar territory there, walking Dax through the various wines he tasted and telling him about wines in general since he had no prior experience with them.

"I'm the last person you should ask on how to actually make a wine. No, next to last. My sister Harper can't tell you anything. She does know a good wine from a mediocre one when tasting, but that's about it. As for me? I can elaborate about the finished product, but I have no idea what goes into the science and art of winemaking. Yes, we harvest the wines. Destem them. Press them. Store them in oak barrels. But that's as far as my knowledge goes. My dad has been our chief winemaker for all these years, and now Braden Clark will be taking over that role soon. I'm just a lowly tasting manager, so don't plan on kidnapping me and forcing me to talk. I have nothing to give up."

His gaze turned hot, so intense that Ivy swallowed visibly.

"I think the old saying that still waters run deep fits you perfectly," Dax said huskily. "I'm ready to know more about you, Ivy." He paused. "I'll see you at Blackwood BBQ in half an hour."

She watched him stroll out and knew her knees were about to give out, so she crouched, wrapping her arms around her legs, dropping her head to her knees. Ivy stayed this way for a few minutes, trying to wrap her head around what had just happened.

Dax had come in for a tasting. They had talked about wine. Yet the entire time, she realized an undercurrent had been present between them, connecting them in some manner. It was a powerful feeling that even with his absence continued to run through her. It was also something she had never felt before.

Her experience with men was sorely lacking and non-existent ever since she'd given her heart to her college sweetheart. Jay Ridley had been like Jay Gatsby, a golden boy who had looks and wealth, and everything seemed to come so easily to him. He'd played tennis for Trinity University and been one of the most popular students on campus, serving as both president of his fraternity and also the student government association. The fact he had even looked at her—much less dated her—had stunned Ivy.

She had fallen deeply in love with Jay, assuming they had a future together because he had guaranteed her they did. Though he never formally asked her to marry him, she believed they would follow through with that step after graduation. Then she had discovered he was cheating on her with a campus beauty, one who made Ivy feel awkward and inadequate. When she finally had the guts to confront Jay, he had acted as if were no big deal. Ivy had cut ties with him.

And given up on men.

She hadn't had time for dating while at the gallery. She certainly hadn't thought about it once she arrived back in Lost Creek. But Dax Whose Last Name Still Remained a Mystery had her blood stirring. It worried her, though, that he was so easygoing. So natural. Because of her experience with Jay, who had a similar nature, Ivy wasn't certain she could trust her fledgling feelings toward Dax, much less trust Dax himself.

Pushing to her feet, she said aloud, "Get real."

Ivy began gathering the wineglasses used in Dax's tasting so she could wash them. She decided to ignore the stupid tingles and quickening heartbeat thinking about Dax brought about. She would go to dinner. Just talk. See if he might become a friend. Or even introduce him to Braden, who was new in town, as Dax was. Maybe they could be the ones to form a friendship.

As she readied the tasting room for tomorrow, Ivy told herself to keep things light this evening. It was just dinner with a new acquaintance. Nothing more, nothing less. Besides, she finally had time to devote to her art. She didn't need to become distracted by a guy with soulful brown eyes.

And extremely kissable lips.

Swearing softly under her breath, she determined not to look at Dax's mouth. She vowed not to kiss him—or anyone else—anytime soon.

She would keep her dinner plans with him, though. He

had been friendly to her, offering her a free drink at his coffeehouse and then stopping by the winery for a tasting. It would do her good to get out of her routine.

Locking up the tasting room, she went to her car. As she headed into town, she called Harper.

"Hey, you on your way home? Braden is doing fettuccini Alfredo tonight."

"I won't be home for dinner. I'm stopping by Blackwood BBQ."

"Oh?"

Ivy heard the note of curiosity in her sister's tone and decided to come clean.

"I met Dax, the guy who opened Java Junction. I stopped by and had a coffee there yesterday, and he actually came out today, and I did a wine tasting for him. He had never had a glass of wine before. It's not often I run into a wine virgin. Anyway, he was headed back to town for dinner and asked if I wanted to grab a bite with him."

"Ivy, that's fantastic!" Harper said enthusiastically. "I'm so glad you decided to go."

"It's just dinner. And it's *not* a date," she clarified.

"Maybe the next time it will be," her sister said, chuckling. "Have fun. See you later. Or maybe not."

"Harper, I will be home after we eat," she insisted.

"Well, no rush. Braden and I will enjoy a romantic dinner. Then we'll probably fall into bed because we're so tired. If I don't see you tonight, we can talk about Dax tomorrow."

She didn't say there wouldn't be anything to talk about

because she didn't want Harper to get started on topics Ivy wasn't willing to discuss.

"Okay. Talk to you soon. And tell Braden to save me some fettuccine."

"Will do."

Ivy slipped her cell into the cupholder, glad that was out of the way. Now that Harper and Braden were a couple, Ivy probably should start giving them more time alone together. It wouldn't hurt to eat in town a couple of nights a week. She could always call Finley and Emerson to see if they'd like to join her. The teachers were their neighbors. Finley had been a sorority sister to Harper at UT, while Emerson had roomed with Finley and was also a fellow teacher and divine baker. Ivy was glad both Finley and Emerson were becoming friends of hers, as well. Braden cooked for the four women one night a week, which had really helped them all to bond over the shared dinner.

She pulled into the restaurant's parking lot and locked her vehicle. Going inside, she saw Dax sitting on a bench, waiting for her.

"Hey." Standing to greet her, he asked, "Did you get everything done that you needed?"

"Yes. How about you?"

"Sean said things were a little slow tonight, so he won't miss my help. I'll leave here and go back to Java Junction to close at eight, though."

She glanced at her watch. It was almost six-thirty. Ninety minutes. Or less, actually. She could do this. A little small talk as they ate. Nothing else.

Dax reached for a tray, handing it to her. Ivy picked up a rolled napkin filled with silverware and set it on the tray, pushing it to where Shy Blackwood stood, meat cleaver in hand.

"Ivy Hart! It's good to see you. Why have you waited this long to come in? I heard you came back last month."

"Believe it or not, I've been busy, Shy." She indicated her companion. "Have you met Dax? He's opened Java Junction on the square."

Dax reached a hand over the counter, and Shy took it. "Dax Tennyson. I hear you have the best barbeque in the Hill Country."

At least now she knew Dax's last name.

"In Texas, Dax. I'd put my barbeque up against anyone in the state."

"How is Ry doing?" Ivy asked.

Shy grinned. "I think he may be putting in his papers and coming home in the next year or so."

"That's fantastic," she said. Looking to Dax, Ivy added, "Ry is Shy's son. He's been in the army ever since he graduated. He and my brother Todd were best friends. "Pausing a moment, she continued. "Todd was killed by friendly fire years ago."

Dax took her elbow gently. "I'm sorry to hear that, Ivy."

"Thank you."

She didn't talk much about Todd. Or her own background. But something told her Dax Tennyson might understand.

Glancing back at Shy, she said, "I'll do the two-meat platter. Make it sliced brisket and ribs."

Shy immediately went to work, his movements a blur before he placed the brisket on her plate and added a side of ribs.

"And for you, Dax?" Shy asked.

"I'll go with the sausage and sliced brisket."

Shy filled Dax's order and handed up both plates to them. "Sides down the line, Dax," he said. "Nice meeting you."

"Come into Java Junction, Shy. Coffee on the house— at least the first time."

The restaurant owner smiled. "Will do."

As they pushed their trays along the buffet line, she said, "You're never going to make any money if you keep giving away free coffee."

He grinned. "But if people like it that first time, they'll be back. Once I have them hooked, there's where the profit comes in." He looked around. "What's good?"

"Everything," she said honestly. "Blackwood has always been my favorite place to eat in Lost Creek. I'm partial to the potato salad and baked beans, so that's what I'll get tonight. The cole slaw is fantastic. The fries are to die for. And you can't go wrong with the mac and cheese."

As he watched her put the potato salad and beans on her tray, Dax said, "I'll get the slaw and fries. That way, we can share."

Sharing food was an intimate thing to Ivy. She started to protest and then decided to let it play out. So what if she took a fry from his plate?

They both filled their glasses with iced tea and got to the check-out at the end of the line.

"It's on me," he told the cashier.

Ivy didn't protest. Dax had invited her and was being generous. She would accept the meal.

Instead, she took her tray to a booth. She'd always preferred the privacy a booth gave as opposed to sitting in the middle of a restaurant, surrounded by other tables. Dax followed, setting down his tray and slipping into the booth, removing his dishes and placing them on the table as she did the same. A bus boy quickly appeared and took the trays, telling them the bread would be coming around soon.

"Bread?" Dax asked, opening his napkin to claim his silverware.

"Someone comes around every few minutes with hot cornbread or yeast-filled rolls. And before you ask, both are heavenly."

He smiled. "Then I'll have one of each."

She laughed. "Just try and have one. The bread at Blackwood's is highly addictive."

Sure enough, a worker appeared with the large basket, asking them if they wanted rolls or cornbread. Dax replied both.

He took a bite of the fluffy roll and sighed. "You weren't kidding. This may be the best roll I've ever eaten."

"Told you," Ivy said, buttering her own and sinking her teeth into it. "This is reason enough to live in Lost Creek."

"I can see that on the Chamber of Commerce website," he teased. "Biggest selling point in Lost Creek? Not the antique shops. Not the winery. But the bread at Black-wood BBQ."

They cut into their meat, and she was surprised how naturally the conversation flowed between them. Dax asked about the town and what it was like to grow up in Lost Creek. He told her about buying the space for Java Junction and learning how to make different coffees.

"I always enjoyed coffee. I started drinking it when I was about eight or nine."

"Seriously? That young?"

"I had a paper route. Having a little caffeine in me made it easier to get up and go. Of course, we didn't have anything fancy like a French press. Or even a coffeemaker. It was instant coffee."

Her nose crinkled hearing that. "Yuck. I've only had instant once. It was..." Her voice faded out.

"Disgusting?" he offered, and she laughed.

"Yes. Very."

"I get that now. But I didn't know any better. We were poor. It was what Mom bought and drank."

"And your dad?"

"There was no dad. At least not one I can remember," Dax explained. "He left before I could form any memories of him. Mom said I wasn't even two."

Instinctively, Ivy reached over and took his hand, wanting to comfort him. "I'm so sorry."

She left her hand a moment and then started to withdraw it, but he put his other hand atop it, keeping it there. "Thank you. I don't talk about it much. Actually, I don't talk about it at all. Mom always cobbled together several part-time jobs, working ninety-hour weeks or more. I did my share, working from the time I was young, trying to contribute to the rent and grocery bills."

A warmth spread through Ivy. Not just from their hands touching, but from Dax sharing this about himself.

"It must have been hard. Did you have any brothers or sisters?"

"Nope. It was always just the two of us." He paused. "I lost her my first year in college. I won an academic scholarship to SMU, and she was over the moon about it. Just so proud she had a boy going to college. It covered tuition, fees, and books, so I didn't live in the dorm. At least until she died. A car struck her as she left the bus stop. I wound up moving on campus and stayed there."

Ivy squeezed his hand. "It must have been hard, being on your own like that. Gosh, I think of what I was like at eighteen. Immature. Head in the clouds. Yes, I'd worked in the vineyards growing up, but I never had a job during the school year. I was too busy with band and classes. And my artwork took up a lot of time."

"I'll bet it did. How long will it take you to paint the mural for the mayor?"

"I think I can be done by late next week."

"What's it like, painting something so large?" he asked.

She laughed. "Since this is the first time I'm doing a mural, it's a learning process. The biggest thing I ever painted before was the run-through sign for the football players to burst through on Friday game nights."

"Then how did you know what to do with this mural?"

Ivy thought a moment. "A huge part of it is instinct. I sketched out some ideas and got approval for one. The rest was simply Googling what to do. I had to prepare the wall first. Prepping the surface took a long time. Other than rain, that brick wall hadn't been cleaned since the building went up. But I needed it washed it thoroughly in order for the paint to adhere. I wanted the mural to have a long lifespan."

"I'll admit that it's been a little hard for me to figure out what it's going to be," he admitted.

"The important thing is to prime the wall and then paint all of the background to begin with. By doing that, the surface has been smoother as I begin the finer details. And I was able to use a paint roller for that, which really cut down on the time."

"That's a lot of work before you really begin the actual painting."

She laughed. "Be sure you tell the mayor that."

"Why? Has he grumbled about the price?"

"No, I'm not charging him."

He looked incredulous. "Ivy, you were chastising me for not charging for a cup of coffee. Think of all the hours you're putting into this mural, not to mention the cost of the paints. Why would you do it for free?"

"First of all, I think giving back to the community is important. I'm depicting different things in the Lost Creek community on it. Second, I haven't truly painted anything in years, not really since I graduated from college six years ago. My job kept me way too busy. It's one of the reasons I decided to quit and move back to Lost Creek. I can manage the tasting room and still have plenty of time for my art. This project is letting me get my feet wet again. And if it turns out well, it's great Ivy Hart advertising."

"Pretty smart," he agreed.

"It's been a fun, interesting way to ease back into art. Yes, I'm also going out and sketching scenery in and around Lost Creek. I've even painting two canvases over the past few weeks. But the mural is testing me, which I like. It's great because I can use the lines of the bricks to my advantage. They're like a grid, guiding me along. I'm having to use all different sizes of brushes, from large to super-tiny ones for the minute details. I'm hoping it will bring awareness not only to what's happening in our community, but I also have my fingers crossed that I may earn a few commissions from people seeing my work displayed."

"It's nice that when you turn off Main Street onto the town square, it's the first thing you see," he pointed out.

"Exactly. So it might not be a Lost Creek resident who hires me to paint something. It might be an out-of-town visitor who does." She hesitated and then said, "The two paintings I've done since I returned home are of the Hill Country landscape. I've always seen an immense beauty in these rolling hills and splashes of color. I think I'm meant to paint these landscapes, in all different seasons and from many different points."

He studied her carefully. "Would you be willing to show me your paintings?"

Ivy hesitated a moment. Her art was so personal to her. Then again, she wanted to get it out there. Maybe Dax might even purchase something she'd done and hang the piece in his coffeehouse. That, too, would be great advertising for her. In fact, she might bring it up—and offer him the painting for free if he would display it at Java Junction.

"Yes. Let's finish dinner, and then I'll take you to my studio."

Dax grinned. "I was going to offer to go back and get some of that blueberry cobbler for us to split. Now, I'd rather leave and see your paintings instead."

It surprised Ivy how much she wanted to show him her work, hoping to receive his approval.

And just maybe, she might have the opportunity to claim a kiss once they had privacy.

7

Dax couldn't believe that Ivy had agreed to allow him to see her paintings. This woman intrigued him. He didn't think she usually shared much of herself. He was looking forward to seeing what she had created on canvas.

They left Blackwood BBQ, and he walked her to the vehicle she indicated.

"My studio is on the square. In fact, it's above the hardware store," she told him. "Just follow me over there."

"I'll park at Java Junction since I live above it," he said. "I'll walk over from there."

"Then take the stairs at the rear of the building. They lead directly to the apartment. I'll see you in a few minutes."

Ivy climbed into her car and started the engine, giving him a wave before pulling out of the parking lot.

Dax went to his truck and drove down Main Street,

turning onto the square where the mural was taking shape. He left his truck and quickly ducked inside Java Junction. Only two customers sat on a sofa in the back corner of the coffeehouse. He made his way over to Sean.

"Any way you could close up for me tonight?" he asked. "Just lock the doors. I'll pull the cash from the register and do any washing up and the floors."

Sean shook his head. "We're not crowded. All the dishes are already done, except for those two and their coffee mugs. I can sweep up and mop before I go." His eyes twinkled. "Are you extending dinner?"

"Yes. Ivy is going to show me what she's been painting," he revealed. "I'm about her, Sean, and I really want to see her work."

"I can close anytime you need me to, Dax," the barista assured him. "Go enjoy yourself."

"Thank you."

He left the coffeehouse and cut across the square, going past the mural to the alley. Spying the staircase, he raced up it and knocked on the door.

Ivy opened it, and he was struck anew by her natural beauty. Most women piled on the cosmetics, hiding any flaws. Ivy only wore a little color on her lips and her hair pulled back in a ponytail, but she would outshine every woman of his acquaintance.

As he entered, Dax said, "Thanks again for letting me glimpse into your world. I know art is very personal, and I appreciate you sharing yours with me."

She closed the door. "I used to be confident about my paintings. I didn't mind anyone seeing them. I was proud to show them off. The long hiatus which I've been on—albeit it unintentional—has had me second-guessing myself. I think any artist has doubts about the work they produce, be it a painting, a book, or a song. I had really thought I would work at the gallery and paint in my free time. I'd hoped to eventually make a living from my paintings, but the gallery was so all-consuming."

She shivered involuntarily. "I worked long hours, days and nights, and most weekends. The little free time I had was spent sleeping or catching up on laundry. I had no time to see friends. Read a book. Go to a movie."

"It sounds as if your boss was too demanding," he said. "I know the type."

Shaking her head, she said, "I won't bore you with the stories, but you're right. I'm glad I resigned and came home. Just getting in the car and driving around for half an hour, seeing the scenery, helps me clear my head and inspires me. Come see what I've been working on."

Dax followed her to a standing easel, where a painting was almost completed. He recognized Lost Creek Lake, a place he'd visited twice. His eyes roamed the canvas, recognizing the exact spot.

"I know this place," he told her. "I've been to the lake a couple of times." He paused, drinking it in. "You've really captured the varying shades in the water. And your detail regarding the trees is incredible."

"Those are Texas live oaks," she said, pointing to a grouping of trees. "And these are Ashe junipers. They're the predominant trees found in the Hill Country."

He gazed at the painting. "I feel such a sense of peace

looking at this," he shared. "It's as if I'm enveloped in calm."

"That's exactly the feeling I wished to convey."

He turned to her. "You hit the mark on this one. How long will it take you to fill in the sky and clouds?"

"Not long. That's the last bit of housekeeping I have to do on it. Here, let me show you the finished one."

Ivy moved to a corner of the room, where a painting sat propped against the wall. She lifted the canvas and set it on an empty easel. He followed her, studying it carefully, noting even the brushstrokes.

"I've never really contemplated a painting," he admitted. "But it's almost like viewing a glass of wine, now that you've educated me on that. I have a finer eye and appreciation. I took in the overall picture first, but now I'm looking at little things about it. Trying to absorb the details with all my senses."

"That's a wonderful way to observe a painting," she praised. "I'll be quiet. Just look."

She stepped back, allowing him to be alone a moment, which was a good thing. Standing almost shoulder-to-shoulder with Ivy, he had caught the scent of vanilla wafting from her and wanted to explore more of it. More of her. Instead, he turned his attention to the painting—and extension of her—and focused on it.

After a few minutes, he said, "It's as if you're telling me a story."

"I think a painting should do so. That's intuitive of you to pick up on that. I read something once which said the Texas Hill Country was like a piece of paper God crumpled up and straightened out again. It's crooked. Rolling. Has tons of dips and creases. It's as if nature took a paint-brush to the landscape and went wild."

He nodded, turning from the painting to her. "I like that quite a bit."

"I'm happy to be back here," she said softly. "The topography is like a playground for an artist. The region has plains, cliffs, mountains, meadows, and valleys. The terrain is full of color in its exposed rocks and boulders. The vegetation is wild and free. We've got abundant water in creeks, rivers, and lakes. We've also got a pretty large number of caverns. And the wildflowers, especially in spring with the bluebonnets, lend such wonderful color."

He gave her a sheepish grin. "I heard about the blue-bonnets, but I didn't see any this spring."

Ivy looked astonished. "How could you not see any bluebonnets? They are scattered along roads everywhere in the Hill Country."

"I got to Lost Creek before they bloomed. Once they did, I was deep into renovating the shops I'd bought, knocking down walls and painting and putting in new flooring. I wore a path from Java Junction to the hardware store, picking up things I needed. I had a ton of help from Scott Bartlett, a cop I met."

"I remember Scott. He was several years ahead of me. A big football and baseball star."

"He recently divorced and needed something to occupy his time so he wouldn't go stir-crazy. Scott is handy with about any task you give him."

"His dad was a carpenter," she told him.

"No wonder. He never mentioned that. But we got along well, and I've hired him as my weekend manager at Java Junction. Cop on the weekdays and coffeehouse king on the weekends."

She laughed. "That's nice. It gives you a break. I know too many owners of stores in town have to work seven days a week."

"I don't mind the work. It's different from what I used to do."

"What was that?" she asked.

"I was an accountant," he admitted.

Ivy burst out laughing. "No way. I think of accountants as laser-focused, silent types, crunching numbers. You're so outgoing and personable." She glanced up and down at his attire. "And I don't picture an accountant wearing distressed jeans and a snug T-shirt."

"I got rid of most of my work clothes," he shared. "Saved a couple of suits and two ties. Just in case I needed them for a wedding or a funeral. Not that I will be going to either anytime soon." He paused. "I was ready for a change. I wanted off the hamster wheel of the business world. I wanted a place where I could breathe and relax. I hit upon the coffeehouse idea because I wanted to provide a place for people to come in and do the same. Sip their coffee. Read a magazine. Meet a friend. Or just daydream. A place to chill."

"I like the atmosphere you've created at Java Junction," she said. "It's laid-back. Comfortable. I can see it becoming a place to meet."

"Mind if we sit and talk?" he asked, seeing the dilapidated sofa.

"Sure." Ivy went and sat on the couch, sinking deep into it. "Sit at your own risk. It came with the place. I gather the last tenant left it behind because he didn't want to pay to move it."

Dax took a seat beside her. Not too close. But close enough to hopefully show he was interested in her.

"I've noticed as business has picked up that I have different groups coming in. The people going to work show up first, needing their jolt of caffeine to jumpstart their day. Then moms who've dropped off kids at school show up next. And there's also a group of old-timers. They gather in the back and stay a couple of hours."

"They used to hang out at the diner," she said. "Your chairs and sofas are probably more comfortable."

"It's not busy for several hours after that, just a few drop-ins. But I'm starting to see a bit of an after school crowd show up. Kids with books opened, working alone on an essay or talking about a group project. It'll be interesting to see what happens when summer comes and if that changes the dynamics being established now."

"Why Lost Creek?" she asked, turning more to face him, placing her arm on the back of the sofa.

He shrugged. "I wish I could put it into words. I wanted out of the big city. I was born and raised in Dallas. While I love it, it's so busy now. The roads are full of traffic no matter what time of day. I got in the car and drove around, not wanting to leave Texas. I'd never visited the Hill Country, and it sounded intriguing. I got here, already knowing I wanted to open a coffeehouse. I wanted a town big enough to support one but not too big.

"And then I stumbled upon Lost Creek. I liked everything about the town. Its layout. The people. When I saw the sign indicating some spaces for lease, I peeked into the windows and my dream started forming. I knew it could become a reality here. I called the number on the sign and met with the owner. Offered him cash to buy the two spaces instead of renting them. He was taken aback but quickly decided to accept my cash offer. Then I moved in and started making the spot my own."

"You have a lot to be proud of, Dax. I think you'll find yourself a part of the community. Have you joined the Chamber of Commerce? You should."

"No, not yet. Good idea." He hesitated and decided to open up to this woman. "I write songs."

"You do?" she asked, looking intrigued. "What kind?"

"Rock and pop."

"No country?"

"Nope. I never knew enough about it to get into it."

"I've showed you my paintings. Maybe you can return the favor and play me a song sometime."

He gazed at her, a deep yearning filling him. "I'd like that. I'm thinking of playing this weekend at Java Junction. Saturday night. Shouldn't be too many people there. I've never played before an audience before, though. I'm nervous as a cat dancing on a hot stove."

"I'll be there," she promised. "If you're unsure, you can look at me for encouragement. I know what it's like to put yourself out there. I'll be your friendly face in the crowd."

He'd told himself to wait. That Ivy would need more time.

But Dax knew if he didn't kiss her now, this moment might never come around again.

Leaning in, he brushed his lips softly against hers. His hand cupped her nape, holding her steady. He applied just a bit of pressure, loving how soft her mouth was. How sweet the vanilla wafting from her skin smelled. He kept the kiss gentle, though, not wanting to scare Ivy off.

He broke the kiss, lifting his lips from hers, his hand still on her nape. Her large, hazel eyes had gone almost totally green, causing desire to shoot through him.

Without a word, she took his face in her hands and pulled him back to her. Their lips touched, and this time the kiss caught fire from the start. His arm went about her waist, pulling her to him as he hungrily drank her in. He teased open her mouth, his tongue seeking her sweetness.

She pushed her fingers into his hair and responded to his kiss. Soon, their tongues warred playfully, as they tasted one another, searching for a connection.

Dax wanted more from her. Much more. But his gut still told him not to rush her. Because of that, he broke the kiss, resting his forehead against hers because he didn't want to completely lose contact with her.

Her hands went to his shoulders, and he realized she was steadying herself.

"That was nice," she said softly.

His hand, still on her nape, tightened slightly, his thumb stroking her satin skin. "Yeah. It was."

He lifted his head, withdrawing his hands from her,

sitting back, taking a deep breath. She did the same, studying him carefully.

"I haven't done that in a long time," she said, her voice shaking.

Dax reached for her hand and squeezed it. "I couldn't tell. I really liked kissing you, Ivy."

She smiled, a smile that was like sunshine warming his back on a summer's day. He reached and tucked a lock of her hair behind her ear, gazing at her, trying to memorize her face.

"Why did you really leave Dallas?"

Her question caught him off guard.

"It was more than wanting to leave accounting and traffic on the streets, wasn't it?" she asked, clearly picking up on things he hadn't revealed.

He sat back, releasing her hand. "I divorced my wife," he said abruptly. "I needed to get away. Make a fresh start."

This time it was Ivy who took his hand. "I don't mean to pry, Dax. It's just not every day a person leaves a lucrative position and turns his life upside down by moving to a place and starting a business so different from anything he's ever done."

Her tone soothed him. It was like a balm poured over him. Dax linked their fingers together.

"I wanted to be a musician," he told her. "I taught myself how to play the guitar when I was a teenager. I wrote songs. I didn't know if I might be any good, though. I never performed in front of a crowd. Instead, I became a DJ."

"A DJ?"

"Yes. I worked a lot of fraternity and sorority parties in college. Also did a ton of weddings and bar mitzvahs. Some Sweet Sixteen parties. I just love music. The energy it can bring to a room. How it can make people feel good about themselves. Make them want to get up and dance. Or tenderly hold one another as they sway to the beat of a ballad."

"Then why didn't you pursue it? Is it because of the way you grew up, not having a lot? I know being a musician can be pretty dicey. You can be immensely talented, but a lot of it is being in the right place at the right time. Artists go through much of the same thing."

He raked his free hand through his hair. "I gave up everything linked to music because my wife wanted a steady income. In fact, she was all about the money. I wanted to please her, so I shelved the music dreams."

Dax fell silent, looking away, but he could feel Ivy's steady gaze on him, as if she were seeing into his very soul.

"She betrayed you. Maybe not physically, but she didn't let you be who you needed to be."

His gaze met hers. "I also wanted kids. She didn't." He left it at that. Dax wasn't ready to get into Shailene's lies. Her affair with Alex.

"If she truly loved you, she would have helped you find a compromise regarding your career," Ivy insisted. "Maybe keep your accounting job—but play on weekends." She paused. "The issue with children, though?

Either you want them, or you don't. Maybe it was better things ended between you when they did, Dax."

He swallowed hard. "I don't think she ever loved me. At least, that's what she told me at the end."

Immediately, she cupped his cheek. Dax leaned into her palm, finding her touch soothing. He savored it a moment and then said, "It was the push I needed. It helped me to see how different we always had been. That there would be no compromising on her part. I realized we'd always done everything her way, and I never got any input. The divorce went quickly, like ripping a bandage off a still-bloody wound. It hurts like hell. And then, it didn't. I felt… empty inside."

He tamped down the feelings roiling through him. "I wanted a clean break and got it. Left Dallas and everything in my past behind. I wanted to become a new person." He smiled wryly. "Or maybe discover the true me buried deep inside, hidden for so long that I couldn't remember who I really am. I'm hoping to do that in Lost Creek. I already feel lighter. Less burdened. I'm ready to play my music and see if it's something I should pursue. I also have thought about maybe forming a band. Just a group who plays on the weekends. I've even been debating names for the band."

"Like what?" she asked, and Dax saw Ivy was truly interested. She showed more curiosity and cared about him and what he wanted to do with his life than his wife ever had.

"Either the Rural Rockers or the Lone Star Rebels. Either sound good to you?"

She cocked her head, repeating both names, giving them each consideration, before saying, "I like both, but I think you need to pull this band together first. Play together. See what you're like as you interact with one another. The name you choose will become obvious. It might be one of those—or something else."

Ivy looked as if she wanted to say more. "Go on," he encouraged.

"Well, I know you said you write rock and pop songs, but you're in the heart of Texas, Dax. If your band—or you —is going to please a crowd, I think you'll need to sprinkle a little country music into your repertoire. Country music gets people up on their feet and dancing. There's something really liberating about it."

"You're right," he agreed, nodding to himself. "I know zero about it, though."

She smiled brightly. "Then I'm the one who can teach you all about it. I grew up listening to it. I know all the classics which you should learn to play, as well as what's hot today."

Dax would be happy to learn from his woman. No matter what she was willing to teach him.

8

Ivy arose early the next morning. Since it was one of her days off from the tasting room, she wanted to get as much done as possible on her mural.

And try not to think about kissing Dax Tennyson last night.

They had sat, after the kiss, talking about Lost Creek and its residents, as well as Dax's music. He was determined to make his debut at Java Junction this coming Saturday night and had asked if she would be in the audience for him. Ivy had agreed to do so, curious as to what his voice sounded like and how he would be received.

She popped an English muffin into the toaster and buttered it when it finished, taking it along with her and eating it as she walked the short distance to the square. Living only a few blocks from her art studio had proven to be convenient.

She wondered what she would tell Harper about Dax.

Her sister would most likely pump her for information about their dinner last night, but Ivy wasn't ready to talk about Dax. Or their kiss.

It had been so long since she had kissed a man, she hadn't been sure she would remember how to do so, but everything came roaring back when Dax placed his lips against hers.

Ivy thought it had been the best kiss of her life.

She didn't want to read too much into it, though, especially since she had learned that Dax was coming off a broken marriage. She was determined not to be a rebound relationship for him, nor did she believe he would want to start up anything serious after being so recently divorced. It would be nice, however, to spend some time getting to know him. It had been a long time since she'd made a new friend, much less had a boyfriend.

"Don't get ahead of yourself, Ivy," she cautioned aloud.

Arriving at the studio, she collected her supplies for the day, making three different trips up and down the stairs as she set up for today's lengthy painting session. With the entire day off and the weather scheduled to be sunny and mild, she wanted to tackle as much of the mural as she could today.

Ivy worked steadily throughout the morning, climbing down from the ladder a few times so she could view her progress. The mural was really taking shape now, and several people passing by called up a greeting to her, asking about it. She was happy to tell them what she was working on, hoping word-of-mouth would spread. While she had no intentions of leaving her parents high and dry by quitting her job as the tasting room manager, eventually, she did hope to make her living through her art. The mural was the first step in that direction, giving her wide exposure in the community.

She was focused on an intricate piece of the mural for over an hour, using her smallest brushes to paint between the bricks. When she finished, she decided to take a break. On her way down the ladder, she sensed someone below her but was still surprised when strong hands caught her waist when she was a few rungs from the bottom. She moved through the air a moment before being set on her feet and turned to see Dax before her.

Ivy's heart thumped wildly in her chest as she looked at him. "Hey. What are you doing out and about?"

He bent and retrieved a large brown sack. "I thought you might be needing a lunch break about now. I went by the diner and picked up something for us to eat. That is, if you have time to stop for a while."

"I was doing that very thing," she told him, her stomach growling noisily, causing them both to laugh. "Let's go up to the studio. I've got drinks in the fridge."

He followed her up the stairs, and she said, "I need to wash up a bit."

Going to the sink, Ivy scrubbed paint from her hands and arms as Dax opened the sack and removed two large Styrofoam boxes and plastic silverware.

"I got today's special. I hope meatloaf is okay with you."

"I've been eating Shelly Blackwood's food all my life.

There isn't anything she makes that I don't like. Well, except liver and onions."

Dax laughed. "That's exactly what she told me about. Your aversion to liver and onions."

Ivy felt her cheeks heat. "You told her lunch was for me?"

"I pop into the diner for takeout pretty regularly. When I placed two orders, Shelly was curious as to who the other plate belonged to."

"Dax, I know you've said you're from Dallas. I'm not sure you understand how a small town works."

He smiled wryly. "Oh, I've learned that gossip spreads faster than a California wildfire. I figure by now, Shelly has told at least five people that I was bringing lunch to Ivy Hart, and those five people have told another five people."

"I'm sorry," she apologized.

"For what? Are you seeing someone, Ivy? If so, I can back off."

Her temper flared. "If I were seeing someone, I wouldn't have kissed you last night. I'm just... I'm just worried that people will begin to couple our names because of this kind gesture."

He took a step toward her, cupping her cheek, his thumb stroking it gently. "Would you object to that? People thinking we're seeing one another?" His deep brown eyes searched her face.

"I... I'm not sure, Dax."

He chuckled. "At least you're honest. But I would like to see you, Ivy. Get to know you a little better."

She reached up, her fingers encircling his wrist and removing his hand from her cheek. "I don't know if that's a good idea. You told me you're coming off a divorce. I'm not someone who plays around, Dax. If you want to be friends, that's fine." She paused. "Friends with benefits? Not a chance."

Ivy thought he would back off. Instead, he framed her face with his hands and gave her the softest kiss she had ever received. It was brief. Sweet. And it made her question keeping him at arm's length.

Dax broke the kiss, his hands still cradling her face tenderly. "My past is just that, Ivy. The past. I'm creating a new life for myself here in Lost Creek. You might say I'm even reinventing myself. I want to get to know you much better. I sense something between us. I'm willing to take the time to explore it if you are."

He hesitated. "If you aren't, tell me now. We can put it behind us and try to simply be friends. But I guarantee you that you wouldn't be some kind of rebound for me. You would be the girlfriend in the new Dax Tennyson's life. He's no longer tethered to anything in his past."

She didn't want to think strictly with her heart and said, "Can you give me some time, Dax? I wasn't planning on getting involved with anyone. I had designated this new chapter for me. For rediscovering my art."

His hands dropped from her face. "Take all the time you need, Ivy, but know that I would never get between you and your art. I understand you're rededicating yourself to it. I would never stand in the way of your professional goals. Ever."

Dax started to turn away, but she caught his hand, pulling him back to face her.

"I don't need any time, Dax. Let's explore this. See where it goes."

A brilliant smile lit up his face, one which caused Ivy to suck in her breath.

"I won't rush you, Ivy. We can let things unfold slowly."

"Thank you. I appreciate that." She glanced away from his intense gaze, immediately spotting lunch. "Why don't we eat? That meatloaf looks amazing."

They sat on the stools, and she devoured her lunch, not realizing how hungry she had been. The meatloaf had just a bit of a kick to it, while the mashed potatoes were smooth and the squash perfectly cooked. Conversation again flowed easily between them, and Ivy realized she had never been so comfortable in a man's company as she was with Dax Tennyson.

He collected their trash and slipped it back into the sack the meal had come in, telling her he would take it back with him to Java Junction.

"Are you going to be working here this afternoon?" he asked.

"Yes. Wednesday is one of my days off from the tasting room. I'll get as much done as I can today on the mural."

"Things are really unfolding now," he noted. "I think this mural will bring a lot of attention to your art, Ivy."

She walked downstairs with him. "Thanks for bringing me lunch. It was a nice break to my day."

He reached for her hand and squeezed it. "The food— or seeing me?"

"Both," she said, laughter bubbling up from her. "What will you be working on this afternoon before you go back to making coffee for customers?"

"I'm tinkering with a new song I started last night," he shared. "If I like it enough, I may play it this weekend. Are you sure you can make it Saturday night to cheer me on?"

"You can count on me," she promised. "Are you going to advertise that you'll be playing and singing?"

He shrugged. "I haven't decided about that yet. Part of me thinks it would be a smart idea. That it would draw in a bit of a curious crowd, and we haven't had a lot of people dropping in on Saturday nights since we opened. A larger part of me simply wants to turn up and play unannounced to whoever is in the coffeehouse at that time. I may have DJ'd in front of hundreds of people, but I've never played a single song for anyone."

Dax's eyes grew darker. "Could I play a few songs for you before then? Either get the Ivy Hart seal of approval or have you let me down gently?"

"I'd be happy to hear you play and sing, Dax."

"Are you free this evening?"

"I can be. I think I should listen to you play at Java Junction after it closes this evening. It would be good to practice where you'll be performing."

"That's a good idea. I close at eight. Would that be too late for you?"

"Not at all," she assured him. "I'll stop by then."

Resisting the urge to kiss him again—and have others on the square witness the kiss—Ivy climbed her ladder again. When she reached the top, Dax waved goodbye to her. Deliberately turning away, she determined to focus on her mural again. She had to work at concentrating because her thoughts kept wanting to return to the handsome man who had kissed her two days in a row. She hoped she hadn't made a mistake by agreeing to see him and told herself if things became uncomfortable in the relationship or if she didn't think Dax was the man for her, she could break it off before things grew too serious. Besides, she doubted he would want to become too invested in any relationship, having come out of a marriage which ended badly only recently.

She worked for another three hours and decided to call it quits, having completed an area of the grid she had been focused on. As she climbed down the rungs, carrying brushes with her, she spied Dax approaching again, carrying a tall drink. Ivy realized how parched she had become and smiled gratefully as he handed it to her.

"I was afraid you wouldn't take another break, and so I brought you one of my teas. It's a raspberry lemon blend. No caffeine in it."

He handed it to her, and Ivy took a long drag on the straw. "Oh, this is delicious," she declared.

"Better than coffee?" he asked, his lips twitching in amusement.

"The iced coffee you made for me yesterday was really good, but this is divine. Thank you, Dax."

"Would you like me to help carry your supplies up to your studio?"

"That would be terrific."

"You go on up. I'll grab the rest."

She took her tea and what she already had in hand and mounted the steps to the studio. Dax made a couple of quick trips, bringing everything to her.

"I'll leave you to cleaning your brushes," he said. "I'm due for my shift at Java Junction now. I'll see you later." He paused a moment. "Thank you for agreeing to listen to me play, Ivy."

"I'm looking forward to it," she said.

"I'll want your honest opinion," he told her. "The good. The bad. And the very ugly."

She laughed. "I promise not to hold back. I have a ton of experience meeting with artists and providing them with feedback on their pieces. I know how to evaluate talent. How to build someone up—or let them down gently. Something tells me that I'll be heaping praise upon you, Dax Tennyson."

He looked as if he wanted to kiss her again. Instead, he shoved his hands into the pockets of his cargo shorts. "I'll see you tonight, Ivy Hart."

When he left, she went to the window and watched as he crossed the square, admiring his long, lean frame. She was anxious to hear his voice and the songs he had written.

And she was eager to spend more time getting to know Dax Tennyson.

9

Dax couldn't believe he'd asked Ivy to come listen to him play. It would be good to have an audience—even if only composed of one person—before he dared to share his music with others. He wondered what she would think about the songs he would play for her tonight.

Especially the one he'd just finished writing about her.

After leaving her studio last night, Dax had been brimming with ideas for a new song. It seemed Ivy had inspired him more than any person or thing which had sparked him to pick up his guitar in the past. He'd rushed home and grabbed his six-string, remembering to hit the voice recorder button on his cell. He'd started using it to capture bits and pieces of melodies and lyrics as he fiddled with different lines and chord changes. Sometimes, watching the video sharpened what he had created. Other times, he paused it because it led him in a new direction.

He'd written the entire song in just under two hours. Nothing had ever come to him so fast before.

Then again, he'd never met someone quite like Ivy.

He could see now why Sean Shackleford had called her a quiet leader. Ivy had a steady presence about her, a soothing influence, and she was open and direct. He tried to capture her spirit in the lyrics and melody and believed he had. Usually, he tinkered with a song for weeks before he was satisfied. Even then, he was always going back and fiddling with lyrics of songs written years ago, like a painter not quite content with how a picture had turned out, continuing to self-edit.

This time, Dax had kept almost everything original to the song, only changing a few words here and there and keeping the basic melody intact. He'd decided to let it sit overnight and return to it this afternoon, not finding any flaws with it and not making a single change. After being with Ivy now, he knew the song was perfect just the way it was.

He only hoped it touched her as she had touched him.

After he'd filed for divorce, he had decided no woman was worth his time anymore. He had invested all he had in his relationship with Shailene, and she had hurt him more than he cared to admit. Dax had been determined that while he started his new life in the Texas Hill Country, he would never tie himself down to a woman again. He didn't mind socializing—and sleeping—with women. Hell, he wasn't a monk. But he did not see himself wanting to be with only one woman ever again.

Until Ivy.

Was he merely intrigued because she was so different from the other women he'd been attracted to over the years? Or was he lonelier than he'd realized and reaching out, trying to make a physical and emotional connection?

The thing is, Ivy was not a one-night stand type of woman. He couldn't see them having sex and either staying friends or parting ways and remaining friendly, nodding to one another when their paths crossed in town. Ivy Hart was special. It didn't matter that he'd decided relationships were a thing of the past. His gut told him if he didn't pursue her, if he let the opportunity of being with her slip through his fingers, it would be something he regretted the rest for the rest of his life.

Maybe he was done with all women.

Except Ivy.

It was hard for him to be pulling this one-eighty, especially since Shailene had burned him so badly. Dax had seen the rest of his life being one where he did what he wanted, when he wanted, beholden to no one. Yet was that truly the kind of life he wanted?

As a boy growing up, he hated the fact that he didn't have any brothers or sisters. Though his mom was busy working sixteen-hour days and had no time to date— much less marry someone—he'd fantasized that she would find a man who loved her for herself. That they would have children, giving him siblings. He could see himself tossing a ball to a little brother or having pretend tea parties with little sisters. It never happened, though, and he'd pushed such foolish dreams aside.

Still, he had wanted children because his soul

hungered for them. He wanted to play with them. Teach them. Love them.

Maybe his attraction to Ivy would cool. Maybe it wouldn't last. But at least it had opened his eyes to the realization that he wasn't meant to spend the rest of his life in solitude. After all, why should he punish himself and never get close to any woman or have children simply because Shailene had not wanted them.

Or him.

Instead, he would act cautiously with Ivy. He'd already promised they would move slowly. If they clicked, he would take it to the next step. And the next. Until she was the one who wanted more—or called it quits. Dax couldn't see himself doing that. Already, he was taken by her. It was more than a physical attraction. More than lust. More than anything he'd ever felt for anyone. These new, fragile feelings he was experiencing for Ivy mingled friendship, respect, and yearning. He simply needed to let it play out. Either it was infatuation and would run its course.

Or it might be love at first sight. A love which would continue to grow.

For now, he simply wasn't calling it anything. No labels. No rules. He and Ivy could make those up as they went along. After all, she was in the midst of changing her entire world, the same as he was. She'd left an incredibly demanding job, one which gave her little to no time to enjoy life. She'd ditched big city living for the slower pace of Lost Creek. She had steady employment, the same as he did, and she was becoming reacquainted with her art. He was once more exploring his ties with music. Together, they could urge one another on, while they fed that creative beast within them.

Dax joined Sean behind the counter. Tying on an apron, he asked, "How are things?"

"See for yourself," the barista said, waving his hand.

He looked across the room, seeing it was a little busier than it had been at this time of day. He hoped by the time school let out at the end of the month, more people would be stopping by Java Junction. Teenagers with time on their hands, looking for a safe place to socialize. More out-of-towners who spent a few days in Lost Creek, sampling wines and shopping. Even some looking to hear a little music.

Then an idea hit him. A good one, at the very least, and possibly a great one. An idea he wanted to share with Ivy, knowing she would approve and be able to add to his vision. Something that would bring the community of Lost Creek together in a unique way and support local artists at the same time. Excitement filled him, and he was eager to share it with her.

A group of women came in, placing orders as only females could. Each order was very specific, with none being a straight off-the-menu drink. Dax didn't mind tailoring their drinks, though. He was here to make people happy, and special orders never bothered him. In fact, he appreciated that some individuals knew exactly what they wanted and weren't afraid to ask for it.

When he reached the last person in the group, she said, "I'm Dianne Farrow from Bluebonnet Montessori. My husband Sam comes in and gets me my morning latte from you."

He smiled. "Nice to finally meet you in person, Dianne. I'm Dax. Will it be a latte?"

She shook her head. "I'm afraid I'm getting to be a certain age, Dax. Women who suffer from insomnia and constantly fan themselves when a hot flash strikes. Do you have something without caffeine?"

"If you're looking to perk up without the caffeine, I'd go with peppermint tea. It's also good for digestive health. But since you mentioned menopause symptoms, you might want to try sage tea. It helps regulate menopause and reduces mood swings."

"Sold!" Dianne said, laughing. "Sage, it is."

"You'll like it," he promised. "It's also got a ton of antioxidants and anti-inflammatory substances in it. Sage tea can really keep you healthy."

"If it can help my terrible mood swings, my husband will be thrilled. So will I."

As he worked on the orders, she asked, "I'm here with members of my book club. We usually meet in someone's home, but Sam suggested we try Java Junction today for a change of pace. Since it was my turn to host, I told the ladies to meet me here. It meant I didn't have to clean up before or after, and I didn't have to deal with preparing drinks. The only thing lacking is the usual snacks."

"I can run a couple doors down and pick up something at The Bake House for everyone," he offered.

"You'd bring something else in?"

"Why not? What's a good book discussion unless you're nibbling on something sweet?"

Dax passed her sage tea to her. "I'll be right back."

"Wait, I need to pay you," Dianne protested.

"Sean will take care of you. I assume with a group of women, chocolate is a must."

She smiled broadly. "I think you are a very smart businessman, Dax Tennyson."

He told Sean he'd be right back and ducked out of Java Junction, heading for Ethel's bakery. He had counted eight women in the group, so he selected four brownies and four chocolate chip cookies, telling Ethel to put them on his tab of morning goodies.

Hurrying back to the coffeehouse, he took the bakery box to the area the book club was now camped out in.

"Dianne mentioned you'll be discussing a book you've all read. I thought you could stand to have a treat as you did so."

He set the box on the table and opened it. "Four brownies and four cookies. Instead of duking it out, I'd suggest you split everything in half. That way, you can get a taste for both."

The women tittered, and he knew most of them, if not all, would be back. To encourage that, he said, "I hope you'll schedule every book club meeting here at Java Junction. You're welcome anytime."

They thanked him, and Dax hoped not only would he see them, but possibly other kinds of clubs might hit upon the idea to make the coffeehouse the place they gathered. He really would need to get with Ethel now in order to have on hand a small selection of sweet treats for this very thing.

A group of teens came in with an older woman, who mentioned she was their drill team sponsor.

"We need to make plans for summer camp and next year's activities," she told him.

"I'm glad you thought of Java Junction," he replied. "What can I get you ladies?"

Dax remained busy for the next few hours, with things only slowing around seven-thirty. Ivy appeared, and he greeted her.

"Coffee or tea?" he asked. "Or do I even need to ask?"

She grinned sheepishly. "Does it reflect badly on you if you're dating a woman who'd rather drink tea than coffee?"

"Not at all. I say stay true to yourself. Would you like to go caffeine-free? Hot or cold?"

"Surprise me," she said.

"I don't want to put you to sleep, so I'll skip the passionflower. I think we'll go hibiscus. It's great hot or cold and really enhances your skin. Not that you need that, Ivy. Your complexion is flawless."

She blushed to her roots. Dax had noticed she turned red at the slightest compliment.

"You know you would make for a terrible poker player," he told her. "Every card in your hand would show on your face."

Her blush deepened. "You've heard of people being an open book. That's definitely me."

He decided to give her the tea cold. It would give her

something to sip on and would last much longer. Hot tea cooled quickly, and he knew she would be at the coffeehouse for a while.

They chatted as he prepared her order. She told him her friends Finley Farrow and Emerson Frost had come for dinner.

"They live a couple of doors down from us, and Braden cooks for us and them once a week. Emerson bakes, though, and she brought the most heavenly German chocolate cake."

"Is Finley related to Sam and Dianne? I'm trying to get my Lost Creek residents straight."

"She's their daughter," Ivy said. "Finley and Emerson both teach elementary school. They roomed together at UT, and Finley and Harper were in the same sorority. Finley also takes photographs on the side. She's been doing senior pictures for students. Not the stereotypical pose in your cap and gown that goes in the yearbook. She takes kids outdoors and shoots them in a more playful way. She also has them bring their uniform if they play a sport or if they're in band. Extracurriculars are big in Lost Creek."

"Says the former drum major."

Ivy blushed again. "Mr. Shackleford must've told you that."

"He said you were the band's drum major two years running and the best leader he'd ever had. That your fellow band members really listened to you."

She looked pleased. "I did my best to be a good drum major and get the best out of everyone."

Dax smiled at her. "You're still doing that, Ivy. I hope you'll also get the best out of me."

Her face flamed, and he laughed. Passing over her glass of tea, he said, "Go take a seat. We'll be closing soon. I have something I want to run by you. I think it's got real potential."

The book club members began rising, collecting purses and books. As they passed, they thanked him for the baked goods.

"We'll be back every month," one of them said. "It's a relief to have somewhere close and charming to meet."

"You're welcome anytime," he said, waving goodbye.

Sean went to collect the empty cups and glasses from the book club members and wipe their tables down, while Dax busied himself behind the bar. Soon, the last customer had left, and all dishes were done.

"Go ahead and leave, Sean. I'll sweep up."

The barista untied his apron. "Okay, Dax. I'll see you tomorrow. Enjoy some quiet time with Ivy."

She waved to her former band director as he left the coffeehouse and then rose, coming to meet Dax.

"Anything I can do?"

"I'll need to sweep and mop, but I'd rather put that off and sing for you. Be right back."

He went to the back of the coffeehouse and up the stairs to his apartment, returning with his guitar. Looking around, he asked, "Where do you think I should be?"

She perused the space. "Here." Ivy walked to an area which had a large wall behind it. "You can push this couch this way. Move this table there. That gives you plenty of room, so you don't feel boxed in."

They moved the furniture, and he pulled up a chair.

"Do you have a stool?" she asked. "If you were up a little higher, people could see you better."

"I don't. But I can pick one up tomorrow. Good idea."

She returned to where she had been sitting. "I don't want to be right on top of you, so I'll sit here." She took a seat. "The floor is all yours."

Suddenly, a wave of nerves struck him. Dax wasn't someone who got nervous. He never had been. But he was about to play songs he'd written for a woman he wanted to impress. He wanted—no, needed—her to like them. To like him.

Taking a calming breath, he told himself that Ivy already liked him. If she didn't think his voice or songs were good enough to perform in public, she would let him know.

Dax sat, anchoring his guitar. Looking up, he said, "This is called *Light Up the Sky*."

His fingers began strumming, his voice clear, as he sang the first song he'd ever written. It was almost surreal, singing his own work aloud, in a place he owned.

With a woman he already cared deeply for as his audience of one.

When he brushed the final chord, he closed his eyes, gathering his courage before opening them and gazing at Ivy. She was already moving toward him, stopping as she reached him. Bending, she captured his face in her hands and brought her mouth to his.

The kiss was tender, her touch light. Dax moved his guitar aside, setting it on the ground and pulling her into his lap. Ivy's arms went about him as his did the same. The kiss took on new life, the passion sparking between them. Yet he didn't want to ask too much of her too soon. Because of that, Dak kept it chaste. Still, he'd never kissed a woman closed-mouth for this long while feeling so turned on by her.

Hungrily, they continued to kiss, his arms tightening about her. He never wanted to let Ivy go.

She was the one to break the kiss.

"Why aren't you doing this for a living?" she demanded. "You have a rare gift, Dax. You should be sharing it with the world."

"For now, my world is Lost Creek," he said simply. "Finding my place in this community. Serving coffee and giving residents a comfortable, clean, friendly place to come to. If I can also entertain them a bit, I'll do that, as well."

"You'll certainly do that. Your song was so poignant. Tender and yet full of life. Can I hear more?"

"If you want to."

Her smile made his heart beat rapidly. "I definitely want to hear more. I feel like I'm Colonel Parker, hearing Elvis for the first time, knowing the world is not going to know what hit them."

He shook his head. "I'm not that good, Ivy.."

"Your voice has a beautiful tone to it, and you also have a wonderful way in phrasing your lyrics. I can't believe I know someone who wrote a song that good."

He met her gaze. "It's the first one I ever wrote."

She looked incredulous. "The first?"

"Yes. Of course, I've fussed with it a lot over the years, trying to get it exactly where I want it."

"I wouldn't change a word. Not one note," she insisted. "Okay. I'm ready to hear more music from you."

In that moment, Dax knew he wanted to wait to play the song he'd written for Ivy. He would play others for her now and perform them Saturday night as he sat in this very spot.

But *Forever's Embrace* needed to stay with him for a while. It was too early in their relationship to let her hear it. He would know when the time was right to play it for her.

She climbed from his lap. "What else you got, Dallas?"

He chuckled. "So, that's my nickname, Professor?"

Ivy smiled flirtatiously. "I suppose it is."

Returning to her seat, she waited.

"This is one I call *Dreams Turn to Dust*."

But Dax knew the new dreams which had taken hold of him—those of building a life in Lost Creek with this woman—were just starting to take shape.

10

Ivy listened as Dax played three more songs for her. With each one, his confidence grew stronger.

Whoever his wife had been, she was a fool to have ever let this man go.

It was not her place to push Dax to reveal more about his broken marriage. Ivy only knew that his divorce had been fairly recent since he had left Dallas after it and come to Lost Creek. The coffeehouse had only been open for about two months, and she knew he had done construction work on its interior before that. She had no idea how long it took for a divorce to go through in Texas, but she assumed his marriage had been dissolved sometime last year.

It worried her—if downright frightened her—to become involved with a man who was still so emotionally raw. The hurt in Dax's eyes when he had shared that his wife had told him she might not ever have loved him had almost done Ivy in. If she felt that way, how much stronger did Dax's emotions run?

There was no hiding the fact that she was strongly attracted to him. He was, without a doubt, the best-looking man who had ever given her a second look. But the connection she felt to Dax went more than skin-deep. She seemed to have found her way into his soul, the same as he had done with her. She found Dax intelligent. Interesting. Humorous. Sensitive.

Could two lost, damaged souls find their way, not only to one another, but discover a path to happiness?

Ivy was willing to give things a try.

She hoped she wasn't drawn to him simply out of loneliness. She realized how empty her life had been since her last relationship ended so dismally. It caused her to lose all faith in men, and she focused her energies on herself and her life goals. She had done well in college and then extremely well professionally at the art gallery. Now, however, she had come home to Lost Creek. The place was like a balm to her soul, and Ivy wondered if she were home to stay. She decided she would give herself not only time to reconnect with her art but equal time to see if she might make a start with Dax.

He finished playing his song and stood, setting down his guitar on the chair. He came toward her and smiled tentatively, taking a seat at the café table where she sat.

"I've bored you enough for one evening. What did you honestly think?"

Ivy had not commented after hearing that first song.

Instead, she had listened carefully to both the music and lyrics.

"Your talent is incredible, Dax," she told him. "Your lyrics really speak to a person's heart. The music you've written to accompany them is the perfect marriage. I told you I love your tone, but you only have a good voice. Not a great one. You make up for it, though, with the emotion you infuse as you sing."

He nodded thoughtfully. "Thank you for your honesty. I haven't sung aloud in a very long time. I might be able to get a little better with practice."

"I know Sylvia Moore, the high school choir teacher, used to give private lessons during the summer when I was growing up. She might still be doing so. It wouldn't hurt to meet with her and take a lesson or two. Do you have any formal voice training?"

"None. I wasn't even in choir in school. I was never involved in any extracurricular activities. I was too busy hustling, trying to make a dollar. I've suspected that my songwriting skills were better than my voice. Do you think I sing well enough to at least perform here at the coffeehouse?"

She reached and took his hand, squeezing it encouragingly. "You should definitely sing here. And if you did form a local band, you would be good enough to perform and sing with it, too. I think you would have a better chance, however, selling your songs to others instead of singing them yourself. Is that your eventual goal? To make a living via music?"

He shrugged. "I'm making this up as I go along, Ivy.

Yes, years ago I did want a career as a performer. I never saw myself having a Top 40 hit. My ambition wasn't that lofty. I just wanted to play in local clubs. At weddings. That kind of thing. Be a journeyman musician and singer and be able to make enough to support myself and my family."

Dax raked his hands through his hair, and she knew he had more to say as he was thinking aloud. Ivy kept silent. She had always been a terrific listener, and she was determined to remain one for Dax.

"I feel I lost out on a lot of years because of Shailene. I do see things from her point of view. I can understand how scary it must have been for her to hear that I wanted to walk away from a lucrative position and salary for the unknown. I realize now that it didn't have to be all or nothing. We should have compromised, letting me see if I could find and play gigs on the weekends, while I kept the day job. She sold real estate and was gone a lot on the weekends, anyway. It wouldn't have cut into much of our time together."

He paused. "Reflecting on the situation in hindsight, I see that I was immature. I didn't have the communication skills necessary to voice what I needed. Shailene was a very strong personality. She had rock-hard opinions and was never one to change her mind about any issue. I see now that we really weren't that good a match, even from the beginning. She didn't listen to me, the way you do. You have from the moment we met, Ivy. That's one thing I truly appreciate about you. You see me for myself. You don't judge. I guess with you being a fellow artist, you understand where I'm coming from. We're both people who put on hold something we love to do. Something that feeds a creative need within us."

Dax's gaze met hers. "I think this will be a much healthier relationship than my marriage because we will support one another and the art we wish to pursue."

"I believe you should sing and play here this coming Saturday night," she encouraged. "I'll also look into whether or not Miss Moore is giving voice lessons, so you have that option to explore."

"Thank you for your encouragement. Your support." Standing, he added, "I'm going to grab something to drink. Singing is thirsty work. Do you want anything?"

"No, I still have half my tea to finish."

While Dax went to the bar, Ivy Googled and found that Sylvia Moore had retired from teaching, but she still was giving music lessons, both voice and piano. She copied the link and started to text it to Dax when she realized that she didn't even have his cell number yet. Again, she hoped they weren't jumping into a relationship too quickly.

He joined her again, setting down a tall tumbler. She looked at it.

"What did you make yourself?"

"It's too late for caffeine, so I went with a chaga tea. Actually, I drink quite a bit of it because it's good for boosting your immune system and keeping down your blood pressure."

"What's your cell number?" she asked, having already set up an entry for him.

He reeled the number off, and she read it back to him to make certain she had it correct.

"I'm sending you a link to Miss Moore's website. She's no longer teaching but has continued to give lessons."

"I'll call her first thing tomorrow morning," Dax said. "If she can work me in, I'll see her. Maybe I should wait until I've touched base with her before I decide whether or not to perform this coming weekend."

Ivy knew his confidence was still a bit shaky, especially because he'd never performed live in front of an audience.

"You're the owner. You're the one hiring the talent. You can go on stage whenever you feel like it, whether it's this Saturday or a month from now."

"Enough about me," Dax said. "I want to talk something over with you. Get your input."

She saw his eyes lit with excitement. "What's this brilliant idea you've come up with?"

"Are you familiar with an art walk?" he asked.

"Of course," she replied. "It's fairly common in smaller towns, ones which have a true artists' colony. College towns, too."

"I thought of having a fusion night. One which brings together live music and art from surrounding talent. We could hang the art on the walls of the coffeehouse. Even sell it. I could also seek musicians in the area to play in an open mic."

"Dax, that is a wonderful idea," Ivy exclaimed. "Mixing the magic of music with art. To be honest, I had actually thought about giving you the painting of Lost Creek Lake to hang here. Another way to advertise my art. These fusion nights could not only help me, they would definitely spotlight other artists in the Hill Country."

She thought a moment. "I know an art gallery opened on Main Street a few years ago. I've never been inside it, much less met the owner, but maybe we could go together and talk with him about this combination of art and music. I'd thought about approaching him when I had half a dozen or more paintings completed, but your idea is too good to sit on. It's also almost summer. Traffic in the Hill Country really picks up during the season, especially on weekends. People travel the region, doing wine tastings and antiquing, scheduling getaways at all of the many bed and breakfasts in the area. You could hold one of these fusion nights several times a month. Once word got out, I think Java Junction would be packed. It's something locals would enjoy supporting, and it would give tourists something fun and different to do while they were in Lost Creek."

They talked about it for another hour, Ivy showing him places they could hang paintings, and then changed her mind, suggesting that artists bring in their easels and display their work in that manner.

"That way, you wouldn't even have to mess up your walls, having to hang different artwork each time. In fact, I'd go with easels exclusively, though your walls are a little blank now and could use a little love."

"I want to buy the painting of Lost Creek Lake from you," Dax said, ignoring her immediately protest. "You're right. My walls are sparse. I thought more about the flooring and furniture and the coffees I'd serve rather than the entire ambience of the place. Your painting of Lost Creek Lake is the first I've seen of yours, Ivy. It will always hold a special place in my heart. I would be honored to put it on permanent display."

"I won't sell it to you, Dax, but I will gift it to you. Take it or leave it."

He slipped an arm around her waist, pulling her close. "I'd be a fool to pass up a free painting from the soon to be famous Ivy Hart," he teased.

His eyes darkened, filled with desire.

Desire for her.

She had never had a man look at her the way Dax Tennyson did. Even though she had been in love with Jay Ridley and thought he loved her, her college boyfriend had never studied her with such intensity. Her body grew warm from the heat of his against hers.

And the heat of her own desire rippling through her.

Ivy had never been one to initiate a kiss, always being the one to accept it and go with the flow, but she wanted this man. Desperately.

Turning, she wrapped her arms about his neck and pulled him down to her.

The kiss started gently but quickly ignited. His arms came about her, holding her flush against him, making it obvious that he wanted her. They kissed greedily, as if they had only been given a handful of minutes and tried to make the most of them.

He broke the kiss. "Want to come upstairs?" he asked, his voice low and rough.

She didn't know exactly what the invitation included.

Certainly, more kissing. Possibly, making love. No matter what Dax had in mind, Ivy was ready to take advantage of this time with him.

Without hesitating, she answered, "Yes."

Suddenly, she was swept off her feet. He carried her behind the barista bar and through an opening, where he mounted a staircase that led to his apartment above the coffeehouse.

Opening the door, he stepped inside, kicking it closed with a foot. The curtains were open, and moonlight streamed into the apartment. She could make out a sofa. A chair. A coffee table.

He didn't turn on a light, instead carrying her to the sofa and sitting, keeping her in his lap. Ivy lost track of time as they kissed. She had never kissed a man this long before. This deeply. This intimately. They still had all their clothes on, and yet she felt as if he made love to her with his mouth and tongue. She felt cherished in a way she never had experienced before.

Dax finally broke the kiss, resting his forehead against hers.

"You taste divine," he said, his voice so quiet she almost didn't catch the words.

Running her fingers through his hair, she said, "I never knew kissing could be this satisfying." She placed her lips against his and kissed him gently. "I've never kissed anyone for this long."

"I haven't either. But I could kiss you all night, Professor."

"Maybe I'll let you," she said seductively.

Their mouths joined together again, tongues mating, euphoria soaring. She liked that they only kissed. She enjoyed it—and she liked discovering what pleased him from the sounds he made. She knew he, too, was learning all about her and what she liked.

He ended the kiss again, and Ivy's head fell to his shoulder. They sat together a long time, her palm against his beating heart. It had been racing but now slowed to a steady pace.

Dax stroked her hair. "I hope you don't mind that we kept it at kissing. I told you we'd go slowly."

"I appreciate that," she told him. "I know we still have a lot to learn about one another."

He looked at her intently. "I'll never rush you, Ivy." His thumb caressed her bottom lip. "I want this to work."

"I do, too," she said quietly, realizing she might actually have a future with this man.

Something she hadn't foreseen, yet she couldn't imagine her life without Dax in it.

"You need to get home," he said, kissing her once more. "That sister of yours will be worrying about where you are."

Ivy snorted. "Harper is in bed with Braden now. She isn't keeping tabs on me."

"It's still time for you to go home. Thank you for coming to listen to me play tonight."

"You shared a part of you no one else has heard. That was brave," she said. "Soon, you'll be sharing your songs with many other people." She brushed the back of her fingers against his cheek. "But I feel special that I was the first to hear you play and sing."

Dax studied her a long moment and then said, "I hope we'll have a lot of firsts together, Ivy."

She hoped for the very same thing.

11

Dax bounded out of bed for his early morning run, surprised he had as much energy as he did. He'd gone to bed a couple of hours later than usual, but he wouldn't have given up a second of that time he'd spent with Ivy. She intrigued him. She soothed him.

And their chemistry was off the charts.

Ivy had told him she'd never kissed anyone for as long as they had done last night. He hadn't shared that the same was true for him. Kissing had always been a gateway to a more physical act of coming together with a woman. Shailene, in particular, had tolerated a few kisses, but she was always ready to rush past that and get down to business.

He still wanted to make love to Ivy so bad that he ached, but he'd been happy kissing her for hours. Completely satisfied.

And that had never been true with any other woman.

Maybe there was something to this taking it slow business. Letting the sexual tension build between them as they became more comfortable with one another. Dax had always been the partner who suggested cranking things up a notch. This time, he decided to give Ivy that power. That, in itself, was liberating.

He ran one of his favorite routes, leaving the square and running through a residential neighborhood, passing an elementary school and houses which had been built four or five decades ago, based upon the maturity of the trees in the yards. Silence surrounded him. Only the pounding of his feet on the pavement kept him company. Not even the birds were awake and singing their morning songs this time of day.

As he ran, Dax let his thoughts drift. To the fusion nights. His songwriting. New coffees he wanted to try. Joining the Chamber of Commerce.

And Ivy.

It seemed something existed inside him now, that with every beat of his heart, it echoed her name within him. He hoped this wasn't infatuation. That this all-consuming feeling of wanting to be with her 24/7 wouldn't flame out. Right now, he wanted to give her—and himself—space. He wanted to see her, but he also wanted them to have time apart in order to create their own art.

Doubling back, he ran up and down a few new streets, spying Ivy's car. He stopped in front of the house where it was parked, running in place, thinking of her sleeping inside. It took everything Dax had not to rush up to the door and pound upon it, getting her out of bed. That might be hard to explain to her sister and Braden Clark, though.

Instead, he returned to the square, pausing as he reached the mural which she had been working on. It was well on its way to completion, with large sections of it finished. He believed Ivy would wrap up the mural sooner than she had estimated. Then again, he wasn't familiar with her work schedule at the tasting room, so he didn't know how much time she had to devote to it. He supposed she worked weekends since that's when more traffic would come through the winery, visitors wanting to do a wine tasting.

He was glad he had done one with Ivy, just to see what she did and said when she shared her knowledge of wines with others. It surprised him how much he'd learned and how ready he was to try a few of the wines again. Maybe since he would be doing the fusion nights, he might need to look into offering a limited selection of wines at Java Junction during those occasions. Then again, he didn't know what hoops he'd need to jump through to secure a license to serve liquor. Maybe he should simply stick with pushing his coffees and teas.

Returning to his apartment, he readied himself for the day, making sure he had Sylvia Moore's phone number ready to go in his cell. Dax liked that Ivy hadn't merely showered him with compliments after he played for her. She had been enthusiastic about his songwriting, but even he could tell his voice was off from years past. Her suggestion to work with a vocal coach was a good one. He only hoped he could schedule an appointment with Sylvia before Saturday night.

Dax went downstairs, greeting Jeanine. Together, they finished prepping the coffeehouse in order to open its doors. Right as the clock showed six, Ethel appeared, bearing the daily boxes of breakfast items. While he had offered to pick them up, Ethel seemed to enjoy delivering the order and chatting a moment before returning to her bakery.

"Here you go, Dax," she said. "How are things moving?"

"Quickly," he replied. "I'm not having anything left. If I did, Sean would probably eat it when he comes in afternoons."

"I'm liking our arrangement," the feisty baker said. "You're paying me a fair price. It's cut down on the number of people I'm serving without costing me money. And I assume your customers are satisfied."

"They are, Ethel."

He paused a moment, thinking her color didn't look good. Having no idea how old Ethel was, he wasn't about to ask and earn her wrath. Still, he would keep his eye on her and if she looked as if she might be going downhill, he would speak to her. Ethel might take his inquisitiveness for pertness, but then again, she might listen to him more since he was almost a stranger. They were friendly with one another, but they weren't truly friends. Sometimes, it took someone objective, outside your circle of family and friends, to get through to you about something as serious as a health issue.

The morning rush seemed a little larger and lasted

longer this morning, which was fine with him. The old-timers were ensconced in their regular places, while the mom groups were scattered about the coffeehouse.

"I need to make a quick phone call," he told Jeanine.

"Have at it," the barista told him. "Things have slowed."

Dax went upstairs to his apartment so he would have some privacy.

Sylvia Moore answered on the third ring. "Hello?"

"Miss Moore, this is Dax Tennyson."

"Ah, yes, the young man with the coffeehouse. I stopped in not long ago to see what the fuss was about. You serve a decent cup of coffee, Mr. Tennyson."

"Dax. And thank you. The reason I'm calling is that Ivy Hart told me you give vocal lessons. I'm interested in scheduling a few with you if you have an opening."

"My schedule is more flexible during the day, Dax," the teacher told him. "At least it is now, before school lets out. Most of my clients are either students who are currently in school or a handful of adults who work full-time and take their lessons at night or on weekends. Would it possible for you to see me during a weekday?"

"Yes, ma'am," he said, falling back on good manners which had been instilled in him by his mother. "I usually work the morning rush and then take off between ten and four. I do put some work in during those hours, but I can be as flexible as you."

"Would today be good, Dax? You could stop by at ten-thirty," Sylvia suggested.

"I can do that. May I have your address, please?"

She provided it to him and then proceeded to give him

instructions on how to get to her house. He could have mapped it on his phone, but he found he liked her very much and didn't mind listening to her. As it was, she was only three miles from Java Junction, so it wouldn't take him long to reach her place.

"I'll see you at ten-thirty then," he told her. "If you don't mind, I'll bring my guitar."

"I'm anxious to hear your voice, Dax. I hope you'll be interested in us working together."

When ten o'clock came, he removed his apron and told Jeanine he'd see her tomorrow. Dax went up to his apartment and retrieved his guitar before heading to his truck. He knew he had a few supplies to order, but that could wait until later.

He turned around, deciding to bring the teacher a treat, hoping she enjoyed coffee. He made her a hazelnut latte and slid a lid into place, leaving to drive the short distance to the former choir teacher's house.

She opened the door, and he was surprised at her appearance. Instead of a little old lady with a white bun, Sylvia Moore wore yoga pants and a flowing shirt. She also had flame-red hair, which he thought might come from a bottle. She wore glasses with a sparkling frame, turning from pink to purple to blue as she moved.

"Good morning, Miss Moore," he said. "I'm Dax."

Her lips twitched in amusement. "I do recall what you look like, Dax. You didn't wait on me and my friend. Sean Shackleford did. Even though you were busy, you were friendly and spoke to us all the same. That goes a long way in this town. I hope Java Junction will be successful. Come in."

Entering her house, she indicated for him to step into a large, sunny room to the right of the door. It contained a piano, a harp, and a drum set, as well as a couple of club chairs.

"I give piano lessons, as well as a few harp lessons," Sylvia said. "And I am teaching myself how to play the drums."

He beamed at her. "Good for you, Miss Moore."

"Oh, Sylvia, please. You didn't go to Lost Creek High School." She paused, appraising him. "Where did you go? And how did you wind up in Lost Creek?"

Knowing this was a part of small town life, he took the chair she indicated.

"I'm from Dallas. Raised by a single mother who worked long hours. I won a scholarship to SMU and majored in accounting. I've held a plethora of jobs, but my favorite one was as a DJ for weddings and parties. I had a few curveballs thrown at me, and I decided I wanted to try a slower pace and different way of life. I drove around Texas and decided the Hill Country was too pretty to pass up. Lost Creek was a no-brainer, Sylvia. The town has charm. As Goldilocks would say, *'It's not too big. It's not too small. It's just right.'* So I decided Lost Creek would be the place I'd open my coffeehouse."

"Have you ever run a business before?"

"Just my DJ business. It was very successful. I worked as an accountant after college, though, so I'm terrific with numbers. So far, Java Junction is doing well. I have no complaints. And I have a way to lure a few more people in, now that the summer season is almost upon us."

Briefly, he told her about the fusion nights, where he'd give local musicians the opportunity to showcase their talents, while artists could display their paintings.

"You might want to add pottery," Sylvia suggested. "We have a good number of potters in the area. Jewelry-makers, as well. Maybe you could set aside a few tables to display those items."

"Excellent idea," Dax said.

"Why are you here if you wish for others to step up to the microphone and sing?" Sylvia pressed.

"Because I also want to perform," he informed her. "I've been writing songs for several years now. I think my voice is decent, but the songs are much better. I wanted to see what you thought of my voice and if you like what you hear, I hope you'll work with me some to get it where it needs to be in order to sing in public." He hesitated. "I've never done that before. I've only sung to my girlfriend."

"Here's how I work, Dax," she said, her tone one of no-nonsense. "There is no charge for this first lesson. You are checking me out as much as I am doing the same with you. I want to assess your range. Identify if you have any problems with your pitch. Work with you on your breathing. Proper breath support is paramount to a singer."

He nodded. "That sounds good."

"If you wish to continue, I'll provide some exercises for you to do at home, between our sessions, which will improve your tone and diction, as well as help with breath control. Usually, I also work with my students on the basics of music theory. However, if you are already writing your own songs, I am going to assume you have a good knowledge of this."

"I have no formal training, Sylvia," he explained. "I bought myself a guitar and taught myself to play. Everything I know about music is instinctual."

She nodded sagely. "I am not one to be a stickler regarding music theory. You might not know the proper musical terms, but I suspect you know the underlying reason behind why you do the things you do. All right, let's work on a few warm-ups now, and then I can assess your voice as you play one of your songs for me."

Sylvia led Dax through both spoken and song-related exercises, with her seated at the piano for some of these exercises. He found it fascinating. By the time he was ready to perform for her, he was glad they had gone through the vocal workout. Already, his voice sounded richer and stronger.

"I've never done anything like that before," he admitted sheepishly.

Her brows arched. "Then it's a good thing you have come to me. What are you going to play for me?"

"*A Brighter Tomorrow*," he responded. "It's more of a rock song. I'd also like to do a ballad for you. *Dreams Turned to Dust*. That way you can assess both styles of music I like to write and play."

"No country?" she asked, sounding surprised.

"No, ma'am. I'm a city boy who gravitated toward rock early on, but my girlfriend says if I'm going to play for people in this area, I better add a few country songs to my repertoire."

"You've mentioned your girlfriend twice," Sylvia pointed out. "Did she move with you from Dallas?"

"No, I met her here in Lost Creek. Ivy Hart."

"Ivy? Oh, she was a darling girl. She and her sister were such good students. On all sorts of committees. True student leaders. Neither of them was in choir, though I do remember Ivy served as the drum major."

"Yes, Sean Shackleford, one of my baristas, has sung her praises to me loud and often."

"And Ivy has heard your music?"

He nodded. "She thinks I knock it out of the park with my songwriting. She also told me I have a good voice. Not a great one. That's why I'm here. To see if you can help me improve upon it."

"Then play *A Brighter Tomorrow* for me, Dax."

He lifted his guitar and pulled the strap over his head.

"You need to stand," Sylvia prompted. "You will have better breath control than if you are seated."

He rose, knowing he better stay on his toes around this woman.

"Do you mind if I record you?" she asked. "Most students never do this for themselves. I think you can learn quite a bit by listening to yourself."

"Go right ahead," he said, and she slipped her cell from her pocket and tapped it, nodding at him to continue.

Dax played the first song. Sylvia had the best poker face he'd ever seen. When she didn't comment after the song ended, he decided to move into *Dreams Turn into*

Dust, playing the ballad in its entirety. After he finished, he removed his guitar, setting it aside.

Sylvia turned off her recording. "How do you think you sounded?"

He frowned. "I thought I was here to get your critique."

"You are. I'm simply interested in what you thought of your performance. Self-evaluation and self-awareness are important if you are to truly improve."

Thinking a moment, he said, "My voice cracked some on the first song. The warm-ups helped, though. As for the ballad, I struggled to hit a few of the high notes."

"Let's listen together and then talk through things."

He covered his embarrassment, having never thought to record himself once he'd written a song, and feeling uncomfortable hearing himself in her presence. Still, he'd come here for help, and Sylvia seemed both knowledge-able—and tough as nails. She wouldn't cut him any slack, which he appreciated.

When the second song ended, Sylvia touched a button, and the room went silent.

"I can forward these files to you. I think a student can learn quite a bit from hearing their own performance. Now, what do you think?"

This time, Dax was more critical of his performance, noting several specific examples, but he pointed out that he thought he'd done better on the ballad than he had with the rock song.

"I agree. You sounded rusty to me. Have you been practicing?"

"I'm putting my cards on the table, Sylvia. I haven't

played in seven years. I put music on hold and allowed myself to be swallowed whole by the corporate world. Despite that, I never totally gave up on my dream to sing and play someday. As I told Ivy, I don't expect to hear myself on the radio. I simply want to entertain people right here in Lost Creek. With that being said, I still want to be the best version of myself that I can be. How can I get better?"

"You're going to need to practice, Dax. A lot. You have a ton of work to do regarding breath control. Your tone is excellent. Your pitch, even better. I detect a richness to your voice, but it's going to take work to bring more of it out. Are you willing to put in the work?"

"Yes, ma'am," he said, eager to push himself.

"I think once we get the rust out of your voice, the rest will come naturally to you. You are a fine composer, however, and your lyrics are superb. I will do everything I can to bring your singing voice to a higher, more dependable level."

He met her gaze. "I was hoping to play at Java Junction this Saturday night. Just a few songs."

She frowned. "Don't. Give me three weeks—and promise me you'll put in the work on your end. After that, I think you'll be ready to sing for the public."

That would take him to the first week in June. Dax decided that Saturday would be the beginning of the fusion nights which Java Junction would host.

And he planned to close out the list of performers.

12

Ivy left home and drove the few blocks to the town square, stopping just outside Java Junction. Dax was waiting for her and climbed into her car, leaning over to give her a brief, sweet kiss in greeting. She knew the gesture was a small one but believed it thoughtful. So many little things about this man appealed to her.

"Ready to visit with Deke Manchester?" Dax asked as he fastened his seatbelt.

She had contacted the art gallery owner yesterday and asked if she and Dax might come by and speak with him about something connecting his gallery with the Lost Creek community. Manchester agreed to visit with them, and they would meet at ten o'clock, when he opened for business.

"I hope he'll be able to put us in touch with several of his clients. Have you been working on the exercises Miss Moore gave you?" she asked.

"I have. Both yesterday and this morning. I'm glad you suggested I make an appointment with her. I can already tell that what she has me doing is going to make a big difference in how I approach my singing."

She had only been slightly disappointed that Sylvia Moore had not wanted Dax to perform at Java Junction this weekend. The former choir teacher had agreed that the music and lyrics Dax had created were excellent, but she thought his voice needed work, especially his breath control. Dax had shared how Sylvia wanted to work with him for a solid three weeks before he made his debut in public.

"I think it will be better for me not being the only act playing when I do perform for the first time," he told Ivy. "With others getting up and playing a song or two, the focus won't be solely on me. I do, however, plan to close out the evening. I'll be ready." Grinning, he added, "Sylvia said she would come and listen in order to give me her evaluation afterward."

"I recall how much other students enjoyed being in her choirs. They brought home more than a few state championships over the years. I'm glad you found her easy to work with and helpful."

"I'll see her again this afternoon, and then we'll do three sessions next week. I've decided the two songs I'll focus on for our first fusion night, and those are the ones I'll be polishing with her."

By now, Ivy had turned onto Main Street. It was only a few more blocks to Manchester's gallery, and she pulled into a parking spot on the street in front of the gallery. She doubted on a Thursday morning it would be busy.

Entering the gallery, she caught her first glimpse of Deke Manchester. He was almost six feet tall and in his early fifties, his dark hair beginning to be threaded with silver.

"You must be Ivy Hart and Dax Tennyson," he said cheerfully, coming to shake both their hands. "Come have a seat," he offered, leading them to a table in the corner of the gallery.

Ivy couldn't help but skim her gaze across the space, noting the various paintings and sculptures strategically scattered about.

After Deke sat, she said, "You have a really fine eye. The artwork exhibited shows that."

"Placement is key to selling art," Deke said. "Most people don't notice that, though. Do you have a background in art?"

"I worked at a gallery in Houston for six years." She named it and Deke nodded, saying he was familiar with it.

"I'm from Denver myself," Deke said, "but I moved to Lost Creek a few years ago after a pretty tourist who came into my gallery caught my eye. Our relationship wound up not working out, but I fell in love with Lost Creek and the Texas Hill Country. I decided to stay permanently and haven't regretted doing so. Tell me about your proposition."

Dax took the lead. "I recently opened Java Junction on the square and had an idea to begin holding fusion nights at the coffeehouse. I want to merge art and music together, setting up easels and table displays of artists' work around my place a few nights each month during the summer. I'll also be pulling in musicians from throughout the area to play. People in the community can come and walk through the art on display and enjoy listening to local talent perform, all while sipping on their favorite coffees and teas."

Nodding, Deke said, "I like it. I went to school at Colorado State in Fort Collins, and the town used to have art walks on a regular basis. Art wasn't displayed in a single venue, however. It was all along a couple of different streets, which encouraged people go inside and view art in different merchants' shops. Everything from a bookstore to an antique shop to a tea company. The local bars would sell wine by the glass, and people would stroll along the street, going in and out of various stores, sipping wine and viewing art. I can see why you would want to confine everything to your coffeehouse, though, especially with different musicians playing."

"We thought it would be a great way to get the community involved in supporting our local artists and musicians," Ivy said. "I'm a painter myself, and I recently moved back to Lost Creek, where I grew up. Because I've been gone from the area about a decade, I no longer am in touch with the artists' community. That's where you would come in."

"We need to find artists who'd be willing to have their work on display at Java Junction," Dax continued. "We'd like for each piece to be available for sale, but if an artist would simply prefer the exposure to the public, that's fine, too."

"As an art gallery owner, I collect a percentage of an artist's sale for having housed their work," Deke said. "Would you be taking a commission?"

"No," Dax assured the gallery owner. "In fact, we could have placards drawn up which reference your gallery. If someone is interested in purchasing a painting or sculpture, we could direct them to you the next day so you could receive your slice of the pie. I don't want to handle any sales. The only thing that I would do is mark a painting off the market if someone wanted it."

Deke thought a moment. "I wouldn't mind being on hand for this first fusion night, along with my different artists. Some will want to show up and talk about their artwork. A few are shy enough and would rather me be there to speak to potential clients for them. What date are you looking at? How many pieces do you want represented?"

"I'm aiming for the first Saturday in June as the debut," Dax said. "Tourist season will pick up with summer. I think I'm going to go for the first and third Saturday nights of the month for June, July, and August. We could also try one weekday night the second and fourth week, just to see if we could stir any interest in the middle of the week or not."

"What we need now is the connection to the artists," Ivy explained. "Can you put us in touch with them? It would be great if you could speak to them before we do, so they would know we have a legitimate proposition for them."

"First, I'd like to come by the coffeehouse and see your setup," Deke said. "That would give me an idea of the space and how many pieces we might display without looking overcrowded. Especially doing this a couple of times a month, you will want to change out the artists being spotlighted each time. I could help rotate both artists and pieces for you. It would give me a new outlet in which to display my clients' work. People who would never think to set foot inside an art gallery might come for a night to listen to music and find that a painting speaks to them."

Ivy was relieved to hear that Deke wanted to place the pieces himself. While she was talented at arranging art, it took precious time. Since it would be Deke's clients represented, she was pleased he wanted to do the placements himself.

"You can drop by anytime," Dax said enthusiastically. "Java Junction opens at six in the morning and closes at eight at night. On fusion nights, however, we'll remain open until ten."

"My gallery closes at six," Deke said. "I can stop by after closing tonight if you don't mind."

"I'm happy to show you the space," Dax said. "I'll set you up with a coffee or tea of your choice."

"Sounds like a solid plan," the gallery owner said. "I'll pull together a list this morning of different artists who might be interested. Once I've seen the size of your coffeehouse, I can then start contacting them."

"If you could firm up the list of artists willing to participate in a week's time, that would be ideal," Ivy told him. "I'd also like for you to choose which pieces will be on display and get pictures to me, I can set up a page on the Java Junction website to give the public a sneak peek. We can also do a little bit of advertising. On our dime, not yours," she assured Deke.

"Okay," Deke said, smiling broadly. "I think this will be an outlet my artists will look forward to. Can we meet again on Monday morning and start ironing out details? That should give me enough time to talk to my clients and have photographs of the art ready to go."

"Monday is good," Dax said, looking to her as she nodded.

"Why don't we meet at Java Junction at nine on Monday?" Deke suggested.

"That works for us," Ivy said.

They shook hands with Deke and left the gallery, returning to her car.

"That went smoothly," she noted.

Dax chuckled. "All except the putting stuff on the website part. Believe it or not, I don't even have a website. It's been on the back burner to do. I know everywhere else has one. I simply wanted to get the doors of Java Junction open. Since customers have been coming in, the website simply slipped my mind. With these fusion nights, however, it would be smart to have a website. I'll have to hustle to find someone who can set one up for me."

"Look no further," she told him. "Besides working at the art gallery, I also have done website and graphic design on the side. I've created Harper's Weddings with Hart new website. I've also been working on updating the Lost Creek Vineyards' website, too. Dad even has me designing some new labels for various wines already in place, and I'll work on designs for the new wines created for this coming year."

"I have no idea what all that involves, but I'll definitely pay you to put together a website for me. Don't even think about doing this for free."

"I'll charge you a fair price, Dax. We can work on the site together this weekend. Once you purchase the domain name and we get a host, they're actually fairly easy to build."

She pulled into a parking spot close to Java Junction.

"That sounds good," he said. "I also need to find some musicians to play. And you did promise to introduce me to country music. How do we go about doing both?"

"Let me think about the musicians. In the meantime, we can go down to Boerne to listen to some country music tonight or tomorrow night." She grinned. "There might be dancing involved."

Dax groaned. "I don't dance."

"Do you have two left feet?"

"I have no idea. Remember, I was the DJ behind the turntable. I always was the one playing the music, never dancing to it."

Ivy started to ask about high school dances and then recalled he spoke about how much he'd worked growing up. She doubted he'd ever attended a dance because of that.

"I'll teach you how to dance," she offered casually. "You already like music as it is. Dancing is merely an extension of enjoying a song. Who knows? It might give you a different appreciation for music and even aid your song-writing."

"When would you like me to pick you up?"

Ivy hesitated a moment. She had not really talked to anyone about the fact that she was seeing Dax. Harper had pressed her after she had gone to Blackwood BBQ for dinner with him, and she had told her sister that Dax was nice and she'd enjoyed his company.

Usually, Ivy told Harper everything. They were only six months apart in age and had been more like twins growing up. For some reason, though, she wanted to keep her relationship with Dax all to herself for a bit longer. Maybe she was being protective of it because of how sour her only serious relationship had turned out, but this one was something special, unlike anyone she'd ever been involved with. Not that she wanted to keep Dax a secret from her sister, family, and friends, but Ivy wanted to savor it a bit longer on her own before she introduced him into the fold.

"Let me swing by and pick you up," she offered. "I know where I'm going, and you can sit back and enjoy the scenery on our way to Boerne."

"What am I supposed to wear?" he asked. "I don't own a pair of boots. I suppose they're mandatory."

"Most people will be in jeans and boots. Do you have a pair of loafers? You can't wear tennis shoes because they don't scoot across the ground easily."

"I do have an old pair of loafers. Jeans and loafers it is. What time? Is tonight good for you?"

"I'll close the tasting room at six. Sarah is working with me, and she would be happy to do all the closing for me. I'd need to run home and change and could get to you by six-thirty."

"It's a date," he said.

And this time, Ivy knew it would be.

13

Ivy finished up a tasting session with a couple about five-thirty. No one else was waiting. She had already told Sarah that she needed to leave at six because she had plans.

"I doubt anyone else will be coming in, Ivy," Sarah said. "Why don't you go ahead and take off, and I'll stay and close out and get things ready for tomorrow."

"You sure you don't mind?"

"Not a bit. It's a Friday night. Go have fun."

"I'll see you tomorrow then," she said since they were both working the Saturday shift this weekend.

Ivy drove home, glad she had a little bit of extra time to get ready. She took a brief shower and dressed in fresh clothes, donning jeans and boots with a black tank top. She freshened her makeup and dabbed on a bit of perfume, excitement filling her. Yes, she had gone out to dinner with Dax the other night but hadn't thought of it as a date. This would be the first time they were out in public as a couple. They might or might not run into someone from Lost Creek but if they did, word would certainly spread that they were together.

Ivy didn't mind that a bit.

It surprised her how much she was already invested in this relationship with Dax. Though they had only known each other for a few days, she believed she knew him better than most of her other friends. He had opened up to her from the beginning. She knew what was important to him, and she had also shared more of herself than she usually did with others. Tonight would be a test, of sorts. She would observe him in public. Most of their time together had been only in each other's company, and not everyone presented the same face to the world that they showed in private. Something told her, though, that Dax was who he was, an open book to others, even though he had quickly let down his walls and allowed her in.

She wondered if she would be able to do the same with him. Not that she'd been hiding any part of herself from him, but she had never really trusted any man after Jay's betrayal. If any man could change her mind, it would be Dax Tennyson.

She brushed her teeth and applied a fresh coat of lipstick in a soft rose shade and then removed her driver's license and a credit card from her wallet and slipped both inside her phone case. Her car key went in a pocket. That way, she wouldn't have to keep up with a purse at the dance hall. She had already texted Braden earlier in the day to let him know she wouldn't be home for dinner this evening, but she went to the kitchen now just to say good-bye, having heard him in there earlier.

He stood at the stove, stirring something which smelled delicious, but looked up as she entered.

"You look nice," he said. "Going out with Dax Tennyson again? Harper said you had barbeque with him the other night."

She felt the blush tinge her cheeks. "Yes. We're going dancing. He's never been, and I promised to teach him how to two-step."

Braden shook his head, laughing. "I don't even know what that is, but I hope you have a great time with this guy, Ivy." He paused, studying her a moment. "You really like him, don't you?"

"I really do," she said aloud, owning it.

"You know Harper and I will want to meet him."

Hesitation fluttered through her. "I want that, too, Braden, but I'm not ready for that to happen just yet. This may seem hard to understand—especially because I share everything with Harper—but beginning a new relationship with Dax? I want something for myself. I don't know if Harper has told you, but it's been eons since I dated, much less had a serious relationship. I don't want to mess this up."

"I get that. You're being protective of something new and fragile. Right now, it's something blossoming between you and Dax. You don't want outside interference. You aren't looking for anyone's opinion. You need to feel your way with him and decide if it's something you want to pursue. Something that might have a chance to last."

Ivy nodded. "You get it. Not many people would have that kind of insight." She hesitated. "I also don't want to steal the spotlight from Harper and you. She went through such a rough time and was gutted by everything that happened with Ath. The fact you came along and seemed to wash away all the ugliness in her life has really made all the difference. I want Harper to enjoy her relationship with you. I want her to heal emotionally with your help. Between Harper starting her own event planning business and seeing you, I'm watching as she blossoms. Right now, I don't want to put anything else on her plate. When the time is right, I'll tell her about Dax and me. For now, though, I want to keep things simple. And quiet."

Braden smiled wryly. "You do realize you're living in Lost Creek again. Even though I've only lived her a short time, I understand the gossip which is churned at the mill here. If you're seen in public with Dax, word is going to get back to Harper."

She thought of how Shelly Blackwood at the diner knew Dax had brought lunch to Ivy and was surprised the gossip generated with that hadn't already reached her sister's ears.

"I know that," she admitted. "And I promise I'll talk to her about it. I'm glad I was able to share what I could now with you, Braden. You've become a good friend to me, and I value your opinion."

"Then I think I might need to get to know Dax. Outside of his relationship with you. After all, we're both the new guys in town. Maybe we'll bond, and I'll make myself a new friend."

Her brother Todd used to be the one who checked out the boys interested in Harper and her. At this moment, a wave of sadness dropped a shadow over her, thinking how Todd's life had been cut short. How he would never dance at her wedding or be an uncle to her children. She looked to Braden, and Ivy saw he was gently stepping into Todd's shoes. That he was not only a friend but a big brother figure to her. Harper was a lucky woman to have Braden Clark in her life.

"You need to go," he urged. "But I will be stopping by the coffeehouse and making Dax Tennyson's acquaintance."

She smiled. "Then I hope he receives the Braden Clark seal of approval."

Ivy went to her car and texted Dax that she was on her way. She pulled up outside Java Junction and found him waiting. Her heart fluttered wildly, seeing how handsome he was in a tan shirt and jeans molded to his legs and butt.

He got in the car and beamed at her. "You look amazing, Ivy," he complimented.

"You clean up nicely yourself, Dallas," she told him. "I've only seen you in shorts and T-shirts up to this point."

"Hey, I told you I kept a couple of my business suits and a sports jacket. If you like this look, you'll go crazy for me in a tie."

She laughed aloud, feeling sheer joy being with this man.

"So, tell me where we're going. You mentioned

Boerne? I actually drove through there when I was hunting for a place to settle. From what I recall, it seems like a nice town."

"It is. Boerne is similar in size to Lost Creek, with about twenty thousand residents. The dance hall we're going to is probably four or five miles north of town, so we won't be going into Boerne itself."

"Okay, educate me on what I need to know tonight, Professor. What should I expect?"

"It's a Friday night, so Renegade Roadhouse will have a decent crowd. They usually have one band which plays both Friday and Saturday nights. Those are the only two nights you can listen to live music there. The rest of the time, they play canned music."

"With a DJ?"

She nodded. "Last time I was there, they did have a DJ, but that was quite a while ago. I'm not sure what the setup is these days, but Renegade Roadhouse is the closest place to go dancing."

"Who are some of your favorite country artists?" he asked. "I need to start boning up on my country music knowledge."

"They'll always be those classic artists and songs. Johnny Cash and *Ring of Fire*. Brad Paisley's *Whiskey Lullaby*. Garth Brooks singing *Friends in Low Places*. *Guitars, Cadillacs* from Dwight Yoakam. Since this is Texas, though, George Strait is absolutely King. You might have heard his *All My Ex's Live in Texas*."

He shook his head. "I've heard the title but not the song. What are some of his songs that you like?"

She reeled off several without hesitation. *"Carrying Your Love With Me. Check Yes or No. Carried Away. You Look So Good in Love.* Honestly? There's not a bad George Strait song. I'm sure you'll hear some of his music tonight. No band worth its salt would play at Renegade Roadhouse and *not* play George Strait."

"I guess that means the bands which play there are cover bands?" he asked.

"For the most part. They may play a song or two which is original, but people like to dance to the tried and true."

"I'm familiar with some country artists' names. Dolly Parton. Tim McGraw. Who are some more recent country singers you enjoy listening to?"

Ivy noticed he'd taken out his phone and jotted down a few songs she'd mentioned. She liked that about Dax. He was thorough. Prepared.

"Once again, being in Texas, I would have to mention Miranda Lambert. Some other contemporary acts that I follow are Dierks Bentley, Big and Rich, Chris Stapleton, Rascal Flatts. And definitely Pat Green and the Zac Brown Band. I also absolutely adore Darius Rucker's voice. That man can sing anything and give you the feels."

"Hootie? Now, that's a name I know. *Cracked Rear Mirror* is a classic album to me. As a DJ, I've played a ton of Hootie and the Blowfish songs."

"He may have been a pop star first, but he's got a solid fan base in country now," she told him. "If you'd like, I can put together a playlist for you."

"That would be terrific," he said. "As you said, if I'm going to eventually perform here, I need to add some country songs to my repertoire. See which acts have songs suited to my voice and range. It'll be different if I play ones in the coffeehouse as a solo act versus if I'm able to pull a band together."

"I did a little research on how to locate local musicians when we hit a lull in the tasting room this afternoon."

Ivy went on to tell Dax how people advertised on community sites within Craigslist and Reddit, looking for others to add to an existing band or creating one from scratch.

"There's also a website which is a national musicians' finder site. It was a lot more specific, looking for exact types to add to an existing group, for the most part. Like a left-handed bass player for alternative rock, for example."

"What I want is something a lot more loosey-goosey," he said. "Just a group who gets together and enjoys playing music. Maybe performing at a wedding or small club on the weekends, if that. Frankly, I think I'm going to put the whole band idea on hold for now, so I can focus on my own singing and songwriting and these fusion nights."

"I was also fiddling around with names for those nights," Ivy said. "If we're going to advertise this on your website—which we'll put together these weekend—we should call it something other than fusion night."

"What do you suggest?"

"I played with a few names. If you don't like any of them, it's fine."

She named five or six ideas she'd toyed with, gauging his reaction to each.

"You put a lot of thought into this," he said. "I liked Sips, Strokes, and Songs, but that might be a little too much of a mouthful. The two I liked best are Harmony & Hues and Brushstrokes & Beats, but I'm leaning toward Harmony& Hues."

"That was my first choice, Dallas," she said, smiling at him.

"Then let's go with it."

They talked a few minutes about the website's design. The colors he wanted to feature, along with the vibe he wanted it to have. Ivy told him she had a couple of fonts in mind to show him, and based upon the color scheme he favored, there would be a nice palette of colors which would be easy to draw from and complement one another.

They arrived at Renegade Roadhouse, where the parking lot was already two-thirds full at seven o'clock on a Friday night.

Dax came around and opened her door for her, and Ivy thought in all the times she'd been with Jay, he had never done so a single time.

"You're still going to make me dance, aren't' you?" he asked.

Grinning, she asked, "What's the point of visiting a dance hall if you don't dance? Don't worry. We can grab a table if one is available. If not, we can stand on the side-lines and let you observe some of the dancers while we enjoy the music and a beer. But I am determined to get you out on the dance floor, Dallas."

Ivy hoped since Dax enjoyed music so much that he

would have a feel for the beat. That made all the difference in dancing.

She slipped her cell into the back pocket of her jeans, and they entered the venue. The band was playing a tune by the Chicks, and the dance floor had two dozen couples moving about it.

"Okay, wine snob. What kind of beer do you drink?" Dax asked.

"I'll take a Shiner Bock."

They moved to the bar, and he ordered two Shiners, paying for them as the bartender handed over the bottles.

Dax threaded his fingers through hers and led them to one of the few empty tables left.

"Who is this?" he asked, and she knew he meant the song the band was playing.

"It's *Save a Horse. Ride a Cowboy*. By Big and Rich. A real boot-scooter."

Taking a sip of his beer, he nodded. "I like it."

They listened to three songs, and Ivy saw Dax observing various couples dancing, his eyes following a particularly good pair.

He turned and met her gaze. "I don't know what they just did. I doubt I'll ever be able to pull it off."

Laughing, she told him, "That's the pretzel. And I won't ask you to even try it on your first night."

"I think I've picked up the basics. Run me through what I should know before I get out there and make a fool of myself." He took another sip of his beer.

"Pretty much everything you see out there is called the two-step, the most popular country dance. Basically, you'll be the leader. I'm the follower. Your left hand will join my right, and your right hand will go around to rest on my shoulder blade."

Dax glanced back at the dance floor. "Not every guy's hand is on a shoulder blade," he commented drily.

"Well, that's where it's supposed to be. Sometimes, couples who are a little more familiar with one another? The guy's hand dips down to the girl's hip. Or even her ass."

He gave her a wicked smile. "I'll start in a proper position, but I can't guarantee where my hand will wind up by the end of the dance."

Ivy laughed, loving every minute she spent in Dax's company. She skimmed the dance floor and picked out a couple.

"See the girl in the white blouse and the guy in the red shirt? Follow them for one complete turn around the room."

Dax watched the couple intently. After they'd made a circle around the ballroom, he said, "Talk to me, Professor. Give me the color commentary as I watch them make a second pass."

"You move your feet four times. Quick, quick then slow, slow. Quick, quick. Slow. Slow."

She repeated the phrase several times, matching it to the rhythm of the couple he watched.

"Okay. Got it."

"Notice how he's not directly across from her. He's slightly to her left. That's so as they slide their feet, they're staggered and won't bump into one another."

"Ah, I get it. A way to protect toes. Smart."

"More experienced couples keep to the outside of the circle, while other, less talented ones stay in the middle."

"Got it. We're definitely middle people tonight. I see everyone goes counterclockwise," he noted.

"Yes. You don't want to alter that and be a fish swimming upstream, fighting the crowd. That's really all there is to it. The two-step is pretty simple. If you get that down tonight, I'll be happy."

"Show me some other stuff couples are doing."

She pointed out a woman wearing a purple blouse and said, "That's a sweetheart dip."

The man dipped the woman several times, and then Ivy chose another couple. "That's called behind the back. Green shirt at nine o'clock? That's the spin out."

"Okay, I won't try anything fancy tonight, but it actually seems pretty simple. All except that pretzel." He pretended to shiver. "That one's beyond me." His smiled turned wicked. "Of course, if you give me private dance lessons, I might be able to figure it out. All that getting twisted and untwisted could prove interesting."

"That'll cost you," she said, laughing.

He waggled his eyebrows. "Can I pay off my bill in kisses?"

Although he was teasing, a rush of desire shot through Ivy.

Flirting, she said, "I will definitely hold you to that." She drained the last of her beer and set the bottle on the table. Standing, she said, "Come on, Dax. It's time to put on your dancing shoes and take a twirl about the room."

14

Ivy moved them to the center ring of the dance floor. Dax had always been a quick study and had watched enough couples to have down the two-step. He had always felt music in his soul, and his body was itching to move to the tune the band would play next. As a DJ, he had known to put on certain songs, ones which would get a crowd up on its feet and out on the dance floor at a wedding or party, but being exposed to world of country music was a new thrill. Already, he was being inspired by the melodies he'd heard tonight.

And inspired by this lovely woman whose hand he now held.

The band struck up another lively song, and he faced Ivy, holding her right hand and placing his free one against her shoulder blade. She wore a tight, black tank top, which meant his palm rested on bare, smooth skin. She had a wonderful, hourglass figure, showed off to perfection by the black tank and worn jeans, which were molded to her every curve.

"Ready?" she asked.

He nodded, counting in his head, and then Dax pushed his right foot forward, along the smooth, concrete floor. For most of the song, he did count the beat, aware of the quick, quick, then slow, slow movement. He made certain to stagger their feet so that he didn't trample on her toes.

Then near the end of the song, everything seemed to kick in for him. He quit counting in his head and merely felt the beat, the rhythm of the song keeping his feet moving in correct time. The tune ended and Dax stopped moving Ivy around the dance floor, but he continued to hold on to her. Gazing into her hazel eyes, he found them an unusual green shade now. The exertion of the dance had her face flushed, making her even more appealing than before.

The band moved into another song, which immediately had the crowd cheering.

Dax leaned toward Ivy so he could be heard and asked, "What's this?"

"*Wagon Wheel*," she replied, smiling widely. "A Darius Rucker song. As you can tell, it's a favorite for people to dance to."

The couples on the crowded floor began moving to the music, many of them singing along. While he hadn't ever heard the song and was unable to join in singing to it, he caught their enthusiasm, maneuvering Ivy around the room with more confidence now.

By the time the third song started, he was comfortable

ALEXA ASTON

with the movements of the two-step and surprised Ivy
with a quick dip. Dax pulled her back up, hearing the
laughter bubble up from her. He needed to hear her laugh.
He craved everything about Ivy. Though he had promised
to take things slow with her, all he wanted was this woman
in his bed—and one uninterrupted night with her in it.

After a fourth song, he led her from the dance floor,
slipping his arm about her waist and moving his lips close
to her ear, where he said, "Dancing is hard work. I need a
drink."

She laughed again, her eyes sparkling. Dax wanted to
freeze this moment in time. The way Ivy looked. The way
his heart beat as he gazed at her. The feeling of complete-
ness which engulfed him, being with her. He'd thought he
had loved Shailene, but after years of being with her, his
feelings toward her paled in comparison to what Ivy
stirred within him. Dax had never bought into the term
soul mate, but Ivy was fast becoming this to him. There
was an easiness between them, almost as if they didn't
have to work at anything. He had never been so comfortable around anyone in his life.

His gut told him he better figure out the way to spend
the rest of his life with Ivy Hart.

He led her to the bar and ordered two more Shiner
Bocks. By now, Renegade Roadhouse was packed, so they
took their beers and found a small opening against the
wall. Dax squeezed into it, placing Ivy in front of him.
One arm snaked about her waist, holding her close to him
as they sipped their beers and listened to the music.

The band took a much-needed break after the song ended, promising to return in a quarter-hour. Voices buzzed about them, but Dax and Ivy didn't need to say a word. He merely held her against him as they finished their beers and handed the empty bottles to a passing server.

She looked over her shoulder. "I'm going to go to the restroom. Be right back."

"Good idea. I'll do the same."

They returned to the dance floor when the band did, confidence brimming through Dax as they began dancing again. He was grateful Ivy had told him to wear loafers because it was easy to glide along the floor in them. He supposed now that he was in Hill Country, he should invest in a good pair of boots. Hopefully, Ivy would take him shopping and recommend a decent pair to him. Even though Dallas was in Texas, the city was cosmopolitan. While he had seen men wearing boots on occasion there, he had always heard the gateway to the west was through Ft. Worth. He'd DJ'd a few weddings in Ft. Worth and recalled how men had worn boots to the reception with their tuxedos.

The next hour passed quickly as they spent the entire time on the dance floor. Dax enjoyed himself tremendously. He tried a few more dips and even attempted the sweetheart and spin out with success, much to Ivy's delight. He did want some quiet time with her, though, and when the band took their next break, he asked if she might be ready to leave.

"I was about to suggest the same thing," she told him. "I'm worn out. I haven't danced that much in ages."

He led her back to the bar again, where he asked the bartender for two bottled waters and paid for them. Dax opened one and handed it to Ivy and then did the same for himself.

They left Renegade Roadhouse and returned to her car. Dax opened her car door and assisted Ivy into the driver's seat before coming around and taking his spot on the passenger's side.

She didn't start the car. Instead, she downed the rest of her water, so he did the same. They set their empties in the cupholder. Ivy also pulled her phone from her back pocket and set it in a tray.

Starting the car, she eased it from the parking lot. Several couples had spilled outside during this break, and Ivy weaved around them carefully, turning onto the highway to head back to Lost Creek.

They didn't speak a word, and it was a comfortable silence. Dax had been on dates when silence had cropped up, and he'd desperately thought of new topics to introduce to fill in the awkward void. That wasn't necessary with Ivy. He wanted to take her hand, but the country road was dark. He knew Ivy was a responsible, conscientious driver, more comfortable with both hands on the wheel. He was glad he hadn't done so when some animal darted across the road in front of them, a blur in the headlights.

"What was that?" he asked, as she swung into the other lane and back into their own.

"Looked like a deer," she replied. "The Hill Country is full of them. They're active at night. You always have to be alert when you're driving after dark."

They settled back into silence until they arrived in Lost Creek, and she eased into a parking spot in front of Java Junction. One light burned inside, illuminating part of the bar.

"Want to come in for something cold to drink?" he asked, wanting to extend the evening. "I know one water wasn't enough for me."

Ivy gazed at him, her eyes large and luminous. "All right."

He escorted her inside the coffeehouse, wanting to take her upstairs to his apartment but knowing if he did, more would happen between them than should at this point.

Dax moved behind the bar. "What would you like?"

"I'll leave it in your hands, but I'd prefer tea over coffee."

He chuckled. "I've got to convert my girlfriend from being a tea drinker to a coffee one, else all of Lost Creek will be gossiping about how my coffee isn't good enough for her."

"Am I your girlfriend, Dax?" Ivy asked quietly.

He leaned over, cupping her cheek. "You know you are. I've told you I want to see you. Only you." A flicker of doubt passed through him. "Have you changed your mind about us?"

"No." She smiled wistfully. "I just haven't been a girl-friend in a very long time."

"I don't think the term girlfriend really fits what we have, Ivy," he said, wanting to convey his strong feelings to her.

This time, he saw doubt in her eyes, and he knew he needed to correct whatever false impression he'd given her.

She spoke quickly, though. "I know. It's too soon." She pulled away from him. "You haven't been divorced that long. You don't want to leap back into another relationship too fast. And I don't want to be your rebound girl. I better go."

Turning, Ivy walked away briskly.

Dax leaped over the bar and rushed after her, catching her wrist and turning her to face him.

"Don't go," he pleaded.

A long moment passed, the air crackling with the electricity between them. Then he felt her relaxing.

"I don't want to make any mistakes with you, Dax," she said, laying her soul bare to him. "I have a lot of tarnish on me when it comes to dating. I'm not sure I even remember how to be in a relationship. I've focused on my career and let personal relationships slide for years."

He released her wrist, bringing his hands up to frame her face. "I don't mean to frighten you, Ivy, but what I feel for you is really strong. Something I've never experienced before. It's hard for me to even put it into words because these feelings are so new to me."

He stroked her cheeks. "I'm not comparing you in any way to Shailene. That part of my life is over and done. It's almost as if I've shed my skin and become a new person here in Lost Creek. Or maybe I'm the person I always have been, layers buried beneath layers, hiding who I was. But I will tell you this. I've never had feelings for anyone as strong as I now have for you. I wake up every morning, and the first thing I think of is you. When something good happens, I want you to be the first person to hear about it. I know we agreed to move slowly, but it's the hardest thing I've ever had to do. All I want is to show you how much you mean to me."

Dax brought his lips to hers for a long, tender kiss. He broke it, his mouth hovering just above hers.

"I want to make love to you, Ivy."

"I want that, too, Dax," she said softly.

"I think we should wait, though," he said firmly. "I want to give us more time. To make certain this is right."

But in his heart, Dax knew it wouldn't matter if a day passed—or a thousand of them. They were destined to be together.

He wrapped his arms around her, kissing her again, long and slow. Ivy fit against him as if she were made to do so, and in a way which told Dax his gut wasn't leading him astray.

Breaking the kiss, he gazed at her. "Let me get that tall tea for you."

He clasped her hand, leading her to a nearby loveseat.

"Stay here. I'll be right back."

Preparing two passionflower teas, he returned to her.

Ivy took one sip. "This is delicious. I don't think I've ever had a cold tea which was this refreshing."

Dax sat next to her, slipping his arm around her shoulders. They talked for half an hour, drinking their teas.

Ivy mentioned getting together in order to build the website, wanting his input.

"When are you working tomorrow?" he asked.

"I'll be at the tasting room from eleven to seven. We have extended hours on the weekends. I know you're busy on a Saturday morning. Maybe tomorrow night?"

"Come over when you get off work. I'll order us a pizza."

"*No* anchovies," she blurted out, causing him to chuckle.

"What do you like on your pizza? That's something I need to know."

Grinning, she said, "Anything *but* anchovies," causing him to laugh again.

"Okay. I'll surprise you then. What do I need to do to prepare regarding this website?"

"Just have a credit card ready to go. Also, be thinking about the name. I can guarantee you that Java Junction has already been taken, so you'll need to put your own spin on the website's name. Each domain name needs to be purchased, and then you pay an annual fee to maintain the rights to it."

"I'll have pizza and credit card in hand tomorrow night," he promised. Dax kissed her softly. "You need to get home."

He walked Ivy to her car.

"Thanks again for teaching me how to two-step. I had a lot of fun tonight, Ivy. I enjoy being with you."

She slipped her arms around his neck and pulled him down to her, kissing him.

"I enjoyed every minute of tonight because I was with you."

Opening her door, she slipped behind the wheel. "See you tomorrow night."

Dax hoped he would see her sooner.

In his dreams...

15

Ivy squealed when Paloma and Arlo entered the tasting room. She rushed to greet them, hugging each of them tightly.

"I'm so glad you could make it," she said. "Thank you for coming. Have you checked into the B&B yet?"

"Yes," Arlo said. "Mrs. Bradley is very kind and introduced us to her cat Spooky. The rooms are lovely." He grabbed her shoulders and kissed her cheeks again. "We have missed you, *mio dolce amico*."

"I've missed both of you, too. Come meet Melanie."

She introduced them to Melanie, who was about to do a tasting with two couples, and then Ivy said, "Let me take you to the new tasting room. It's really coming along."

Waving to Melanie, Ivy drove her friends the short distance to the new structure and led them inside. She walked them through where the tasting bar would stand and then led them around the space, thankful no construction workers were present today. The crew was working simultaneously on the new event center and tasting room, and so she supposed they were at the event center now.

"Here is where there will be additional spaces for tastings. Long tables where a group can gather and be walked through various wines. We'll display award-winning wines in this area." Moving along, she added, "This is where there will be an area of tables for those who've completed their tastings to gather and sip on wines. There will be a bar located nearby for them to order fruit and cheese trays, along with wine by the glass or bottle."

Walking them further along, Ivy said, "This area is the gift shop."

"What kind of merchandise will you carry?" Paloma asked.

She indicated the shirt she wore, bearing the Lost Creek Vineyards logo. "Definitely shirts, such as this one, in an array of colors. T-shirts and sweatshirts, as well. We'll also have aprons. Ball caps and visors. All with the vineyard's logo. Barware such as cork stops and corkscrews. Wine charms. And plenty of different wine glasses."

Being from Italy, her friends were quite familiar with wines and the various types of glasses used with reds, whites, and rosés.

Paloma thought a moment. "How about bibs? Those would be cute."

"I love that idea," Ivy said, pulling out her cell and jotting a note.

"You've mentioned visitors come to the Hill Country to shop," Arlo said. "What about a Christmas ornament? Round ones could have the winery's logo on them. Or you could do tiny plastic wineglasses with the logo."

"Christmas ornaments are a great idea," Ivy exclaimed, opening the note she'd just closed and adding ornaments beneath where she'd typed bibs. "See, I needed the two of you here to spark new ideas."

"Besides wanting our fabulous company," Paloma teased.

"I have missed you. But come see the rest."

Ivy took them outside, explaining this would be where a covered patio area would stand. It would also have a bar outside.

"Harper wants to encourage people to make Lost Creek Winery a weekend destination, beyond the events held in the new center," she explained. "We've been talking with different merchants in town, such as The Cheese Connoisseur, and we'll offer different plates and picnic items for purchase, as well as wines. We'll have picnic tables scattered in that area. Eventually, Harper wants to bring in local bands to play on Friday and Saturday nights."

"It is all very exciting," Paloma said. She took Ivy's hand. "You seem very happy."

"I am," she assured her friend. "I didn't realize what a rut I'd gotten into at the gallery. I was there every day of the week. It was soul-sucking, and I didn't even realize it. Here, though, I've been able to make huge contributions to the design of the new tasting room. I've also made a few suggestions for Harper's event center. We think both venues will open in November. Possibly sooner."

"More importantly, are you painting again?" Arlo asked.

She nodded. "I'm definitely painting again. I have a few things to show you at the apartment I'm renting. I'm using it as a studio and renting a house with my sister and her boyfriend. I'll take you there soon. For now, come back to the tasting room with me. It's almost closing time there. I want you to try some of our wines."

They returned to the tasting room, where Melanie had finished up with the couples' tasting.

"It's almost six," Ivy said. "Go ahead and leave. I'll handle closing. Right now, I'm going to introduce my friends to some of Lost Creek Vineyards' best wines."

She took the next half-hour to share some of her favorites which the winery produced.

"You know we practically drank wine in our bottles," Arlo said. "We know good wines when we taste them. What your family is producing is top quality, Ivy. I am impressed."

"I agree," Paloma said. "Arlo has always favored reds, while whites have been my go-to. I actually enjoyed the reds we sampled, and I am crazy about your blends."

"We're becoming known for those blends," she shared. "We also have a new viticulturist from Napa who has been working with the vines this season. My dad has always been our chief winemaker, but he'll be promoting Braden to that position and stepping aside to concentrate more on the advertising and marketing end of the business."

Her friends offered to help her wash and dry the wine glasses they'd used, so Ivy allowed them to do so while she dealt with other housekeeping details. Tomorrow would be the first Saturday she hadn't worked since her return to Lost Creek, in part because her friends had come to town and also because she was going to help prepare for tomorrow's first fusion night at Java Junction.

When everything was set up for the tasting room's opening the next day, they left. Paloma rode with Ivy, while Arlo followed in his car. She took them to Black-wood BBQ, where they feasted on ribs, brisket, and pork. Paloma fell in love with the jalapeño chicken and shrimp poppers Shy brought to them.

"These are amazing," she raved, calling Shy back and having him explain how to put together the bacon-wrapped wonders.

"I can barely move," Arlo said, patting his belly. "I haven't eaten this much in a long time, but it was all so good. I would eat here three times a week if I lived in Lost Creek."

After they ate banana pudding for dessert, Ivy took them to the town square. She parked behind the hardware store but had them walk around to the side, where her finished mural was on display.

"You did this?" Arlo asked, his eyes roaming the brick wall. "It is amazing, Ivy."

"Thank you. I'd never taken on a project of this magnitude before. The size alone was a bit frightening, but once I got down the perspective, it went really fast."

"How much do you ask to paint something like this?" Paloma asked.

"Nothing. I thought it would be great advertising. Plus, visitors to town almost always come to the square to shop." She indicated the bottom, right corner. "See, I signed my name. We have a gallery in town, and I've spoken briefly with its owner about the possibility of carrying some of my paintings. I'd like to complete several more before I do so, though."

"Speaking of those, I want to see what you've done since you've left Houston."

"This way."

Ivy led them up the back staircase. She'd finished four paintings since she'd returned to Lost Creek, all of them landscapes of the Hill Country. Two leaned against a wall. Another sat on the coffee table. The final one remained on an easel and was the one she planned to display it at Java Junction tomorrow night, along with the painting of Lost Creek Lake. That one was her gift to Dax, and he would hang it on the wall in the coffeehouse permanently.

Her friends went to each of the four paintings, studying them carefully. Ivy worried her bottom lip as they did so. Arlo and Paloma were no pushovers. If they praised her efforts, she would know she was on the right track.

Finally, they completed their viewing. Paloma threw her arms about Ivy.

"These are so good!" she declared. "They speak to me, Ivy. It is your soul on the canvas."

"I agree," Arlo seconded. "I can tell this place is home

to you. It's evident in every brushstroke. And your colors are amazing. I have never seen a sunset such as this."

She grinned. "Well, we get them all the time here in Lost Creek. I have felt inspired, returning to my roots. I've taken my sketchbook and simply driven around, capturing different scenery. It gives me a lot of options as I decide what I'll be painting next."

"May I see it?" Arlo asked. "Only if you wish to share it, that is."

"Of course."

Ivy retrieved the sketchbook, handing it to him. Arlo sat on the couch, Paloma beside him, turning the pages, murmuring and nodding. The siblings looked at one another, some silent communication passing between them.

Paloma spoke up. "Do not contract with this local gallery owner," she begged. "Let Arlo and me sell your paintings."

She shook her head emphatically. "No, I'm sorry. I can't have them displayed where I once worked. I don't want a single penny going into Lawson Everhart's pocket. I refuse to have him represent my work."

Arlo beamed at her. "But that is the beauty of how life works out, Ivy. Paloma and I only have a week left to go working for Lawson. How else do you think we managed to take the time off to come and visit you this weekend?"

"Really? You both found jobs somewhere else?"

"I am going to San Francisco," Arlo revealed. "Paloma has found a position in Dallas."

"That means we should have two different outlets for

your work," Paloma told her. "Your native Texas and the west coast. I think you should keep painting for now. Let us become established at our new galleries. Then we can each show the directors examples of your work. A Dallas exhibition should come first, don't you agree, Arlo?"

"Yes, because Ivy's paintings are of Texas. It would give her firmer footing. Then we could broaden your audience with my gallery in California."

Excitement filled her. "You really think I could have showings at your new places of employment?"

"You are that good, Ivy," Arlo confirmed. "Landscapes are very popular with clients. You know that. I think here in Texas people will clamor for your work. It will be familiar places to them, but your take will be fresh and exciting."

"But you need a decent number of paintings before I would think to approach my new boss," Paloma said. "You yourself know how many paintings you would look at with artists, picking and choosing only from their very best, as you selected the paintings for a showing."

"I will certainly keep working," she assured the pair. "I do have one more mural to paint, though. That will probably take me two weeks or so."

"Where? What will you paint?" Paloma asked.

"I don't know if you looked around the places on the square, but a coffeehouse is diagonally across from where we are."

She led them to the window and pointed out Java Junction.

"The owner has asked me to paint a mural on his brick

wall. I'm going to focus on Texas wildflowers. Bluebonnets, of course, will be the most prominent ones featured. They are the state flower and so prevalent here in the Hill Country. But I'll include others, too, such as Indian paintbrush, Brown-eyed Susans, spotted beebalm, and lantana."

Retrieving her phone, Ivy pulled up a few websites so her friends could see the beautiful colors of Texas wildflowers.

"We don't see these in Houston," Paloma said. "They are all gorgeous. Such variety of colors. You must paint these wildflowers, Ivy. Not only on your mural but in your landscapes, as well."

"Oh, I plan to. I believe everything I paint from now on will be rooted in Texas and what is found in nature here." She paused. "I have something I want to invite you to attend tomorrow night. I asked you to come this weekend specifically because of it."

"What is it?"

"I've been seeing the owner of the coffeehouse. The man who commissioned the mural outside his place. We've come up with an idea to bring music and art together, and we're calling it Harmony & Hues. Harmony for the music. Hues for the artwork. I'm sure you've done an art walk before. Instead of going from store to store, all the art will be located inside Java Junction. People can come view paintings and sculptures and also listen to some local talent perform."

"This idea is very interesting," Arlo said.

Paloma snorted. "We can talk about the idea later. I want to hear about this man."

Ivy laughed. "His name is Dax Tennyson. He's from Dallas. He quit his accounting job and wanted a simpler life, which is how he ended up in Lost Creek. He opened Java Junction back in March. The fusion nights will be held a couple of Saturdays each month during the summer, in order to take advantage of the local tourists coming through. If they become popular, they'll continue into fall."

Once again, Ivy tapped a few keys on her cell, calling up the new website she'd designed for Java Junction. She went to the Harmony & Hues page and handed over her phone.

"You can see the different art which will be displayed tomorrow night," she explained, "as well as pictures of the artists who created them, along with brief biographies."

"I will need to study this," Arlo said. "And we most certainly will come tomorrow night. Not only to see your art on display but to meet Dax."

Her face softened at the mention of his name, and Paloma laughed. "Look at you, going all dewy-eyed just hearing his name. I cannot wait to meet your Dax, Ivy."

She glanced at her watch. "It's almost closing time at Java Junction. Dax told me to bring you by for a cup of coffee and a chat."

Paloma's eyes sparkled. She slipped her arm through Ivy's. "I thought the glow surrounding you was due to the fact you were painting again. I think your art is only a part of your new happiness, Ivy. I already like this Dax. Let's go meet him in person."

16

Nerves were about to get the best of Dax. He had awakened with them, and they had continued to swell within him as the day progressed, moving toward a crescendo which he hoped would not shatter him in front of those who had turned out for Harmony & Hues tonight.

He walked about the coffeehouse now, looking at the placement of art, which Deke Manchester had arranged. The gallery owner obviously knew what was aesthetically pleasing, and each bit of art on display was being shown in a flattering way. Deke had even suggested to Dax where to hang Ivy's painting of the lake. Pausing in front of the landscape now, Dax thought of the lake's calm waters, hoping it would soothe him.

After a moment of deep, slow breathing, he continued to move about Java Junction, taking in all the art on display, from paintings on their easels to a few sculptures and a table of jewelry.

People were just starting to enter the coffeehouse again. He had closed it from four to six in order for Deke to work his magic, as well as giving some of the musicians a chance to run through their brief sets again.

He was the only one who had yet to play.

Dax had done so to an empty coffeehouse the last two nights, however. After Ivy and her friends Paloma and Arlo had left last night, he had locked the doors and fetched his guitar, running through the two songs he intended to sing this evening. The time spent with Sylvia had been well worth it. Already, Dax heard a quality in his voice which had been missing in the past. With no formal voice training, he hadn't known a thing about the exercises and warmups a singer should do before a performance. He had reported faithfully to Sylvia three times a week over the past three weeks and knew his voice was more than ready for tonight's challenge.

He'd decided to give people between six and seven to enter the coffeehouse and view the art on display. At seven, the first act would go on. Dax had found a few from Craigslist, as Ivy had suggested. Others had been drawn from Sylvia's students. A dry run of the musical portion of Harmony and Hues had been held three nights ago, and everything had gone smoothly. If everyone played and sang exactly as they had during rehearsal, the first fusion night at Java Junction would be a roaring success.

Moving to Deke, Dax asked, "Everything good from your end?"

"Absolutely," the gallery owner responded. "This was a fantastic idea, Dax. Something the town needed in order to support the arts. I hope not only tonight is a success but that you'll continue Harmony & Hues nights well beyond summer."

"We'll have to see how it goes, Deke. Thank you again for staging the art for me."

"Happy to do it. Now, let's hope it sells."

Dax checked in at the barista bar next. Scott Bartlett assured him that everything was under control.

"We have plenty of coffee and tea," his weekend manager assured him. "Jeanine and Sean are busy, as you can see, and I'll pitch in, too." Scott glanced to his right. "Looks like I'm needed now. Good luck, buddy."

Scott slapped Dax on the shoulder and moved behind the bar, greeting the next customer in line.

He went to Ivy now, who was talking with two women who looked to be close to her age. One had brilliant aquamarine eyes and blond hair. The other had raven hair and gray eyes.

"Hey," he said, slipping his hand against the small of Ivy's back and kissing her on the cheek.

She pinkened slightly, and Dax wished he could take her upstairs and really kiss her the way he wanted to.

The two women eyed him with interest as Ivy said, "Dax, let me introduce you to two friends of mine. Both of them teach elementary school in Lost Creek. This is Finley Farrow and Emerson Frost."

Shaking hands with both, he asked Finley, "You wouldn't happen to be related to Sam and Dianne?"

She smiled. "They're my parents and the reason I got into education in the first place."

"Finley also is a terrific photographer," Ivy shared. "I've used her to shoot photos for Harper's website. She'll also be available to photograph weddings and other events once the center opens. Harper is also trying to convince Emerson to be Weddings with Hart's exclusive cake baker."

"That has to be monumental task," he said. "Wedding cakes are so tall and intricate."

Laughing, Emerson said, "They can be, but I enjoy the challenge each cake brings. I work on weekends at The Bake House. In fact, I've put together the boxes of bakery items you sell here at Java Junction. Ethel is appreciative of your steady business."

"How would you have time to teach and work weekends for Ethel and still bake wedding cakes?" he wondered aloud.

"I haven't given Harper an answer yet," Emerson told him. "It's a lot to think about, and I am loyal to Ethel."

Arlo and Paloma arrived, joining their circle. Dax greeted the siblings and asked what they'd been doing today.

"Besides buying wines at Lost Creek Winery?" Arlo asked. "Paloma has bought out entire shops on the square," he joked.

"Lost Creek is a charming place," his sister said. "I cannot help it if I find so much appealing to me." She indicated what she wore. "I found this." Raising her arm, she showed off the bracelet she sported. "And this."

"If you like that style of jewelry, something similar is on display in the corner," Dax informed her. Smiling, he added, "It is for sale."

Arlo clucked his tongue. "Here we go again. Come, Paloma. Let us view the art, including this jewelry."

After they left, Finley said, "I was invited tonight by one of my former students. I teach fifth grade, and a student I taught the first year is singing with her sister this evening."

"You must mean Carolyn and Marcy. Their harmonies are angelic," Dax said. "And Marcy is a fine guitarist in her own right," he praised.

Emerson said, "We also need to stroll through the art. Nice to meet you, Dax. Hope we can visit with you and Ivy later."

Once the two departed, he removed his hand from Ivy's back and entwined his fingers with hers. "Your friends seemed interested in us."

"I'd mentioned to them that we were seeing one another, but I'm sure they'll be grilling me now." She squeezed his hand. "I will definitely let them know you are taken."

"Do me a favor, will you?"

"Anything." Ivy glanced around. "I think everything looks perfect tonight. What else do you think needs to be done?"

"No, it's something I want you to subtly bring up with Emerson. It's about Ethel. She hasn't looked well to me recently. She's a feisty, proud woman, and I don't really know her well enough to pry and see if anything is wrong or not. I'd like to help her in any way I can, however."

"I'll see if Emerson knows anything," she promised. "Emerson had become Ethel's right hand since she started working weekends at the bakery. I know that's why she's hesitating about quitting and filling orders solely for Harper. If anyone will know anything about Ethel's health, it will be Emerson."

He brushed his lips against her cheek again. "I better go mingle. The table in the center, where you first listened to me play, is marked reserved. It's for you. I want to be able to look out and see you there."

"You are going to be wonderful tonight, Dax. I know it."

Dax circulated through the coffeehouse, seeing that the line moved briskly as coffees and teas were ordered, greeting those he knew and meeting others for the first time.

Sylvia appeared at his elbow. She had come to the rehearsal on Wednesday and given a few of the singers a note or two. Sylvia hadn't questioned Dax when he did not perform alongside the others.

"You've got a lovely crowd tonight," she said. "I've already strolled along the art on display and have decided I may have to purchase something for myself."

"You know to go through Deke?" he asked.

"Yes. I'd already seen everything available on your website, but I wanted to view what interested me in person. We'll see if I get the work I want or if I'm outbid."

"No bidding tonight," he informed her. "At least this time around. All you need to do is agree to the price Deke has set, and he'll mark it as sold. You can go into his gallery tomorrow and pay for and pick up your artwork."

"I really like the painting of Lost Creek Lake hanging on your wall. I saw Ivy painted it."

"She gifted it to me. It's the first painting of hers which I saw."

"I hear she's going to be doing another mural for you, similar to the one she did for Charles Bennett."

"Yes. I run by that mural every day and thought it would be special to have something along Java Junction's wall, as well. Ivy told me she wanted to run with Texas wildflowers. We sat and looked at photographs of different ones, and she let me help decide which flowers to be included."

Sylvia took Dax's hand. "I know you're nervous, but you have been faithful in doing your exercises. I've seen tremendous gains in your voice since you first came to me. Remember, you want to enjoy yourself this evening. This first fusion night is one of celebration. You've written and will perform two wonderful songs. Relish the fact you have a venue where you are bringing the Lost Creek community together through Harmony & Hues. Be open. Vulnerable. Those gathered tonight will enjoy your music."

"Thanks for the pep talk, Coach," he teased.

Half an hour had passed, and Dax decided to address the crowd. He moved to the microphone and turned it on, tapping it to gain the attention of the room.

"Hello, everyone. I'm Dax Tennyson, owner of Java Junction, and your host for the first Harmony & Hues evening. I hope you'll take time to move around and view all the art on display. Every piece here has been created by an artist in the area. Deke? Wave at me."

The gallery owner stood and waved his hand.

"Deke is in charge of sales this evening. If you're interested in purchasing anything on display, speak with him. We'll start the music in another half-hour. I think you're in for a real treat as you listen to some very talented musicians and singers perform for you." He grinned. "And don't forget to grab a coffee or tea!"

The crowd chuckled, and Dax turned off the mic, circulating again, seeing how crowded Java Junction had become. He hoped the fire marshal wouldn't close him down.

Locating Marcy and Carolyn, the sisters who'd been recommended to him by Sylvia, Dax asked, "Are you two ready to roll?"

They nodded, brimming with enthusiasm, and Carolyn said, "Thanks again for giving us this opportunity to perform."

"I'm glad you were able to come tonight. I want to feature different people each fusion night, but I hope you'll agree to make a return later in the summer."

"We'd be honored to do so," Marcy said.

"It's almost time to start. Be ready to take your stools."

After having Dax stand at lessons, as well as insisting he stand on his feet while he practiced, this past week Sylvia had allowed him to perch on a stool as he played and sang. He could easily see the difference in sitting and standing and made a few adjustments in his breathing. Tonight, he believed he'd be more comfortable on the stool, though.

Once again, he took the mic, seeing every seat filled and a good number of people standing along the walls. A thrill shot through him. This was his hometown now. The place where he had started a business.

And the place he wanted to settle down—with Ivy.

The thought didn't startle him. It was merely a natural progression of his feelings for her. Yes, it was not too long ago since they had met, but Dax knew the feelings he held for Ivy weren't fleeting ones.

He loved her. Completely. Deeply.

And he would tell her tonight. Through his songs.

"I want to thank everyone again for turning out tonight for Java Junction's first fusion night, as well as thank a few people. First and foremost, my staff, who serve up coffees with a smile every day and hopefully brighten the lives of many of you here. Scott, Jeanine, Sean. You're the best."

The baristas waved to the crowd, who gave them a round of applause.

"Deke Manchester selected and arranged all the art you see here this evening. Sylvia Moore coaches several of the performers and contributed sage advice. And finally, Ivy Hart, my girlfriend, who supported and encouraged me as this idea to marry music and art came together. Ivy's the one who came up with the name Harmony &

Hues. I'm grateful for that—and for having her in my life every single day."

More applause sounded, and he looked at Ivy, who blushed profusely. Still she blew him a kiss, which prompted a few in the crowd to whistle.

"We're starting off with a sister act. Carolyn is a sophomore at Lost Creek high and Marcy is a senior. Alone, they each have a wonderful voice. Together, their voices blend and become something truly special. Ladies?"

The siblings took to the area designated for performing as Dax stepped away. They sang an old Everly Brothers song, *All I Have to Do is Dream* and moved on to *Wicked's Defying Gravity*, their voices soaring, bringing down the house.

Dax, who had stood to the side, hurried up and said to the crowd, "Can you believe how talented these high schoolers are?"

The enthusiastic applause was evidence enough how appreciative the crowd was.

Six more acts followed. A forty-year-old plumber. A high school biology teacher. An EMT. Each musician received a warm welcome. While it was obvious none of them were professionals, they each possessed talent and communicated their love of music through their voices and instruments. Some sang country. Some did pop. One guitarist played the blues, B. B. King and Johnny Winter songs.

Finally, Dax knew his moment had come.

He took a seat on a stool, lifting his guitar strap over his head, adjusting the mic to the proper height.

"Java Junction is sponsoring Harmony & Hues tonight, and I want to thank you for the large turnout," he began. "You're stuck with me now as I finish up this evening's entertainment. I think we've heard some great music tonight, and I'm here to play you a few songs that I've written. I've never sung in public before. Never had the chance. But I hope you'll like what I've done."

He launched into *Dreams Turn to Dust*, a mournful ballad about opportunities not taken and risks which didn't pay off. Despite the sadness permeating the song, he received a strong round of applause at its conclusion.

Knowing his voice would be even better on his next selection, Dax begin strumming his guitar, performing *A Brighter Tomorrow*. The hopefulness in the song rose to a peak as his voice, rich and strong, hit the final note. Again, he received a tremendous amount of applause.

During each song, he had looked to Ivy, who wore an encouraging smile on her face. Now, Dax knew the right time had arrived.

To perform the song he had written after meeting her.

"I've got one more song to play for you to finish out our first fusion night at Java Junction. We'll be holding these the first and third Saturdays of the month during the summer, with the second and fourth Wednesdays also spotlighting local talent, be it art or music."

He swallowed. Looking straight at Ivy, he said, "I wrote this song is for a very special lady in my life. It's called *Forever's Embrace*."

Ivy's eyes widened. Her lips parted slightly.

Dax sang from his heart, pouring everything he had into this song, this moment.

Forever's embrace, our love will endure,
A bond so strong, forever pure.
You've changed my life, our hearts aligned,
In forever's embrace, our love entwined.
So let's dance through life, hand in hand,
Together we'll conquer, forever we'll stand,
You are my everything, my journey's end,
With you, my love, I've found my one true friend.

His voice broke slightly near the end, the strong emotions rushing through him as he told Ivy how much he loved her.

Forever's embrace, darling, you're my saving grace,
The love that lights up every space.
You've colored my world, erased my pain,
With you by my side, I'm forever changed.

He ended the song, tears blinding his eyes. For a moment, the hush remained, no sound uttered. Then applause rang out. People came to their feet, cheering him.

But Dax only had eyes for Ivy.

Removing his guitar strap, he set down the instrument and moved toward her. She was the only one in the room who had yet to stand, overwhelmed by his public declaration of love.

When he reached her, Dax took her hands, pulling her to her feet. Tears streamed down her cheeks.

"I love you," he said simply. "I needed you to hear it through my song."

Her arms went fast about his neck, and Dax enveloped her in his, holding her close.

She whispered, "I love you, too," in his ear.

His heart sang. His spirit felt light. Free. Ready to start a new life with this amazing woman.

Dax kissed Ivy, oblivious to the cheers ringing about them.

17

I vy watched some of the last stragglers leave Java Junction. Dax told them goodbye and headed her way.

Finley and Emerson had remained with her. She'd been glad her friends had stayed. They now each sipped a cup of herbal tea. Arlo and Paloma had already said their goodbyes. They would be leaving early tomorrow morning to return for their last week in Houston. She promised to stay in touch with them, sending them photos of any paintings she completed.

"Well, that was a tremendous success," Emerson said.

"You're right about that," Deke said, joining them. "Every piece of art sold this evening, down to the last piece of jewelry." He looked to Ivy. "Your landscape brought the highest price of the evening."

She had allowed Deke to place one of her paintings on display, telling him he could take his usual commission if it sold. Ivy had wanted to see if she would be able to move a painting or not. So many people who lived in the Hill Country already had art representative of the area.

"That's good to hear," she said.

"I could've asked more for it and gotten it," the art dealer told her. "I think you undervalued your work, Ivy. Let me know if you have anything else on hand. I'd be happy to display it in my gallery."

"Thank you, Deke. My friends from Houston whom you met will probably be representing me in the future. I may have something to contribute to a future Harmony & Hues night, though. We'll see. I still need to get started on Dax's mural. That's going to take me a couple of weeks to complete."

"Just let me know," Deke said. "Thanks again for including me in your fusion nights."

They said goodnight to him, and Ivy saw Dax and his workers were cleaning up.

"Why don't you both head home?" she told her friends. "I think I'll stay and see if Dax needs any help."

Finley gave her a knowing smile. "Oh, I think Dax could use your help with quite a few things."

She couldn't stop her face from flaming. Finley hugged her, saying, "I'm teasing you, Ivy. I think Dax is a great guy."

"I'm happy for you, Ivy," Emerson said, also joining in the hug. "I hope you two have a bright future together."

Her friends left, waving goodbye to Dax as they left the coffeehouse.

Ivy had yet to be alone with Dax. She headed toward him now, asking, "What can I do?"

"I don't think anything," he replied. "I've taken the sound equipment to the back and stored it for the next fusion night. All the dishes are now washed. Scott has already swept up. He and Sean said they'll mop." He paused. "Looks like I'm free the rest of the night. Are you?" he asked softly.

"Are you asking for now—or literally all night?"

Dax sighed, taking her hands in his. "I'll take whatever you choose to give me. Five minutes. Five hours. Anything in-between that. The ball's in your court, Professor."

"Can we play it by ear?" she asked, wanting to commit to him, yet a little fearful of doing so.

"Want to come upstairs for a nightcap? I've got this great bottle of wine from a local winery that you might enjoy."

She laughed. "A glass of wine sounds perfect."

He took her hand and called out to the others. "Thanks for everything. You guys rocked it."

"I'll lock up," Scott said. "Goodnight."

Dax took Ivy upstairs. She had been in his apartment before, but this time her heart beat so fast, she was afraid it was loud enough for him to hear.

He closed the door, telling her to have a seat while he poured them a glass of wine.

"Red or white?" he asked. "I've got both. Lost Creek Vineyards doesn't produce a bad one."

"Red," she suggested, preferring the more mellow tones in a red.

He opened a bottle and got out two wineglasses, filling each one about half full. Bringing them with him, Dax handed her one and kept the other as he sat on the sofa next to her. Ivy took a sip, feeling the wine's smoothness on her tongue.

"What? No sniffing or swirling? No aerating? Have you forgotten everything you preach?" he asked in mock horror. "Well, what's good for this goose is also good for this gander." He also took a long pull of the wine, his eyes closed as it went down.

Then he opened them, the chocolate brown color warm as he gazed at her intently.

"We should talk about things," he said.

Ivy nodded. "Okay," she said, hearing how small her voice sounded.

Dax took her glass from her hand, placing it on the coffee table before them. "I didn't mean to startle you. Or embarrass you. I took a risk playing *Forever's Embrace* like that."

He raked a hand through his hair, sighing aloud. "I hadn't planned to perform it tonight. I only had practiced the other two songs with Sylvia and on my own." He hesitated. "Yet when I looked at you Ivy, all I wanted to do was share with you the feelings I have for you. I'm sorry it was in such a public way. It was something I should've saved for when we were alone together. Saving it for now would've been smarter."

She placed her hand on his knee. "I'm not upset with you, Dax. Don't think that. If I gave you that impression, get rid of it. Did the song surprise me? Yes—but in a good way. Your lyrics were so moving. I felt cherished with every note."

He leaned forward, taking her face in his hands. "That's how I wanted you to feel. I have never written a song for or about anyone. Ever."

"When did you write it?" she asked softly.

"The first day we met," he admitted.

She drew in a quick breath. "Seriously?"

Dax nodded. "It's as if I knew that first night, Ivy. That we were meant to be. I was drawn to you in a way unlike I've ever experienced with any other woman. Something in your soul speaks to mine. The best way I could express my love was through a song."

"But the first night?" she pressed. "Dax, we barely knew one another."

He shrugged. "Maybe we knew one another in a previous life, Ivy. Something in my soul recognized something in yours. The song just poured from me." He paused. "I was afraid to play it for you. Afraid for you know how fast I'd fallen for you. I was scared you wouldn't think my feelings were genuine. Or that I was simply doing whatever it took to get you into bed."

Taking her hand, he brought it to his heart, placing it flat against his chest. "Can you feel it beating? Every beat speaks your name to me, Ivy. Every breath I take carries you inside me. And yes, the depth of these feelings frightens me a little. I know it wasn't that long ago when I was married to someone else. I wouldn't admit to myself that we'd been drifting apart for years. The divorce brought clarity to me, though. I think I was too young to have gotten married. I should've just lived with Shailene. I think we both would've figured out pretty quickly that it was more lust than love."

He brought her hand to his lips, kissing it tenderly. "I mean what I've told you. I'm free of my old life and taking up my new one here in Lost Creek. This town spoke to me when I drove into it. I'm happy to sink roots here." Kissing her hand again, he brought it to his cheek. "I feel I'm a better man when I'm with you. Better than I ever have been. I love you, Ivy. I want a life with you. I'm not foolish enough to ask you to marry me now. We still have a long way to go, getting to know one another. But I know your heart. Just as you know mine. And I want to show you how much I love you."

Dax kissed her then, a kiss that told of days to come. One that promised Ivy he spoke the truth.

She captured his face in her hands. Breaking the kiss, she told him, "I love you. Part of me is terrified admitting that aloud. Another part of me thinks I've gone stark-raving mad. That it's too soon to feel the way I do."

Gazing into his eyes, she added, "But the biggest part of me silences all those doubts and fears. It tells me that you can't set up a timetable for love. That it happens when it's supposed to." She swallowed. "I do love you, Dax. I want to give you the world."

"I don't need anything but you," he said, his mouth covering hers.

His arms went about her, and Ivy lost herself in his kiss. She relished his taste. His masculine scent. The feel of his runner's body pressed against hers.

They kissed for a long time, desire building within her. When she broke the kiss and placed two fingers against his lips, she could see the flames of desire in his own eyes.

"I want to make love with you, Dax. No, I need to. Now."

Ivy kissed him again before he could answer. Bolder than she had ever acted before, she began unbuttoning the shirt he wore, slipping her palms inside, feeling the immense heat coming off him.

He placed his hands atop hers, pulling slightly away, staring at her. "Are you sure, Ivy?"

With complete faith in him—in them—she said, "I've never been more certain of anything in my life, Dax."

That was all it took. His mouth seized hers again, his fingers pushing aside the straps of her sundress. He broke the kiss, his lips trailing along her throat and down the slope of her neck to the top of her bare shoulders, where he pressed fervent kisses, causing her core to tighten. She finished unbuttoning his shirt, pushing the material off his shoulders, helping him to shrug out of hit.

Her eyes roamed over his chest and the six-pack she was seeing for the first time.

"I should have separated you and your shirt long before now," she said, boldly leaning down and licking his nipple, an incredibly un-Ivy-like thing to do, but something had compelled her to do so.

Immediately, Dax groaned, his hands tightening on her elbows before he released them. His arms went around her, his hands finding the long zipper of the sundress. He started to unzip it and then brought them both to their feet. He turned her in his arms, wrapping them around her middle, holding her to him as he had that night at Renegade Roadhouse. His lips nibbled her nape before his tongue licked the length of it, trailing along her shoulder, causing delicious shivers to run through her.

Dax released her, his fingers returning to the zipper, slowing moving it down her back. His tongue followed the same path along her back, going lower and lower. Ivy now trembled with desire. He pushed the dress over her hips, and it dropped to the ground. Strong arms enveloped her again as he kissed her neck. One arm pinned her to him as his free hand grazed down her belly, his touch light. It went lower, his fingers slipping into her underwear, stroking her. She moaned softly. One finger pushed inside her, causing her to whimper. Dax's lips continued to feast on her shoulders and neck as another finger joined the first. Ivy began moving against it, wanting more.

Then his fingers plunged deep inside her, caressing her, causing her body to tremble uncontrollably. She murmured his name as she moved against him, his arm still holding her tightly against him.

"Dax," she managed to say. "Please. More."

His lips moved to her ear. "I'll give you everything you want, Ivy. Everything. And more."

His fingers worked a magic she'd had never felt. Something built inside her, something wicked and wonderful. Suddenly, it was as if her body erupted. Light exploded through her, and she continued to move. The most exquisite feelings rushed through her, and she heard herself calling Dax's name, over and over.

Then she went limp as spaghetti. His other arm went about her, securing her so she didn't fall into a puddle on the ground.

It hit her that he'd brought her to orgasm. Ivy had never experienced one before. Jay had never been one for foreplay, only interesting in seeing to his own needs. She had been too timid to ask for more from him whenever they had sex, and she had been too shy to masturbate. Once she'd ended her relationship with Jay, she had put aside the need for physical pleasure.

But she'd certainly experienced it now.

Ivy reached a hand up, stroking Dax's cheek. He responded by nuzzling her throat, causing desire to quickly build within her again.

"Maybe we could take this to your bedroom," she said over her shoulder, feeling sexy for the first time in her life.

Quickly, he whirled her in his arms, his mouth coming down hard on hers, the kiss hot and demanding. They did something that vaguely resembled the two-step, with Dax lifting Ivy from the confines of her dress around her ankles, pushing her along the floor and into the bedroom.

He didn't turn on a light, which she was grateful for. His fingers tucked into her underwear, pushing them down and over her hips. She stepped out of them and got to work on him, removing his belt and unbuttoning his jeans. Dax helped her push them down to his ankles, then he turned and perched on the bed to remove his tennis shoes and socks. Ivy helped get everything off him, and he stood once more, looking like a statue of Adonis from one of her art books, perfectly formed in every way. Muscled chest. Flat belly. Beautifully sculpted legs.

And a cock eager to claim her full attention.

Fearlessly, Ivy grasped it in her hand, her thumb stroking the sleek, hard shaft.

Dax placed his hand over hers. "Keep doing that, and I'll explode."

She smiled. "I think I'd like to see that."

"Not until I've done some exploring," he replied, lifting her onto the bed and lying down beside her.

They kissed again. While they're mouths fused together, their hands roamed each other's bodies, stroking, seeking, becoming familiar with every nook and cranny. He moved to her breasts, his tongue outlining the rise of them, his teeth and tongue teasing her nipples. When he blew on her nipples and then sucked her breasts, she went wild with the sensations he caused.

Ivy did her fair share of exploration, kissing his neck and pecs, working her way to one of his nipples, her tongue circling it teasingly before she grazed her teeth against it. She was doing things she had never done before.

And enjoying them immensely.

Dax kissed her everywhere. Her brow. Her elbow. Behind her knees, which proved to be quite ticklish. Then he pushed off the bed, opening a drawer in the nightstand, removing a small foil packet. She hadn't even thought about a condom, her brain in a haze of desire.

"I can't wait any longer," he said, his breath coming harshly.

"I don't want you to," she told him, her fingers playing with his abs, watching them bunch at her touch.

Tearing the packet open, he removed the condom and placed it on his cock, which looked far too large to go inside her. Still, she innately trusted him.

He pushed her back into the pillows, hovering over her now, kissing her deeply. She felt his fingers again, pushing into her, caressing her, making certain she was ready for him. Then he removed them and pressed against her. Ivy took a deep breath and relaxed completely as he drove inside her.

She gasped, full and stretched, getting used to him. When he began to move again, she eagerly met each thrust. Their dance of love was heated. Frenetic. Fulfilling. Incredible.

His mouth took hers as their bodies came together, her orgasm building again because he'd brought his hand between them, playing with her even as he thrust wildly. He moved his finger in a circular motion, causing her to explode again with heat and light. She cried out his name and he called hers, as well, collapsing atop her, driving her into the mattress. Ivy welcomed his weight. She welcomed him.

How had she ever lived without Dax Tennyson in her life?

Slowly, he pushed back up on his elbows, his large hand cupping her cheek, giving her a sweet, tender kiss. He brushed her hair from her face.

"I love you, Ivy Hart. That was the most extraordinary experience of my life."

Dax's arms slipped under her and he rolled, bringing her with him as he turned on his side. They faced one another now, and she knew she wore the same sappy smile he did.

"I love you," she told him earnestly. "You made me feel like a princess. A very aroused, sexy princess, but a princess, nonetheless."

He laughed softly. "And you make me feel like the king of the world, Ivy." He brushed his lips against her brow. "I don't think *Forever's Embrace* did you justice. I may have to write a new song about what it's like to make love to you."

"Just don't sing that one in public."

Kissing her again, he said, "I think you'll always be my muse, Ivy Hart. I plan to write quite a few songs about you and how much I love you." He grinned. "But I'll keep those intimate details to myself. Like that small freckle just above your right nipple."

She swatted him playfully.

He removed his condom and turned her so her back was now pressed against his chest.

"I'm exhausted. Let's get a little sleep."

"Okay."

Ivy closed her eyes, blanketed by Dax's warmth.

And love.

18

D ax awoke at his usual time, his body curled around Ivy's.

Last night had been life-altering.

It wasn't just the sex, either. He had felt the chemistry between them, and it had proven to be correct. Their lovemaking had been explosive. Yet it wasn't merely the physical act of making love to Ivy which had changed between them. It was where he stood emotionally.

Coming to Lost Creek, Dax had wanted a clean start. He had ripped off the bandage that was his old life—job, marriage, philosophy—in order to become the person he wanted to be proud of for the rest of his life. He hadn't known Ivy would play such a huge role in this trans-formation.

He no longer wanted to go it alone. He understood now that his life would be better—*he* would be better—if

Ivy were an intricate part of it. Dax only hoped she felt the same way.

She shifted in his arms. Suddenly, warm lips pressed against his chest, stirring desire within him. Soon, they were making love again, this time slowly. Tenderly. Lovingly. When they climaxed at the same time, joy filled him, along with a very possessive streak.

This was his woman. His future.

They lay together in the aftermath, limbs tangled, kissing, not being able to get enough of one another.

Finally, Ivy asked, "What time is it? I know you get up early to run."

Reluctantly, he lifted an arm from her and reached for his phone by the bedside. "It's five after six."

"You open Java Junction at seven on weekends. I should be going."

When she began to untangle herself from him, his arms tightened about her.

"Five more minutes."

"I would stay here five days if we could," she told him.

They spent that time kissing deeply, and contentment poured through Dax, knowing he finally felt complete because of the commitment they'd made to one another.

Ivy was the one to pull away. "I need to let you get moving. I've already disrupted your running routine."

He kissed her. "You can disrupt my routine every day of the week. I think I got enough of a workout with you, as it is," he teased.

Forcing himself to relax, he allowed his arms to fall away, freeing her. She rose from the bed and began dressing. Dax watched, flashes of last night and this morning playing before his eyes.

He climbed from the bed once she was dressed, enveloping her in his arms and kissing the top of her head.

"I assume you're working at the tasting room today."

"Yes. Yesterday was the first Saturday I've taken off since I've been the manager. Weekends are busy for us, however. I need to be there all day today."

"You have plans for dinner?"

"Yes. Some guy I've been hanging out with lately. I just can't seem to shake him."

Dax laughed, kissing her. "You want to come over once you've closed up? I don't really cook. Except for breakfast."

"Ooh, I love breakfast for dinner. Can I bring anything?"

"Just yourself, Professor."

Kissing her a final time, he let her go so they both could begin their day.

At the door, she said, "I'll see you tonight. About six-thirty."

He caught her elbow. "I love you, Ivy. Thank you for last night. And all the nights to come."

Those hazel eyes gazed up at him, making him feel complete in a way he never had before. "Thank you for making me feel special, Dax. Sexy. No man has ever made me think I was sexy."

"You've dated a lot of idiots then."

Laughing, she said, "I agree." Then she sobered. "I love you, too."

Once Ivy was gone, he showered and shaved, dressing in his usual T-shirt and shorts before heading downstairs. He thought he might take a page out of the Lost Creek Vineyards playbook and think about both him and his employees wearing Java Junction T-shirts. He didn't usually work weekends, allowing Scott to take over both those days, knowing it was important to create that work/life balance and not get caught on the hamster wheel ever again as he had in his Dallas accountant days.

Today, though, was different. Dax believed the coffeehouse might do more business than usual. He'd learned gossip was the life of a small town, and the citizens of Lost Creek would want to talk about last night's Harmony & Hues.

When he reached the barista bar, Scott was already busy brewing the gallons of coffee which locals picked up for various Sunday school classes meeting on Sunday mornings. He knew Ethel did her fair share of business with the same crowd, providing donuts for pickup.

"And here I thought you were just some coffeehouse owner," Scott said, spying him. "Who knew the boss could sing and play so well? Seriously, Dax, your music is really good. I can't believe you wrote the songs you performed." He paused. "I'm happy for you, buddy. Not just for the success of fusion night, but also because of Ivy. I don't know her well, but her family has a stellar reputation in this town. Bill and Cecily Hart are good people. I know Ivy and Harper are, too."

"Nothing like telling your girlfriend you love her in front of a huge crowd," Dax said lightly.

Scott grinned. "Oh, I'll bet you scored major points for telling her you loved her in a song you wrote for her. You'll be playing that song for Ivy for years to come."

It was a little hard for Dax to wrap his head around that idea. Ever since he'd opened Java Junction, he'd lived in the moment. Yet he knew he wanted a future with Ivy. How he would go about asking her to share it with him was another matter. Maybe he better write it in a song. He seemed to know exactly what to say through his lyrics.

The morning rush hit heavier than the usual Sunday. Some of the customers were headed to church. Others were grabbing their caffeine before hitting the lake for a day of fun in the summer sun. He recognized many faces from last night, all assuring him how much they'd enjoyed attending Harmony & Hues and how they couldn't wait for the next one to roll around. He decided he should have a few signs printed up to put in the coffeehouse's window to advertise the next event. Maybe a few of the other local merchants along the square and Main Street might also place one in their windows to spread the word. He would talk it over with Ivy and have her design something for him.

Deke stopped in, ordering an Americano, saying, "We need to talk about last night, Dax. Do a port-mortem."

"I agree. I would say now, but things are hopping."

Deke indicated the newspaper tucked under his arm. "I'll sit in a corner and read the paper. If you have a few minutes to spare, come over."

It surprised him when Sean and Jeanine showed up. Both baristas wore their aprons and joined Scott and the two teenagers who worked the Sunday shift.

"What are you two doing here?"

"I figured things would be busy this morning," Sean said. "Thought you might could use an extra hand or two."

"I don't think all of us will fit behind the bar," Dax said, laughing.

"Then get off your feet for a few minutes and let us pitch in," Jeanine said.

"I think I'll take your advice."

"What can I bring you?" Scott asked.

"Just a regular coffee," he replied. "One sugar and a splash of milk. Thanks."

Dax went and joined Deke. The gallery owner asked if Dax had received any feedback this morning.

"Quite a bit. All of it positive," he shared. "A lot of people who've stopped by this morning came last night. Those who weren't are realizing they missed out on something special. It was already standing room only last night. Frankly, I don't know how we're going to be able to cater to everyone who wants to attend next time."

"That's what I wanted to talk to you about," Deke said. "Actually, Ivy is the one who mentioned it to me last night."

She had said nothing to him. Then again, they had been busy with other things.

"What's the idea?"

"Ivy thought we needed to move the event outdoors. To the gazebo in the center of the square. That way, we wouldn't have to limit the amount of art on display. It would take investing in some good sound equipment in order for the singers and musicians to be heard."

The idea excited him. "I'd be happy to make that investment. We wouldn't have to limit the number of people in attendance if we hold it outdoors. I'm sure it'll take some kind of permit to hold a public event, though. I can look into that."

"If Texas is anything like Colorado, you'll have to apply for the permits in advance. It might be too late to do so for next week's Wednesday fusion. Still, you could apply for the other ones since we already know the dates. You could still provide coffee and tea for people. It might be smart to speak with Rob Owens. He owns Hill Country Hangout, the sports bar. I know Rob has a food truck he takes to events in the area. I'm sure he'd be willing to set up on one of the ends of the square."

"This is terrific, Deke. I'll get on this first thing tomorrow morning once the city offices open. Have you decided any of the pieces to be shown this upcoming Wednesday?"

"I started thinking about that after three pieces sold last night, Dax," Deke said, chuckling. "I should finish pulling a list together from the gallery and get that email with pictures to Ivy by the end of the day. She can load those photos to your website. You might want to contact that jewelry maker. Her stuff sold out even faster than my clients' paintings and sculptures did."

"I'll do that today," he promised.

Deke finished his coffee. "Let me know if you want to meet anytime tomorrow to finalize things."

"I'll holler at you as soon as I've spoken to someone with the city. That way, you'll know whether you're setting up at Java Junction again or outdoors."

Dax sat for another hour, sipping his own coffee as multiple people stopped by, telling him how much they enjoyed the previous evening or how they looked forward to attending future Harmony & Hues nights. The crowd finally dwindled, but he knew they would continue to do a steady business after church let out. He sent Sean and Jeanine home, thanking them both for pinch-hitting this morning and then took their place again behind the barista bar.

"While we've got a minute to breathe, let me ask you about something," Dax said to Scott. "You saw how crowded last night turned out to be."

"To be honest, I was waiting for the fire chief to show up and close the doors," Scott admitted.

Dax explained the idea of moving fusion night to the town square, saying, "Deke thinks it would be a better way to display the art. The musicians could perform in the gazebo, and that raised platform would give them better visibility to the crowd. We could still sell our coffee and tea. Deke suggested Rob Owens set up his food truck, too."

"I like that idea. Better crowd flow. A little elbow room. But you'll need some permits."

"That's why I thought I'd talk to you first and get an

idea how to go about filing for those. I thought as a policeman, you could point me in the right direction."

"My aunt handles that at city hall," Scott explained. "Let me give her a buzz." He tapped his cell phone. "Hey, Aunt G. You stopping by Java Junction on the way home from church? Good. Listen, Dax has a few questions to run by you. Coffee on the house if you answer them for him. Okay. See you soon."

Scott ended the call. "Aunt Gladys stops by with a few friends every Sunday. She's my favorite relative and is really the one who, besides you, helped me get through my divorce. Aunt G fed me and listened to me, while you gave me something to do with my hands and kept me busy during the roughest part of it. She'll get you squared away."

Ten minutes later, a group of five women came through the door. Scott greeted them and introduced Dax.

"Gladys Bradshaw, this is Dax Tennyson, my boss."

"You were part of the book club that came in with Dianne Farrow."

"I was. Java Junction is going to be a godsend to our group. I love my book club ladies, but we'd gotten to a point where everyone was trying to outdo everyone, making more and more elaborate treats to eat and finding exotic coffees to brew. This way, we can come into Java Junction, grab a cup of coffee or tea and something sweet, and actually talk about books."

Scott passed his aunt a coffee. "Your favorite. Go sit with Dax."

He led Gladys to a table for two in the corner. "I want

to talk to you about the fusion night we held here last night."

Gladys brightened. "Oh, yes. I already had plans with my bridge club or I would've been here, but I heard all about Harmony & Hues at Sunday school this morning. What a lovely idea, spotlighting local talent."

"Thank you. What we ran into last night is that a lot of people attended. More are expected at the next one. I'd like to start holding them in the gazebo in the middle of the square. That way, people could even bring lawn chairs or sit on the grass. Do their art walk and listen to the music. Hopefully, stop in at Java Junction beforehand and pick up some coffee. I need to know how to go about renting the gazebo from the city and any permits I might need."

"The good thing is you're not holding what Lost Creek classifies as a community event. Those are more for a community carnival or fun run. That type of thing, where we have requests to close off public parking and streets and tents are erected, is a little more complicated and expensive. I assume your singers and musicians would play in the gazebo, so no stage would be erected."

"Yes, that's the plan."

"Then I would classify this as more of a rental of outdoor facilities. You're merely hosting your event at a public space. The good thing is that the rental application for this only takes three days to process. You do have to submit your application a minimum of seven business days in advance, though."

"Okay. That'll cut out this coming Wednesday's fusion

night. Then again, I'm not anticipating the crowd on a weeknight that we had on Saturday."

"If you stop by city hall tomorrow morning with a date of your future art walks, I can get those on the city's calendar and reserve the gazebo for you. You do have to apply for a separate permit for each instance, but I can speed things through for you with only one application to cover all the nights this summer. If you go beyond summer, we'll need to talk again."

"Thank you for fast-tracking things, Gladys."

"The city does require a fee of one hundred dollars for every four hours of use. If you use less time, it's still the same fee. If you go over the specified four hours, it's an additional seventy-five dollars per hour."

"I'm not worried about the money," he told her. "I'm wanting to give back to this community because they've welcomed me so warmly."

"You can write a check or pay by credit card," she explained. "Pay for one event at a time or all together."

"It'll be easier for me if I do the one payment." Dax was fortunate he had the funds to do so. He knew others trying to set up a series of events weren't so fortunate.

"Can you stop by at ten tomorrow morning?" Gladys asked. "I'll have the applications printed out for you and ready to go."

"I have a ten-thirty voice lesson with Sylvia Moore. I think she'll let me bump that."

"Oh, this won't take ten minutes of your time, Dax," Gladys assured him. "I'll make certain you make it to Sylvia's on time."

He shook her hand. "Thank you for helping me with this matter, Gladys. I'll see you in the morning."

Scott told Dax he could handle the rest of the day, freeing Dax to head out for a run. As he pounded the pavement, a new song began to form in his mind. He cut his run short and returned to his apartment, quickly showering, humming the melody in order to keep it going. Sometimes, the music came to him first. Sometimes, the lyrics were what appeared.

He quickly toweled off and dressed, turning on his cell's video to record as he grabbed his guitar and began tinkering with the chords.

By the time Ivy arrived, he had the music completed, as well as one verse and the chorus in place. He played it for her, delighting in her excitement.

"I can't believe you've written this much today. Does a song always come so quickly to you?"

"Not really. And remember, I've had a long layoff from songwriting. I'm having to understand what my new process is."

He set down his guitar. "I can work on it again tomorrow. Right now, I need my Ivy time."

He pulled her into his lap, and they made out like teenagers after a Friday night football game. Dax wondered if he would ever get his fill of this woman.

Breaking the kiss, he said, "We've got two things on the agenda tonight."

She arched a brow. "Oh, we have an agenda?"

"We do. Eat. Make love. I'll let you choose the order."

The dimple in her cheek flashed. "That's a no-brainer, Dallas."

Ivy took the hem of his shirt and yanked it over his head, tossing it aside. Laughing, Dax did the same with the Lost Creek Vineyards shirt she wore. Beneath it was a black, lacy bra with a convenient front clasp. His hands quickly opened it, pushing the material aside so he could feast on her full breasts. As he did, she wriggled out of the bra, making very Ivy-like noises which let him know he was definitely on the right track.

Dax began sucking on one breast, kneading the other, as she moved in his lap. Her hands pushed into his hair, and she held him close to her. The vanilla scent wafted up from her smooth skin, teasing him. He licked in a lazy circle around her nipple, each time shrinking the size of the circle, coming closer and closer. Then he flicked his tongue across it, her whimper causing his own desire to flame. He began sucking again, hard, hearing her mewl. Her hips rose moving against him, and then she cried out. Dax sucked even harder, hearing her cries of satisfaction.

She stilled. He lifted his head, seizing her mouth, drinking from her greedily.

Ivy broke the kiss. "I had an *orgasm* just then. And all you did was tease my breast!" she added, wonder on her face.

"I've heard that can happen to some women."

She grew serious. "Dax, I'd never had an orgasm before last night."

He frowned. "Never?"

"Never. This is all so new to me. I think… I think the

difference is because I love you. You have all my heart, Dax. Every bit of it."

He kissed her gently. "You have mine, too, Ivy."

Her eyes gleamed with mischief. "Why don't we shed the rest of our clothes and go have some more fun, Dallas?"

"I like how you think, Professor."

Dax carried Ivy to the bedroom.

They forgot all about dinner.

19

E ven though it was her day off from the tasting
room, Ivy drove to her art studio long before
the sun rose, ready to put in a few hours on her
latest painting. During these past few months, she had
been getting up early to paint, spending mornings
working on her art before reporting to the tasting room
for her day job. She did so because the rest of her hours
were spent with Dax.

Summer was almost over, and only one more
Harmony & Hues night remained on the calendar. The
town of Lost Creek and summer visitors had generously
supported the series spotlighting local musicians and
artists. Ivy had only sold one additional painting at the
event, holding back everything else as Paloma and Arlo
had suggested. Paloma was driving down for the final
Harmony & Hues and would arrive on Saturday morning.
That's why Ivy was eager to finish the painting she now

worked on, hoping it would be among those Paloma chose to take back with her to Dallas.

Ivy had regularly texted pictures of her finished work to both her friends, and they all had high hopes that she would be able to quickly sell what she had worked on this summer. She still didn't think she had enough paintings for an exhibit, but she would place herself in Paloma's hands regarding that. Paloma got along well with Jameson Polk, her new boss in Dallas, and felt once Polk saw Ivy's work, he might even offer to represent her.

She reached the studio and tossed on a smock so she wouldn't get paint on her clothes. She wanted to keep them fresh because Dax would pick her up at eleven this morning. They would be picnicking at Lost Creek Lake, which had become a favorite spot of theirs. They had rented kayaks and paddleboats at Hill Country Sports, owned by Finley's brother Ches and his wife Sally. Ches was still trying to talk them into renting a fishing boat, but Ivy didn't want to think about having to bait a hook and clean fish afterward. Fortunately, Dax had never been fishing, being a city boy, and for now they simply ate their fish on a plate.

Sometimes, she found it hard to recall what her life had been like before Dax Tennyson entered it, though she was glad they had not met before she returned to her hometown. In Houston, she wouldn't have found time to pursue a relationship with him, her responsibilities at the gallery keeping her too busy.

Ivy became lost in her painting and was startled when she heard a knock at the door. It was far too early for Dax to show up since he would be working his usual Wednesday morning shift at Java Junction. Curious as to who was here, she set down her brush and went to the door. Opening it, she found Harper waiting on the doorstep.

"Hi. Can I come in?" her sister asked.

"Of course," Ivy said, motioning for Harper to enter.

Harper said, "I haven't been a great sister to you this summer. I've been distracted by starting up my own business, supervising the construction of the event center, and having my head in the clouds because of Braden. Beyond our weekly dinners with Finley and Emerson, you and I rarely see one another." She paused. "I want to do better in the future."

Harper embraced her, and Ivy felt the love flowing between them.

"You've had a lot on your plate," she told her sister. "It's been the same with me. I told you that I'm trying to put together enough paintings for Paloma to see if she can persuade her boss to hold a showing for me in Dallas. Or at least have him agree to represent me and sell some of them. Between painting and working at the tasting room, I've been swamped." She hesitated and then added, "I've also been seeing quite a bit of Dax."

Ivy knew Harper wanted her to elaborate, but she really had no idea where to start. Instead, Ivy said, "Come look at some of the art I've been working on over the past few months since I've been back in Lost Creek."

"I've already seen some of it in the square. You know I rarely go into town, skirting past it when I head to the winery each day, but I recognized your murals on the square on my way here just now. I stopped and looked at both before knocking on your door. Ivy, I didn't know you had done these. Why didn't you share that with me?"

"You've been incredibly busy." She took Harper's hand and squeezed it. "I also know how rough it was to have the rug pulled out from under you. You thought you were going to be married. Instead, you faced a deep betrayal by two people you loved. I wanted you to find your mojo again, Harper. Have the time to heal and look to the future. And you've done that. I'm in town a lot more than you are, and folks are excited about the event center's opening. People are checking out your website, as well. I've been keeping tabs on those stats, the number of visitors hitting the site, and traffic is increasing daily."

Ivy paused. "As important as Weddings with Hart has become to you, I understand how Braden is someone you wanted to spend most of your free time with. He's great, Harper. I look upon him as a good friend and big brother. I think the two of you together rock."

Her sister's face softened. "I'm lucky. I could have moped around for months. Years. Coming back to Lost Creek to start my own business has kept me busy, though. The fact that Braden and I found one another and are so happy together is merely icing on the cake. I love him so much, Ivy. Way more than I did Ath. Having experienced what I have with Braden, I doubt my marriage to Ath would have lasted. Or it would have—and I would never have known the absolute joy I've found with Braden."

Ivy showed Harper her paintings. She had almost

fifteen completed now, once the one on her easel was finished, and that would only take another couple of days before it was done.

Harper flipped through the stack of canvases leaning against the wall. "These are incredible, Ivy. I always knew you had talent. Maybe I took it for granted when we were growing up. It was just an Ivy thing. A part of you. You must have really suffered during those years in Houston, not having time to paint."

"Now that I'm back to painting again, it lets me see how unhappy I was the years I walked away from my art. I had always thought I'd return to painting at some point, but that day never arrived in Houston, thanks to Lawson Everhart being a slug and making me do his job and mine. The horrible event which happened to you was the catalyst which woke me up. It enabled me to quit my job and come back to Lost Creek. I'm finding myself here, Harper. Both as an artist and a person. It makes me wonder why I ever left Lost Creek in the first place."

"Well, there was this little thing called college that called us away," her sister pointed out. "I know what you're saying, though. This place is special. Maybe we appreciate it more now for having left it. We're both returning home and see Lost Creek with mature eyes now. I can't imagine living anywhere else. I know Mom and Dad were proud of what we did in the years after college, but they are so happy to have both of us home again. I'll admit that I have felt slightly guilty, knowing neither of us wished to take over the winery. Now, however, you're involved with the tasting room. I'll be managing the event center. And Braden is in charge of the wines. I feel we have all major areas covered."

Harper smiled. "I'm glad I stopped by this morning. It was wonderful to see the paintings you've been working on. You've been gone a lot, but then again, so have I. I promise to spend more time with you in the future. For now, though, I've got to do whatever I can to ensure that Weddings with Hart is kicked off with a bang. Have you been to the event center or tasting room lately? They're really coming along."

"I have. I think they'll both be finished before the deadline. Probably within the next two weeks, I'll start interviewing for staff to work the gift shop. It's going to be great. We both have a lot to be proud of, Harper."

Ivy walked her sister to the door, and they embraced again. "Thank you for stopping by, I'm glad you like what I've produced. It's nice to have the Harper stamp of approval."

"I'm wild about all your paintings, but especially the one of Lost Creek Rock. I've shared the legend of it with Braden. It's always been such a mysterious, romantic place. You captured its essence beautifully."

After Harper left, Ivy went to the painting of Lost Creek Rock, thinking of the stories about Ekta, the beautiful Native American daughter of a tribal chief and how Tarak and Tosawhi fought to the death, seeking her hand. Ivy separated the painting from the others Paloma would review, setting it aside. This would be her wedding gift to Harper and Braden. She didn't know when they would marry, but her gut told her it would happen sometime soon. They were certainly soul mates. While most people might think things had happened between them too quickly, Ivy understood both had suffered painful breakups in the past before they had found one another. She didn't see either of them wasting time when they could be together. It wouldn't surprise her if they married by the end of the year.

She loved Lost Creek Rock, though, and decided she would paint it from a slightly different angle, wanting it to be part of the collection Paloma's gallery would hopefully sponsor.

Ivy went back to her current work-in-progress, getting more done on it than she had expected, knowing she would be able to finish up on it by tomorrow. She came to a good stopping point and cleaned her brushes and put away her paints, knowing Dax would be here any minute. She was proud of the fusion nights he had sponsored this summer, bringing attention to so many different painters, sculptors, potters, and jewelry makers, along with various musicians. Though he had thought to put the idea of forming a band on hold, Dax had found he had much in common with a few of the musicians who had played on several of the Harmony & Hues nights.

That had led to him recently forming a band, which practiced Tuesday nights after Java Junction closed and Sunday afternoons in the drummer's garage. Ivy had gone to the three Tuesday night sessions, watching the band start to feel its way as they got to know one another musi-cally and personally, finding their strengths and weak-nesses. The drummer had a decent voice and sang lead on a few of the songs they'd practiced. For the most part, Dax was their lead singer and guitarist. The band also included a bass player and keyboardist. They had worked on a few of Dax's original songs, as well as covers from rock to country. Ivy was thrilled that Dax had fallen in love with country music. His voice was a natural fit for it.

She heard a light tap on the door and went to answer it, pulling Dax inside the apartment, where she gave him a slow, lingering kiss.

"You keep kissing me like that, and I'll forget all about the picnic we're supposed to go on," he flirted.

"I've been painting since a little after six this morning, and I didn't take time for breakfast," she told him. "I need food in me." Smiling seductively, she added, "Before I need *you* inside me."

He pulled her to him, laughing. "Aren't you a little saucy minx," he said, kissing her again before releasing her. "Food's in the truck. So is a blanket. All I need is the girl to complete everything I need for a successful picnic."

"This girl is all yours," Ivy said, wrapping her arms about his neck and kissing him again.

She locked the studio's door and accompanied him to his truck. As Dax drove the short distance to Lost Creek Lake, Ivy went through the items in the picnic basket.

"Sandwiches. What kind?" she asked.

"Ham and turkey on one. Roast beef for the other. And before you say anything, I know you like both, so I had the deli cut them in half. So we can have half of each."

"Smart man. Ooh. A cheese plate. Someone's been to The Cheese Connoisseur."

"I'm hooked on that place, thanks to you. I added the berry pack to my order. You should find raspberries, blueberries, and blackberries, along with crackers for the cheese."

He patted a cooler sitting on the floorboard behind him. "A bottle of wine and waters are chilling in the cooler. The wine is that red blend we both like."

"My, Dallas. You are definitely wining and dining me today."

He reached for her hand and brought it to his lips, pressing a tender kiss against her knuckles. "I want the best for my girl."

They reached the lake and parked. The late August day was hot. While she saw a few boaters out on the lake, the picnic area was abandoned.

"Want a table, or we can find a spot in the shade over there."

"It's not a picnic unless you eat on a blanket," she declared, gathering the blanket in her arms.

Dax took care of collecting the rest, and soon their feast was spread before them. They skipped from topic to topic, mostly talking about the final fusion night coming up in three days.

"Are you sure you should bring them to an end?" she asked. "They've turned out to be so popular."

"I think we've featured enough artists and musicians in the area for now. You don't want to oversaturate your market. Deke has signed several new clients from these nights, so their work will be available at his gallery. As far as musicians go, I'm going to feature different musicians on Wednesday and Saturday nights at Java Junction throughout the fall and winter. Only one artist per night, so they can really delve deeply into their inventory of songs."

"Will you perform any of those nights?"

He nodded. "Singing in public is now in my blood. I'm comfortable with it. I'll continue taking one voice lesson a week with Sylvia, just to keep me on my toes. She's a great sounding board, and I'll play my new songs for her, as well as polish some older ones and even a few covers. Sylvia actually came to band practice on Sunday."

Ivy giggled. "I would've liked to have been a fly on the wall to hear her comments. Too bad I work Sunday afternoons."

"As always, she didn't pull any punches. But that's what I like about her. She doesn't criticize just because it's expected. Yes, she does give notes for us to work on, but she's also effusive with her praise when she thinks it's deserved. If I ever need a female singer, I may twist her arm to make a guest appearance with us. As it is, I've talked her into performing a duet with me Saturday night."

"That's terrific. Have you decided what to name the band, Rural Rockers or the Lone Star Rebels?"

"I shared those two names with the other band members. We're still deciding."

"I know you're just starting to get your feet wet with the band, but Harper will be needing some live entertainment to play wedding receptions, so keep that in mind."

"You said her center should be open by November?"

"That was the target date. Surprisingly, the construction manager has indicated it might be a month sooner. Then Harper will start booking events right away."

"We would need another few months to really gel before I'd be comfortable asking people to pay to have us play their receptions and parties. Maybe by the end of the year—say, December—I could pitch to Harper. Have her come listen to us play and see if we're what she might be interested in."

"She will be," Ivy encouraged. "Although I've only been to a handful of your practices, everyone is talented. It'll just take time for you to come together."

Dax slipped his arm about Ivy's waist. "You build me up every single day. Make me feel good about myself and this life I'm now a part of in Lost Creek." He gazed at her, his love for her obvious in his eyes. "I'm the luckiest guy in the world. I have Java Junction. I've got new friends. And most important of all, I have you, Ivy. You're at the center of everything I am. Everything I do."

He kissed her deeply, a kiss full of unspoken promises and a passion which burned just below the surface.

Capturing his face in her hands, Ivy said, "I love you more than I ever thought possible, Dax Tennyson. My life is richer and fuller than it ever has been. All because of you."

He tucked a lock of hair behind her ear. "I'd make love to you right now on this blanket, but I don't want to give any of the boaters or fisherman out there a free show. How about we head back to my place? I'm melting in this heat. We could both use a shower."

"So, you want shower sex, Dallas?"

His smile turned wicked. "And then some, Professor. If I can't get you to scream my name at least half a dozen times, I'm not doing something right."

She arched her brows. "Half a dozen? Someone has an extremely high opinion of himself."

Grinning, Dax said, "We'll stop counting at six." His smile broadened. "But I'll bet the number when we finish is higher. *Way* higher."

He pushed himself to his feet, holding out a hand and pulling her to hers.

"Let's see just how good you are, Mr. Tennyson. For me, I think it'll be a win-win."

20

Ivy received a text from Paloma, telling her that their flight from Dallas to San Antonio had been delayed due to a mechanical problem. The flight had been rescheduled to leave later in the morning. It would not reach San Antonio until a little after eleven.

Disappointment filled her. Paloma had called Ivy last night to let her know that instead of driving, she would be flying, and Jameson Polk, her new boss, would accompany her. Paloma had shared the pictures Ivy had texted, and the gallery director wished to see Ivy's paintings in person. Her friend said Polk had seemed taken by her paintings and shared that she believed he would ask to represent Ivy. They would also be attending the final Harmony & Hues before flying back to Dallas Sunday morning.

Since they would be delayed in arriving, it would take them probably two hours to disembark, pick up their rental, and drive to Lost Creek. Knowing the winery would be busy this last Saturday of the month, she texted back for them to meet her at the tasting room. She would do a tasting with Polk, since Paloma said he had expressly asked for one, and then hopefully she'd be able to sneak away for an hour to show the gallery director her paintings.

Paloma responded, telling Ivy they would see her at the tasting room, going straight there instead of to the B&B where they had reservations. Ivy only hoped she would be able to share her artwork in person. Her first priority, though, was to the tasting room. She was not going to let down her parents and employees during such a busy time. Thanks to the fusion nights, more visitors had been coming to Lost Creek, and the winery had benefited from these extra visitors. Ivy made certain the brochures she had designed for Weddings with Hart were prominently displayed in the tasting room and also told tasters of the expansion taking place, urging them to return soon.

Her cell rang, and she saw it was Dax. Answering, she asked, "Is your morning crazy?"

He chuckled. "Crazy in a good way. Business is booming at Java Junction. It's all hands on deck this morning. I assume the crowds will keep coming while I'm out assembling the sound equipment in the gazebo this afternoon. Deke said with so many artists participating in this last fusion, he'll be setting up the art walk extra early. At least all the tenants on the square are benefitting from the heavy foot traffic. But I was calling to see how you're doing. Are you ready to show off your paintings to the bigwig coming in?"

She explained how Paloma and Polk were running behind schedule. "I'm only hoping I can slip away from the tasting room and show him my work in person."

"You *make* time to do it," Dax said firmly. "If you're swamped, you call in reinforcements. Your mom. Your dad. Braden. Any of them are knowledgeable enough and can do a quick tasting or two during your absence."

"I'd hate to pull them away," she said, waffling.

"This is too important, Ivy," he emphasized. "I don't want you to blow this opportunity."

"I won't. Thanks for your support."

Ivy thought if push came to shove and she couldn't leave the tasting room, she could give Paloma the key to her studio and allow her friend to take her boss to view the paintings. She and Paloma had FaceTimed quite a bit, discussing each painting once Ivy completed it, so Paloma could easily point out the best features to Polk and give him behind the scenes stories if he asked for them. That would be the best compromise. Polk might not even want Ivy around while he perused her work.

She moved about the studio now, propping different canvases against the wall, staggering them so each could be completely seen with no overlap. She set up three easels in order to display what she thought were her best efforts on them before leaving for the winery.

As she'd expected, the tasting room had a steady crowd. She, Melanie, and Sarah all had different groups in play from the time they opened at eleven-thirty. Several mentioned they would be attending Harmony & Hues tonight, and she believed the series would end on a high note, with the largest attendance they'd had.

Close to two o'clock, she noticed Paloma enter with a distinguished gentleman who appeared to be in his mid-sixties. Bright blue eyes stood out in his tanned face. He was the only man in the tasting room wearing a suit and tie. She acknowledged Paloma with a smile, and her friend led her boss over to a display area where different Lost Creek Vineyards wines were featured. Fortunately, Ivy was near the end of a tasting and finished up her final remarks to the two couples with her. They had been enthusiastic in their responses, and between them, they bought a dozen bottles of wine. Melanie had finished her previous tasting a few minutes earlier, and she told Ivy she would ring up the sales, allowing her to greet the newcomers.

Paloma brightened as she headed toward them, kissing Ivy on both cheeks, saying, "Ivy Hart, I want to introduce you to Jameson Polk."

They shook hands and Polk said, "Paloma has sung your praises, Ivy. She also said you worked together at a Houston gallery."

"Yes, I served as the assistant director."

"So, Lost Creek called you home again?"

"You could say that. I was ready for a transition, one which would allow me to return to painting on a regular basis. The tasting room manager at my family's winery was retiring, and I've always had a nose for wine. It was perfect timing. My schedule allows me to paint for several hours most mornings before the tasting room opens."

"I've already seen the photographs of your work. Paloma shared those with me. I wouldn't have made the trip down to the Hill Country unless I saw great potential in you." Polk smiled. "I'm a Hill Country boy myself, though you probably wouldn't think that, seeing how I'm dressed. I was born in Uvalde. Went to SMU and stayed in Dallas after graduation since the gallery I'd interned at offered me a position. I hear your family's wines are top notch. Paloma has insisted I do a tasting with you since she knows how I'm fond of wine."

"Do you have time to do so?" she asked. "I know you're running behind schedule because of the delayed flight. I can give you my keys and you can look at my paintings."

"Our return flight to Dallas doesn't leave until nine tomorrow morning," Polk said. "I have the rest of the day free to sample Lost Creek Vineyards' wines and view your paintings, as well as attend the fusion night Paloma spoke of. Besides, if I'm in the Hill Country, I want wine and barbeque. Those are the essence of the region."

His words caused Ivy to chuckle. "Then I suppose we should get started, Mr. Polk."

"Jameson. Mr. Polk is my father."

She had them move to the tasting bar, asking his preferences in wine.

"I stick with all levels of red," he shared. "I will drink a rosé when the weather is warm, though. Let's focus on your reds today."

Ivy spent the next forty-five minutes walking Jameson

Polk through different reds produced from their vine-yards, giving him a thorough, detailed explanation about the wines and answering his questions with ease. She also had him taste a couple of blends, especially the one Dax had grown fond of, which consisted of a Syrah, Merlot, and Cabernet Sauvignon mix.

When they finished the tasting, Jameson looked pleased. "I've been to numerous wine tastings over the years, but I appreciate your knowledge and ease in describing Lost Creek Vineyards wines. Every bottle I tasted should be available at the finest restaurants in Dallas."

"My dad has gotten some of our wines placed in the better steakhouses in Dallas and Ft. Worth. He's been our chief winemaker from the beginning, but he's stepping aside from that role, turning the winemaking reins over to a winemaker from California. Dad will focus more on marketing in the future. Our wines have won numerous awards, including international ones, and I know he wants to put them on the tables of more restaurants in Texas and beyond."

Polk removed a card from his inner coat pocket and handed it to Ivy. "Give this to your father. Have him call me the next time he comes to Dallas. There are people I can introduce him to, hopefully smoothing the way a bit."

"That's very generous of you, Jameson. His name is Bill Hart. Dad has a trip planned to Dallas at the end of next week. I'm sure he would like to give you a call before he comes in. Hopefully, you could arrange a meeting between the two of you. If you let me know which wines you enjoyed now, I'll have Dad bring a few bottles of each when he drives up."

The gallery director told her his two preferences, and Ivy assured him he would receive several bottles of each. Her gut told her Polk had valuable connections that could make a difference as her father worked to get the family's wines into more restaurants.

"Are you ready to see Ivy's paintings now?" Paloma asked.

Ivy looked around the tasting room. Things had slowed a bit, and only one couple waited to begin a tasting at this point.

Sarah stepped to her and said, "We've got this, Ivy. Go ahead. You won't be gone that long."

"Thank you," she said gratefully, not only wanting to explain some about her art to Polk but hear his feedback.

She told Paloma to follow her into town because she would need to return to the tasting room after their visit.

Driving the ten minutes into town, Ivy's stomach knotted. She told herself Polk would either like her work or he wouldn't. If he didn't think he could find a market for it, he wasn't the only gallery director in the State of Texas. She could pursue other avenues, starting right here in Lost Creek with Deke Manchester. Her feminine intuition told her, though, that what she was now producing was good. Better than good. Ivy had high hopes that she could make a living through her art—and that Jameson Polk was key to her future success.

They parked behind the hardware store and mounted the stairs, Paloma pointing out the mural which Ivy had painted. The sun was bright this afternoon and would show off her paintings well in strong, natural light. She admitted the pair and closed the door behind them, letting Polk move from one painting to the next. He didn't comment as he studied each painting, causing more nerves to rattle through her.

Finally, he turned to her. "What would you wish to tell me about your art in general, Ivy?"

"The Hill Country is embedded in my soul," she began. "The landscape in this region is so varied. Hills. Valleys. Unique rock formations. Caverns. The land alone is breathtaking in and of itself, but I enjoy inserting the vegetation and wildlife into my work, as well."

She moved to one of her favorites, completed last month. "Bluebonnets speak to the heart of Texans. I particularly like this field of bluebonnets with the morning sun rising, kissing each flower with a ray of sunshine."

Stepping to another, she said, "I've always been intrigued by sunrises and sunsets. The spectrum of colors which come alive in the sky during those brief periods of time. That's apparent in this picture of the sun setting over Lost Creek Lake. Bodies of water do run throughout the Hill Country, despite its barren landscape. I've spent many happy times tubing along the Guadalupe River and swimming in this very lake. I love to paint water in various forms, capturing its varying shades and movement."

She waved her hand, indicated the body of work in the studio. "As you can see, my focus is on my roots. I think just as the Hill Country speaks to me, it does to others, as well. Not only Texans, but lovers of nature and its varying beauty."

Swallowing, Ivy found her mouth dry. "Do you have any questions for me? Or any feedback on a particular painting?"

A slow smile spread across Polk's face. "I'm one of those Texans whose heart will always be in the Hill Country. I may have lived in Dallas for over four decades, but this region holds my heart in its hands. I think your use of color is dynamic, Ivy. Your brushstrokes are impeccable. I see everything here has been done in oils, save for this one picture of Lost Creek Lake. Do you work in watercolors very often?"

"I'll be honest, Jameson. I didn't paint for several years. My previous employer kept me so busy that I barely had time to make my bed, much less sit before a canvas and indulge in hours of painting. Since I recently moved back to Lost Creek, though, I've rediscovered my passion for painting. Yes, I have worked with watercolors before, and I plan to continue experimenting with them, but the bulk of my work will continue to be done in oil. I used to always enjoy charcoal, but I feel it doesn't do the Hill Country justice, with all its incredible colors embedded in the landscape."

"I wish to represent you and definitely will commit to a showing of your work, Ivy. I haven't been as enthused with a Texas artist in many years, but I see something special in your work." His eyes roamed the room a moment. "It looks as if you have fourteen or fifteen canvases. For a show, I would want a minimum of twenty-five paintings. Thirty would be better. How long would it take you to produce the additional paintings?"

She thought a moment, doing the math in her head. "I've completed a little over two paintings a month since I've returned to Lost Creek. I still have my job at the tasting room, and I do know it's important to have a balance between work and spending time with family and friends. I could probably be ready with another ten paintings by the beginning of February, but that would mean you would need to accept every painting I gave to you. There wouldn't be extras to sort through with that tight deadline. You could give me more time, and I could give you a better variety to select from."

"I can't see myself rejecting anything you paint, Ivy. I don't say that lightly. Paloma told me you were in charge of selecting and placing paintings exhibited at the Houston gallery. You know from experience that it's always good to have extra canvases to look upon, but I don't need them in this instance. I'll take whatever you can give me by the first of February."

Jameson extended his hand, and Ivy took it, shaking.

"We can draw up the legal paperwork when you come to Dallas in the near future," he said. "I do wish for my gallery to represent your work. We can agree on a period of time regarding our agreement, as well as the commission I'll take for your exhibition."

Pausing, he studied her a long moment, and Ivy felt her cheeks heat. "I also think you should consider coming permanently to Dallas to paint. See what inspires you there. If you leave your job at the winery and start painting full-time, you would produce more art in a timely fashion. Would that be possible, especially with the guarantee of an exhibition at my gallery?"

Ivy was torn. She felt a deep responsibility to her parents because they had allowed her to take over the tasting room. Especially with the new expansion, she would be needed more than ever here in Lost Creek.

And that didn't even include factoring in her relationship with Dax.

How could she go to Dallas to paint and still see him? A long-distance relationship with the man she loved had no appeal. Yet Jameson Polk was giving her the opportunity of a lifetime.

"For now, I need to remain in Lost Creek," she said firmly. "I have obligations to my family's business."

"Yes, Paloma told me of the expansion. How there will be a much larger tasting room and your sister is opening an event center on the winery's grounds. But while family obligations are important, Ivy, you must be true to yourself and your art."

"It's tempting to come to Dallas, Jameson, but I need to stay in Lost Creek for the foreseeable future. Inspiration surrounds me here. If you can't commit to a showing of my work early next year, I completely understand. I can always find different representation."

He shook his head vigorously. "No, Ivy, I want to show your work and represent you. I merely believe unless you choose to dedicate yourself to your art full-time, you are wasting your potential. I do, however, respect your commitment to your family and their business. Keep sending photographs of your completed artwork to Paloma. In fact, I will have her drive down here one day next week to collect what you've already finished. That will give you extra room in your studio, and I can also began thinking of the show and how I will assemble it."

"That would be terrific, Jameson. The only painting which needs to remain with me is the one of Lost Creek Rock."

Disappointment filled his face. "Why?"

"That painting goes to my sister when she marries, which should be soon. I can, though, paint something very similar. Approach the rock from different angles. Lost Creek Rock is a huge part of this town's history, and I can see myself painting it many times in the future. Have you heard the legend surrounding it?"

"No, I can't say that I have. In fact, I wasn't familiar with it. I only know of Enchanted Rock."

Ivy briefly related the tale of the tragedy between the two lovers, and Polk gobbled it up.

"Yes, I do want more than one canvas of Lost Creek Rock. Being able to share this story with clients is a wonderful way to tease potential buyers."

"I need to get back to the tasting room," she told the pair. Looking to Paloma she asked, "When will you be down here to pick up the paintings? Will you bring the specialty wrap and custom crates for shipping, so they'll be protected?"

"I can return any day that's convenient for you, Ivy, and I'll have everything necessary to make certain your paintings arrive without a scratch on them. You know I have experience with shipping art. I won't let you down."

"Why don't you make it Monday or Wednesday? Those are my two days off from work."

"Monday works for me," her friend said.

Glancing to Jameson, she added, "I know you're ready to get some barbeque in you, but I do hope you'll make time to stop by the final Harmony & Hues night. It will be the largest display of art since we started the fusion nights."

"Paloma assured me I'll want to pick up a painting or two for the gallery. Who knows? I might find another talent to sign on this trip."

The trio left her studio, with Paloma saying they would check in at The Inn on Lost Creek, followed by a trip to Blackwood BBQ.

Ivy returned to the tasting room, having been gone just an hour. She did another tasting for a family of four. By then, it was five o'clock.

"Why don't you head to the square?" Sarah asked. "We'll finish up here. Dax will be wondering where you are."

"I think I'll do that," she said, eager to share with Dax the positive outcome of Jameson Polk viewing her art.

When she reached the square, a crowd was already gathering, even though Harmony & Hues wouldn't start for another hour. Ivy parked behind the hardware store and walked to Java Junction, not having seen Dax at the gazebo. She waved at Scott and Jeanine, working behind the barista bar, and they both pointed up, letting her know Dax was in his apartment. Cutting through the storeroom, she went up the interior staircase and knocked at his door.

Dax opened it, his guitar in hand. When he saw her, he pulled her to him, the kiss unexpected but wonderful.

"Tell me everything," he said, stepping back into his apartment, and Ivy followed.

"Jameson liked everything he saw!" she said, her enthusiasm bubbling over. "He's going to hold a showing for me, probably in mid-February. I've got a lot to paint between now and then, though. He wants between ten and fifteen more paintings from me by then."

He frowned. "That's a lot of work. Then again, maybe traffic in the tasting room will slow some once fall ends."

She had told him how Lost Creek still received a good number of visitors through October since the weather was usually mild.

"Maybe you can move from working at the tasting room five days a week to four," he suggested. "That extra day of painting would help. And if we need to cut back on seeing one another, I—"

"No," she interrupted. "I want to see more of you. Not less."

He raked a hand through his hair. "You have a ton on your plate, Ivy, especially with the new tasting room opening soon. You have workers to hire, and that includes those in the gift shop, since you'll be taking on the responsibilities of that since the two will occupy the same building. Ordering the merch. Keeping track of sales."

Wrapping her arms around his waist, she said, "*You* are my priority, Dax. Everything else is a distant second."

He kissed her. "I like being your number one, Professor, but we need to talk about this more once tonight is over. Right now, I need to get back to the gazebo."

Taking her hand, he led Ivy downstairs and to the center of the town square. She watched him talking with different musicians who would be performing tonight and decided to see if Deke needed her help. As she hunted for Deke, Ivy decided it wasn't important to mention to Dax about Jameson's suggestion that she move to Dallas, even if it might be temporary. It wasn't something she planned to do, so she didn't feel she was hiding anything from him.

So why did she feel guilty keeping it to herself?

21

Dax checked in with a few of the people who would be performing this evening. He had asked the most popular acts from previous Harmony & Hues nights to return for this final fusion of the season. Everyone invited had agreed to appear this evening, even Joe Morgan, who was a college senior and returned from his civil engineering studies at Texas State in San Marcus.

He had thought to possibly DJ the six to eight slot when people viewed the art and gathered in the town square, nibbling on something they had picked up and sipping beverages from Java Junction. Instead, he had decided to simply put together a playlist. Having upbeat music play over the loudspeakers would lend a party vibe to the atmosphere and keep him from being tied down at a turntable those two hours. In putting together his selections, he made certain to include several popular country songs. Dax had grown fond of the musical genre and had his fledging band rehearsing a few country covers. If they were going to perform at any events in this area, they would definitely need country in their repertoire.

Looking over the residents and visitors who now gathered in the square, he was pleased that the square's merchants had taken to the idea of holding Harmony& Hues outdoors this summer. Many of them extended their Saturday hours in order to accommodate the evenings. Tonight, all would be open late for this final fusion night.

Since it was a minute until six, he decided to address the crowd, moving up the gazebo stairs and picking up the microphone, turning it on.

"Good evening, Lost Creek!" he declared, getting a rousing response. "I'm Dax Tennyson, your host for Harmony & Hues."

The crowd began to settle down, giving him their full attention.

Dax continued. "Ivy Hart and I had an idea a few months ago about celebrating local talent, supporting both artists and musicians, coming together a few times a month to do so. Tonight is the last fusion night of the season. Hopefully, we'll be back for more next summer. In the meantime, you'll be able to hear some of the same singers and musicians at Java Junction, my place, on Wednesday and Saturday nights. If you're interested in performing, please touch base with me."

He surveyed the crowd and smiled. "I want to thank the people who live here in Lost Creek and those who are visiting it for making Harmony & Hues such a success.

You've got the next two hours to complete your art walk and see what's available. If you're interested in buying a piece, let Deke Manchester know."

By now, Deke knew to be close to the gazebo, and he bounded up the stairs, waving at the crowd.

"You can't miss Deke," Dax said. "Not in that bright yellow Hawaiian shirt."

The crowd laughed as Deke traveled back down the stairs.

"All the merchants on the square will be open until eight o'clock tonight, so I hope that after you've seen all the art, you'll stop in and do a bit of shopping. The sports bar and diner are open for takeout if you want to bring your food outside, and we have a taco truck parked at the north end of the square. I know you'll all get thirsty at some point, so head over to Java Junction and grab yourself something cool to drink. In the meantime, enjoy yourselves. The musical portion of the evening will start at eight. Thank you."

Applause filled the air as Dax put on the music, which lent a true party feel to the event. He worked his way through the crowd, proud to know so many of the people in attendance. Although he'd only been in Lost Creek since January and opened for business since March, he felt like a part of this community. He spoke to the mayor. The police chief. The president of the local bank. A doctor. The high school principal. The head football coach. Everyone was friendly and supportive, asking him to make sure he brought back Harmony & Hues next spring or summer.

Spying Ivy with Paloma, he noticed the older man with them. He assumed him to be Jameson Polk. Dax weaved through the crowd, making his way to them. He kissed Ivy's cheek and then turned to greet Paloma.

"Glad you could make it back to Lost Creek, Paloma. I hope you're enjoying your new gallery and Dallas."

"Very much, Dax. Thank you for texting me the list of restaurants. I've tried all but one of them. Let me introduce you to my boss." She turned. "This is Jameson Polk. He went to SMU as you did."

Dax grinned. "Go, Mustangs!"

Jean Bradley came up, drawing Ivy and Paloma's attention away, so he focused on Polk.

"I hope you'll have time to walk through all the art on display, Mr. Polk. I know you've already seen Ivy's paintings and know how talented she us."

The gallery director smiled wryly at Dax. "So, you're the reason Ivy doesn't want to come to Dallas."

It was as if the older man had sucker punched him. "What are you talking about?" he asked, taken aback.

Polk strolled away, stopping at the next easel on display. Dax followed, his heart pounding wildly in his chest.

"Ivy Hart is one of the most talented artists I have met. I have over forty years in the business, so I know what I'm talking about."

"Ivy and I did discuss your conversation with her," Dax said, carefully measuring his words. "She told me you were interested in representing her work and would put on a show for her early next year. She didn't have time to share any of the details with me."

Polk's gaze met his. "Don't get me wrong. I'm a Hill Country boy myself, but I don't think Ivy needs to waste her time here. She's only painting part-time now because of her job at the tasting room. I told her she needed to move to Dallas and devote herself to painting full-time. I guarantee I can sell every canvas she gives me."

Again, Dax felt as if he'd been bashed by a sledge-hammer out of nowhere. Why hadn't Ivy mentioned this to him? Then again, he'd been in a rush when he'd seen her and said they could talk more about Polk after tonight's Harmony& Hues ended.

Carefully, he said, "Ivy is very close to her parents and sister. She has a lot of responsibility as the manager of Lost Creek Winery's tasting room. I don't know if you're aware of it, but the winery is undergoing a huge expansion now. The tasting room will triple in size and also include a gift shop. Ivy will be responsible for both of those enterprises. It's not something she can easily walk away from. Her parents would need to replace her with someone they trusted. Someone who has her remarkable smell and taste for wines, as well as her vast knowledge. Ivy doesn't take her duties lightly. Right now, she's enjoying the balance of working at the tasting room and still having time for her art."

Polk frowned at him. "Should Michelangelo or Da Vinci have worked at another job and merely dabbled with their art? While I don't mean to compare Ivy to two artistic legends, I believe her talent is being wasted by not dedicating herself fully to her art. Yes, she told me of the winery's expansion and even mentioned she wished to have a balance between work at the winery, her painting, and her private life. That she needed to spend time with family and friends."

Polk paused. "I can see a big part of that is devoted to her relationship with you. Don't hold her back, Dax. If you have something that will last, it can stand up to a separation for now. Ivy needs to be in Dallas, focusing solely on her painting and the upcoming show where I will feature her work. This will be her big break. I can introduce her into and give her access to a world she has only dreamed about. Something tells me you are the only person who could convince her of that."

From the corner of his eye, Dax saw Ivy and Paloma headed toward them. Jameson Polk must have spied them as well because he pointed to the painting in front of them and began talking about the artist's technique.

Dax tuned out the man as Ivy slipped her hand around his.

He loved her. She was his life. But he wanted what was best for her. Lawson Everhart had stolen most of Ivy's twenties, making work demands on her that left her no time to paint. Even Dax could see how talented Ivy was with a brush. If he didn't persuade her to go to Dallas and pursue this opportunity, he would be as guilty as her former boss of preventing her from spreading her wings and taking the art world by storm.

Squeezing her hand, he thought how different his life would be without Ivy in it. If she were truly going to commit to her art, she didn't need to be in some long-distance relationship which took away her focus and time.

Much as he loved her, Dax understood it was time to let her go.

He turned to her. Smiling brightly, he said, "I'm going to keep circulating. You're still coming over at the end of the night?"

Her smile caused his heart to sink. "I plan to be with you *all* night, Dax Tennyson. Knock 'em dead when you perform."

They parted and he moved through the crowd, stopping and chatting here and there, his gut churning painfully as he went through the motions. When eight o'clock came, Dax took the stage again, cutting off the music. That was the signal for everyone to have a seat. Some had taken to bringing lawn chairs, while others sat on blankets or the grass itself. A few even perched atop the hoods of their cars parked around the square.

He pushed aside his feelings, owing the best of himself to those gathered, and looked out at the crowed. "We've got a great lineup for you tonight," he said into the mic. "Some of your favorites from the season will be performing. We're kicking off our last fusion evening with Carolyn and Marcy Tompkins, two talented sisters who will get this party started. Ladies?"

As the pair took the stage, Dax hurried down the gazebo steps. He would concentrate on the music and not his heart, which was painfully shattering with each breath.

Each singer and musician wowed the crowd, and Dax

was pleased he'd brought something good to this community, a place he would still be a part of once Ivy left.

Sylvia joined him. "Are you all right, Dax?" she asked, concern in her voice.

"A little sad, seeing Harmony & Hues come to an end," he lied. "Ready for our duet?"

He bounded up the steps and thanked the previous performer, saying, "Before I came to Lost Creek, I hadn't sung in front of a live audience. I'd written some songs and thought I might perform them in my coffeehouse. Ivy was smart enough to recommend that I take some lessons with Sylvia Moore. I know many of you shared many hours in the high school choir room with her. Sylvia has taken me under her wing, giving me voice lessons, building my confidence. She's a talented singer in her own right, and I've asked for her to sing with me this evening."

The former teacher climbed the gazebo stairs, and Dax gave her a bear hug.

"We're doing one of Sylvia's favorite songs tonight. *Islands in the Stream.*"

They had rehearsed their duet several times during the last two weeks, and their voices blended together as well as Dolly Parton and Kenny Rogers in their original recording of the tune. By the time the song ended, the crowd's enthusiastic response had Sylvia blushing. She waved and moved down the steps.

Dax waited until they fell silent again. "I'd like to close out the night with a song I performed at the very first fusion night."

By now, he had located Ivy, who smiled at him. "This one's for you, Ivy."

He sang *Forever's Embrace*, knowing it would be the last time he would ever play it. Dax got through the song without his voice breaking, but he knew he would never be able to sing the lyrics again, live or otherwise.

He sounded the final note, and the crowd cheered for him. At a moment when he should have been celebrating, he was at the lowest point in his life. Still, he hid his feelings from everyone.

And Ivy.

"Goodnight, Lost Creek! I'll see you next summer—or hopefully, at Java Junction every morning."

Dax lifted the guitar strap over his head and set the instrument on a nearby bench. He began unhooking the sound equipment. Scott appeared and helped him bring everything back to the coffeehouse over a few trips. Sean was in the process of closing, along with three other workers. Ivy had followed them and pitched in, picking up a broom and sweeping the floor.

With everyone helping, they wrapped up things within a few minutes, and Dax escorted Ivy up to his apartment, allowing Scott to lock up.

Her cheeks were flushed with the excitement from the evening. "That was definitely the best turnout we've had all summer. Deke told me sales were brisk. And Jameson asked to represent one of the potters. All in all, it was a spectacular way to end the series."

He framed her face with his hands, wanting to freeze this moment and the way she looked in his memory.

Kissing her softly, he relished the taste of her. The subtle vanilla scent on her skin. The feel of her curves pressed to him.

Breaking the kiss, he said, "A lot of the success goes to you. We wouldn't have had a Harmony & Hues without your contributions. Your idea to move it outdoors was genius."

"I'm glad the community supported the idea—and those artists who contributed to it. But enough about fusion. I'm ready to fuse our bodies together, Dallas."

She yanked his mouth down to hers, and the sparks between them ignited. They kissed hungrily as they tore at one another's clothes. He lifted her in his arms, taking her to the bed and tossing her atop the mattress, quickly following as his body covered hers. They made love greedily, gobbling one another up, desire engulfing them in flames. Dax tried to memorize Ivy's every curve, knowing it would be the last time they were together.

When they climaxed, it was an achingly beautiful moment.

He collapsed against her, kissing her for a long time before finally rolling to his side, their limbs entangled. His hand stroked her hair as she rested her cheek against his chest.

"I wish I could have known my parents," she said, her words surprising him. "I think they would have been proud of the woman I've become."

She turned her head to look up at him, stacking her hands beneath her chin, resting atop them. "I call Bill and Cecily Mom and Dad, but they're actually my aunt and uncle," she explained. "My dad and Bill were brothers. We were driving up from Houston to spend Thanksgiving with them. A truck driver fell asleep at the wheel and hit us head on."

"Were you hurt?" he asked, stroking her hair.

"No. I was only six months old and facing the rear, buckled into my car seat in the back seat. My parents were killed instantly. The police told Bill and Cecily that the car seat saved my life. I had a few bruises, but other than that, I was fine. They adopted me."

"When did they tell you about the accident?" he asked.

"I was young. About four or five. They never wanted it to be a secret. I had a picture of the three of us—my parents and me—which I kept on my nightstand for a long time. They've always treated me as one of their own. Harper and Todd were my siblings. Bill and Cecily have been my parents in every sense of the word. I do think about my birth parents every now and then, though, and wonder what they were like. What our relationship would have been like. Would I have turned out the way I did growing up in their household? Would I have had brothers and sisters?"

Dax pressed his lips to her brow. "I'm sorry you never got to know them."

"I've always felt loved. That's what Mom and Dad said was most important. I do think of Cecily and Bill as my parents, but I thought it was something you should know about me."

After Ivy had opened up to him, he hated to hurt her now, but Dax felt he had no choice.

"Anything else you want to tell me?" he asked softly.

He sensed her body tense for a moment before she replied. "No."

"What about Jameson Polk asking you to come to Dallas?"

She startled, quickly sitting up. "What? He told you that? He had no right to share that with you!"

Dax pushed to a sitting position. "Why didn't *you* tell me, Ivy?"

Moonlight poured in the window, illuminating her face, showing how flustered she was.

"There was nothing *to* tell, Dax. Other than Polk is interested in my paintings. That he wants to represent me and hold a showing for me."

"He said that you're wasting your time in Lost Creek, Ivy. You're playing at painting." Taking a deep breath, he slowly let it out. "He's right. You're too talented to only paint part of the time. You have tremendous potential."

Anger flushed her cheeks. "Oh, so now you're an art critic? You want to tell me how to manage my career?"

"You may not have a career if you don't listen to Polk," Dax insisted. "He's been in the business a long time. He sees something special in you. In your work. Don't blow this chance and stay in Lost Creek just because of me."

She crossed her arms protectively. "I'm not staying just for you. I have obligations to my family. To the business." Her mouth set stubbornly.

He shook his head. "The winery was getting along just fine before you came home. Your parents can find a new tasting room manager."

Her eyes filled with tears. "I *love* you, Dax. Why are you pushing me away?"

Though his heart was breaking, he firmed his resolve. "Because it's the best thing for you. You let your art remain dormant within you for too long, Ivy. This your chance. An opportunity that might not come along ever again. Hell, Polk could wind up pissed at you and black-ball you if you don't listen to advice. I don't want that to happen."

He took her hands, even though she tried to pull away. Bringing them to his lips, he kissed them tenderly.

"Take the leap of faith, Ivy. Go to Dallas."

"But… what about us?"

He swallowed painfully. "There is no us anymore. I refuse to hold you back. I need to let you go."

"Even though we love one another?" she asked, her voice small.

"*Because* we love one another," he told her. "Ivy, this is the hardest thing I've ever done."

"We can try long—"

"No," Dax said firmly. "You don't need to waste time on me. Making phone calls. Driving back to Lost Creek every weekend. We need a clean break."

This time she jerked her hands hard, freeing them. "What if I don't want that?"

"It's the best thing for you. For your career. Let's just be happy for the time we've shared."

She moved from the bed, angrily cursing under her breath as she gathered her clothing. She hurriedly slipped into her clothes, avoiding looking at him. When she finished, she faced him.

"I believed in you. In us." Her eyes pleaded with him to take back what he had said.

"And I believe in you." Echoing her words from earlier in the evening, Dax said, "Knock 'em dead, Ivy."

Hurt filled her eyes, along with tears, which now streamed down her cheeks. Wordlessly, she walked out the room.

And out of Dax's life.

22

Ivy hadn't slept. Her eyes were almost swollen shut from the tears she'd wept.

Dax had ended things between them. It was over.

She wanted to hate him. Rail at him. Punch him. But none of those would change the fact that they were done.

All because of her art.

She paced around her studio, looking at the canvases as the manifestation of betrayal. It took all her willpower to sit on the lumpy couch and not claw at the paintings, tearing them to shreds. That would be foolish, though. Months of work would be down the drain. Besides, each painting was like a child to her. A piece of her. An investment of her time. Her soul placed upon a canvas. She couldn't destroy them.

But she could certainly give Jameson Polk a piece of her mind.

Going into the miniscule bathroom, Ivy washed her face, holding a cold cloth to her eyes, hoping to reduce the swelling. She needed to confront the gallery director before he left Lost Creek for his flight in San Antonio. Knowing he and Paloma must be leaving soon, Ivy went downstairs to her car and drove to The Inn on Lost Creek, Jean Bradley's charming B&B. She pulled in, seeing the rental Paloma had been driving yesterday, and waited in her car.

Not ten minutes later, her friend appeared, carrying her weekender on her shoulder. Polk also came into view, wearing the same suit coat from yesterday. He'd changed his shirt and sported a different tie. Ivy climbed from her car, reaching Polk just as he placed a carry-on in the trunk of the car.

"Ivy!" Paloma exclaimed. "What a surprise. I didn't think we'd see you this morning."

Her eyes narrowed as she looked at Polk. "I need to speak to you. This has nothing to do with Paloma—and everything to do between you and me."

He turned to Paloma. "Get in the car, dear. I'll be with you shortly."

Paloma looked confused. "What—"

"In the car," Polk said again, more firmly this time.

Paloma looked to Ivy, and she nodded. Thankfully, her friend climbed behind the wheel, but it was obvious she was concerned, still looking at them over her shoulder.

"Don't take anything out on Paloma," Ivy warned. "She has nothing to do with this. *You* are the one I have a problem with."

Polk sniffed. "I see Mr. Tennyson spoke to you. Good for him. I wasn't certain if he had it in him or not."

Anger seared through her. "You had no right to discuss my personal business with Dax. And I'll have you know that he is the best man I have ever known."

"He seems lovely, Ivy. And if you believe I overstepped, then I apologize. I merely spoke with him about your vast potential and the prospects which lay in front of you, especially if you will stop being so pigheaded and commit fully to your art."

Keeping her voice even, she said, "I have put both heart and soul into each painting I've completed since I've moved back to Lost Creek. It's obvious if you look at my canvases. But I'm not a factory, Mr. Polk. I can't produce, produce, produce. Art is woven into every fiber of my being, but I will never allow it—or anything else—to consume me. I enjoy my role as the Lost Creek Winery's tasting manager. I have a wonderful time meeting new people and introducing them to the intricacies of wine. I've contributed numerous ideas to our current expansion, and I plan to be a part of my family's winery for many years to come."

She paused, collecting her thoughts. "I am a better painter *because* I do other things I enjoy. See people and share experiences outside of my art. Art can drain its creator. Deplete him or her. Use up an artist until nothing is left. I need balance in my life. And love."

Apparently, her words had no effect on him. Ivy shook her head. "You've ruined the most important relationship in my life, Mr. Polk. I can never forgive you for that. I no longer wish for you to represent me. I am withdrawing from the planned exhibition next year."

His eyes gleamed at her. "We had a binding, oral contract, Ivy. In Texas, a verbal contract is enforceable."

She stared at him. "You forget whom you are talking with, Mr. Polk. I was involved in contracts with all the artists whose works my gallery in Houston displayed. The Texas Business and Commerce Code mandates that a contract must always be placed in writing if the sale of goods includes a price greater than five hundred dollars. Since my paintings would have gone for far more than that, you don't have a legal leg to stand upon."

"Touché, Ivy," he said, inclining his head in respect. "I am disappointed that you no longer wish to work with me. Perhaps after you have calmed down, a cooler head will prevail."

Knowing she would never agree to have her work represented by this man, she demanded, "Will you black-ball me?"

He looked hurt. "I would never do such a thing. In fact, more than anything, I still wish to come to an agreement with you. I see how honorable you are. Very few people are so these days."

She shook her head. "I can't work with someone I don't trust. If you would go behind my back on this issue, what else might you do?"

"I see," he said brusquely, seeming to understand that she wished to sever all ties with him.

"Please, don't take out your anger with me on Paloma."

He frowned. "And lose the best employee I've ever

hired? Have no fears on that front, Ivy. Paloma's employment is not in danger." He hesitated. "I do hope you will reconsider working with me. My door will always be open to you."

She shook her head, angry that he still continued to push. "No. Once trust is broken, it can never be won again."

Polk cleared his throat. "Would you be opposed to me passing along a couple of names to you? Dealers you might place more faith in than me?"

Ivy thought this was just a way to get around them working directly together. "Have Paloma text me their names and numbers. I can't guarantee I will contact them," she said coolly.

He smiled grimly. "I wish you the best of luck, Ivy. I hope one day to see your paintings being shown. In Dallas and beyond."

Polk got into the car and signaled to Paloma to drive. Before the car passed Ivy, her cell chimed. She walked back to her car, checking the screen after she climbed behind the wheel. The text was from Paloma. She must have typed it while watching Ivy and Polk and hit send as her boss got into the vehicle.

> What is going on??? I thought you were happy with your arrangement with Jameson. I know there's a story here. I can't talk around him. I'll call you once I'm home.

Ivy sighed. She would happily give Paloma her side of

the story, knowing Jameson Polk would most likely give her friend his own, heavily edited version.

In the meantime, Ivy had not only chosen to give up an opportunity most artists never received, she was also without the man she loved.

Could her relationship with Dax be repaired?

She still loved him. She believed he still loved her.

But would he accept that she had squandered the chance to be represented by one of the most revered names in the Dallas art world? Dax would feel guilty— even blame himself—for this wasted shot at getting her foot in the door, thinking she rejected it for him alone.

No, she had considered other things besides her relationship with him. Ivy just had to make Dax understand that.

Because she wasn't certain she could ever pick up a brush again if she didn't have Dax's love and support.

Ivy didn't want to go home and be like a dark rain cloud raining on Harper and Braden's morning. She decided to stop at The Bake House and pick up something to eat before returning to her studio.

It was barely six-thirty by the time she arrived, but two people were already in line ahead of her. The bakery had a sweet scent hanging in the air, and she inhaled deeply.

Emerson finished with a customer and smiled at Ivy, but her smile faded quickly.

"What's wrong? You've been crying," her friend said, worry filling her face.

Nodding, she said, "I need a little pick-me-up. Lots of sugar and butter. What do you suggest?"

"A dirt bomb," Emerson told her. "It's like a cinnamon sugar donut and a muffin had a baby. Or maybe a chocolate cinnamon babkallah. I've been playing around both these recipes. This is first weekend Ethel has let me put them out for sale."

"One of each," Ivy said. "And a coffee, too." She wanted something to drink and knew the bakery didn't serve hot teas.

As Emerson placed the dirt bomb in a bakery box, she paused. "You aren't going to Java Junction for that?"

"No." Tears welled in her eyes.

Emerson set down the box and came from behind the counter. She wrapped her arms around Ivy.

"I'm sorry. I like Dax. I like the two of you together. We stayed open late last night because of Harmony & Hues, and I propped open the door after closing as I cleaned up so I could hear the music." Emerson paused, looking directly at Ivy. "I heard the song he sang for you. Ivy, that man loves you."

She sniffed. "We've... hit an impasse."

Another customer came in and went to the cooler, pulling out a carton of milk.

"I know you've been trying to let Harper enjoy being in her bubble of happiness. But you should talk to her. Or go to Finley. She's at home now. She has a photo session at two and said she was staying home this morning to grade papers and do laundry. Go talk with her, Ivy."

Emerson went behind the counter, smiling at the new customer who'd stepped up behind Ivy. "Be right with you." She added another bomb and two of what she'd called the babkallahs to the box, closing it and handing it to Ivy before pouring her a tall coffee and slipping a lid onto it.

"I'll text Finley and let her know you're on your way," Emerson said, not giving Ivy an out, for which she was grateful.

When she tried to pay for the bakery items, her friend shook her head. "Go. We can talk later."

Ivy left the bakery and drove home, parking in the driveway. As she got out of the car, she saw Harper and Braden halfway down the block, dressed in running clothes, turning the corner. She decided to shower first and texted Finley that she'd be over in about twenty minutes.

The shower revived her, and her eyes no longer looked so puffy. She pulled the shower cap from her head and shook out her hair, dressing quickly and running a brush through her hair before brushing her teeth. By the time she retrieved the coffee and bakery box, Harper and Braden still weren't home, for which she was grateful.

She walked the few houses down to Finley and Emerson's rental. Finley sat in the porch swing, pushing off with her toe. She held a red pen in her hand.

"Grading spelling tests," she said, looking at Ivy carefully. "Want to come inside? It's about time for me to move my sheets from the washer to the dryer."

"Sure."

Ivy followed Finley inside, heading to the kitchen and placing the bakery box on the café table. She got out plates and set the pastries on them, putting her coffee beside her plate and taking a seat.

Finley appeared, the pen and papers gone. She poured herself a tall glass of milk and joined Ivy at the table.

"How bad is it?" she asked. "I see Emerson prescribed a double dose of medicine." Finley bit into the bomb.

Ivy did the same, savoring the cinnamon and sugar rush. She chewed for a moment, wondering how to explain everything.

"It has to be something with Dax," Finley ventured. "Tell me what you can."

Ivy explained how Paloma had brought her boss from Dallas to view Ivy's work and how Polk had praised it to the rafters.

"He made me feel like the next It Girl in art."

"He's not off the mark, Ivy," Finley said. "I've seen your stuff. You're really, really good. And that's coming from one artist to another. I wouldn't dare put myself in your class, but as a photographer, I've got a good eye. I know good art—and that's what you produce. It's powerful. Evocative. I was raised in Lost Creek, so I have a tremendous fondness for the landscape of the Hill Country, but I believe anyone would be moved by your paintings, no matter where they call home. If this guy was so keen on you, where's the breakdown? I can't see Dax being jealous of you getting that kind of attention. He's always appeared supportive to me."

"*Too* supportive," she replied, not bothering to hide her bitterness. "Polk suggested I quit the tasting room and move to Dallas. Paint full-time."

Finley frowned. "No, he's wrong about that. You're too loyal to your family to do so. Besides, you've invested a lot of yourself in this expansion. You'll have the best and largest tasting room for miles, plus you've had great ideas for the gift shop. You're meant to run both places. And I know how your art is better because you've got balance in your life."

"Exactly," she said, nodding her head. "You get it."

"What side did Dax come down on? Polk's, I'm assuming."

"Polk pretty much said Dax and everything in Lost Creek was holding me back. Keeping me from being the artist I could be. Preventing me from dedicating myself entirely to my painting. Dax bought his pitch—hook, line, and sinker." Tears sprang to her eyes again.

Finley took her hand, squeezing it. "And he was being noble and stepping aside, so you can go be this famous, wealthy artist."

She nodded, taking the napkin Finley handed her and pressing it against her eyes.

"Dax is wrong. Polk, too. I need balance. If I don't have it, the art will devour me. Deplete me. And then it will suffer."

"Did you explain that to Dax?"

"No," she said quietly. "I was too angry by that point. I felt Dax was throwing away what we have together. Sacrificing our relationship so he wouldn't hold me back. I was so angry, I just left."

Finley's gaze met hers. "Then you're going to have to make him understand, Ivy. He's hurting as much as you are. And he loves you. I'm sure of that. You need to really talk to him. Don't let him shut you down or push you away. You need to fight for the two of you—and your art. I know your heart won't be in it without Dax."

She blew her nose with the napkin. "Thanks for getting it, Finley. Thanks for listening."

Her friend grinned. "Thanks for bringing the pastries." She rose and went to the pantry, returning with a large bag of potato chips. "Let's balance the sweet with the salty."

Ivy laughed—and for the first time since she'd walked out Dax's door, she felt hope shining within her.

23

Dax pounded the pavement of the empty streets of Lost Creek, despondency filling him. He hadn't slept after Ivy walked out. He hated to have forced her out that door, but he knew it was the best thing for her and her career. She had great things ahead of her and didn't need to continue looking back.

He ran twice as long as he usually did, to the point of exhaustion, hoping if he wore out his body, he wouldn't feel the anguish filling him. Returning down Main Street, heading to his apartment, he realized no amount of pushing himself beyond his limits would ever make the truth go away.

He loved Ivy Hart. And he would never love anyone else again.

Deliberately, Dax focused straight ahead, not looking at the gigantic mural he would see every day of his life.

The one which would remind him of the woman he would never forget.

In his apartment, he stood in the shower stall so long, the water finally ran cold. It was important to keep busy, but working the Sunday morning after the final Harmony & Hues was the last thing he could face doing. He couldn't smile at all the customers congratulating him on the series. Not when his soul had been shattered.

Grabbing the keys to his truck, Dax went downstairs and drove aimlessly for hours through the Hill Country. It seemed that every vista he passed reminded him of Ivy. They had taken many trips in his truck, driving around and stopping so she might sketch a place. His throat swelled with unshed tears, wanting her desperately, knowing she would always be just out of his grasp.

Dax drove into San Antonio, a place he'd never been before, and got out to stretch his legs, walking along the lengthy Riverwalk. Being a Sunday, he saw couples everywhere, strolling hand-in-hand, or families corralling laughing children. He hadn't dreamed ahead enough to think about the children he would have with Ivy, but it would have been a natural progression of their relationship. Now, he knew he would always be alone. By choice. No one would be able to bring the sunshine into his life the way Ivy had.

He returned to his truck, driving again through the Hill Country. When his stomach grumbled loudly, protesting that he hadn't fueled it, he pulled in at the next town's Dairy Queen. One bite into his Hungr-Buster, Dax found he couldn't swallow. He tossed it in the trash.

Driving on, he went through many of the small towns he had passed through when choosing the place to settle and start Java Junction. He couldn't imagine staying in Lost Creek with Ivy gone. There would be too many reminders of her. Maybe he could go from town to town in the region, starting up a Java Junction in each of them, even beginning a Harmony & Hues series in every different place. Scott Bartlett would be the perfect manager to take over in Lost Creek for Dax. The cop was personable and efficient. Dax could see himself staying in a place for several months and then moving on, leaving a new Java Junction behind.

One thing he knew for certain. He would never perform live again. At this point, he couldn't even imagine picking up and playing a guitar. Eventually, he hoped he might seek solace in his music. Now, he was too raw to want to do so.

Finally, he came full circle, with Lost Creek the next town he would hit. Passing Lost Creek Winery, he turned in, as if he had no willpower, and drove past the tasting room. Since it was almost seven, he knew Ivy would have already closed and headed home. No cars stood in front of the building. He cursed aloud for even allowing himself to be here. Quickly, he left the winery, hoping no one had seen him.

Instead of returning to an empty apartment, Dax drove to Lost Creek Lake. It had been a favorite place of his and Ivy's, and he wanted to be close to her in the only way he knew how. It would give him a place to think about starting a Java Junction in places such as Burnet and Boerne.

When he pulled into an area to park, he slammed his foot on the brake.

Ivy's car sat in the parking lot.

Quickly, he scanned the area, spying her at the water's edge. The noise his truck had made had drawn her attention, though, and she stared at him.

He didn't want any animosity between them. Or any awkwardness. Dax decided to be the man Ivy believed him to be and pulled into a parking spot. He would wish her the best, hoping they could end on a better note this time.

She watched him get out of his truck. As he moved toward her, the ache which had filled him all day now throbbed painfully. Still, Dax pushed forward, meeting Ivy halfway.

"I hoped you would come here," she said softly, her eyes brimming with unshed tears.

"I'm sorry we left things the way did between us," he told her. "I hope that we—"

"Wait," she said, placing her palm flat against his chest.

Her touch almost had him coming undone. A rush of emotions filled him, and he had to take a step back and break the contact between them.

Hurt filled her face, but she pulled herself together and stoically said, "I need to say some things to you."

He started to speak, and she held up her hand to silence him. "No, let me finish. I have to get this out."

Ivy stepped away from him, and Dax blindly followed

her. She climbed upon a picnic table, sitting atop it, resting her feet on its bench. Dax joined her, making sure he didn't sit close enough to touch her. Still, her vanilla scent seemed to swirl about him.

"I was angry when I left you." She smiled ruefully. "If I'm being honest, I still am. Because the one thing I've always appreciated about our relationship is how well we've communicated with one another. We did a lousy job of that last night. I should have been up front and told you what Jameson Polk had suggested to me."

She hesitated. "But you were guilty of being judge and jury regarding the two of us."

Dax kept silent, neither reacting nor responding, giving Ivy the space she needed to say whatever she wished. He owed that much to her.

"You chose to end our relationship without consulting me, Dax. That hurt. A lot. I had always looked at us as equal partners, and suddenly, you took the wheel and drove the car off a cliff. You claimed you were doing it because it would be best for me, but did you ever ask what I might want for myself?"

Guilt flooded him as Ivy studied him with her large, hazel eyes.

"I'm sorry. You're absolutely right. I demanded you paint full-time so you could reach your potential. Because I did think it was best for your career. Ivy, I didn't want to hold you back. Not with the kind of opportunity Polk was presenting to you."

She reached for his hand, threading her fingers through his. Warmth enveloped him.

"I've already lived for several years with a job which consumed my every waking moment. I promised myself that I would never let that happen again."

Ivy's gaze met his. "I like my life exactly how it is, Dax. I need the balance in my life I have now. Yes, I believe I'm a talented artist. That I can sell my paintings. But do I want to paint ninety hours a week, with no life beyond that?"

She shook her head. "I enjoy being a part of my family's business. Sharing my knowledge of wine with people who come in for tastings. It's a great outlet for me. I've always been a bit reserved. Meeting people at the tasting room brings out a side of me I really like. One which makes me happy. I've hit upon the perfect balance of being able to paint mornings and work in the tasting room afternoons."

Squeezing his hand, she said, "But more importantly, I have you in my life. I am the artist I am *because* of you, Dax. And Lost Creek. I need to live in the Hill Country, not a cosmopolitan city such as Dallas. My roots are here. Inspiration surrounds me. If I hit a point where I'm stuck? I can just jump in the car and drive around, soaking up the landscape. The Hill Country is my inspiration. If I left it, my desire to paint would wither. And if I left you? I would be leaving behind my heart and soul."

She touched her fingers to his cheek. "I don't want to leave Lost Creek, Dax. I don't want to leave you. I'm fulfilled living here. Painting here. Being with family and friends. I've discovered that true artistry is rooted in passion. In authenticity. In human connections.

"And my greatest, strongest, most lasting connection is with you."

Tears filled his eyes. "I was becoming a better man because of you, Ivy. Because of my love for you and what we had together. I'm sorry I was such an ass and mansplained that you needed to go to Dallas to succeed."

"You were pretty much like a caveman, weren't you?" The corners of her mouth turned up in a knowing smile.

"I was," he agreed, smiling back at her, his heart soaring. "We're in this together—for better or worse. If you will have me, I promise never to pull a stupid stunt like that again. Anything that comes up, we talk it out. We talk it to death. But we make all decisions together. As equals."

They moved toward one another, lips touching. Dax poured all the love he had for this woman into the kiss, wanting to assure her that he wasn't going anywhere. Ever.

He broke the kiss, grinning at her. "I suppose we hold the record for shortest breakup in Lost Creek Texas."

She laughed, a musical sound which he would never grow tired of hearing.

"Not by a long shot, Dallas. Harper and Danny Tucker hold that record. They broke up between third and fourth period in ninth grade. After fourth period, they got back together at lunch."

"Tell me the story," he encouraged, scooting close to her and wrapping his arm about her waist, savoring that intoxicating smell of vanilla.

"Well, Harper was in Spanish third period when Tandy Johnson told her that Danny had been kissing one of the

JV cheerleaders that morning before homeroom. If anything, Harper values loyalty, and she about blew a gasket. She fired off a note, breaking up with Danny. Gave it to me at our lockers since I had fourth period biology with Danny. She told me to give him the note and tell him they were done.

"I delivered her message and handed him her note. He unfolded it and began writing one of his own after he'd read it." Ivy chuckled. "Of course, being a guy, Danny had no idea how to fold it up intricately and just folded the page, shoving it at me, and telling me to give it to Harper."

"The perfect messenger," he said, giving her waist a squeeze.

"When the bell rang, I went to lunch and found Harper at our usual table. I handed over Danny's note, and she read it, her face going from stone to a smile. Harper stood and looked across the cafeteria, where Danny ate with the other freshman football jocks. He stood and began walking toward her."

"Ah, a reunion in front of the entire school," Dax said. "How romantic."

"Everyone in the cafeteria figured out something was going on. Things got super quiet. Harper deliberately stopped right beside Tandy's table—and dropped Danny's note on top of Tandy's sandwich. By then, Danny had reached Harper, and they locked lips in what became known as The Kiss. Capital T. Capital K. *The Kiss*."

"I like Harper's style," he said.

"The assistant principal and some coach pried Harper and Danny apart as the entire cafeteria cheered and hooted. As they were led out, Harper looked over her shoulder and hollered, telling Tandy that people would forget The Kiss, but they would never forget what a liar Tandy was and how she'd deliberately tried to break Harper and Danny up."

"I'm guessing Tandy wanted Danny for herself," Dax said.

"She did. She had actually told Danny earlier the same morning that Harper had been spotted kissing the JV's quarterback and was going to break up with Danny. Tandy encouraged Danny to be the one who made the first move so he wouldn't be humiliated. She even offered to be the shoulder he cried upon. Danny had been smart enough to see through the ruse and had blown off Tandy. She was so upset, that's why she told Harper Danny was cheating on her. Anyway, The Kiss became legendary at Lost Creek High School."

"Since Harper is with Braden and not Danny Tucker, what happened to their romance?" he asked, loving Ivy's narration of the incident. Loving being with her.

Loving her.

"Danny's parents divorced three months later. He and his mom moved to Oklahoma since she had relatives in Ada. Harper ran into him in Dallas at the Texas-OU game —or the OU-Texas game—as Danny called it. He introduced Harper to the girl he was with, and she knew all about The Kiss. When Danny hugged Harper goodbye, he whispered in her ear that he'd found the girl he was going to marry. A year later, after college graduation, Harper attended their wedding."

"And Tandy?"

Ivy shrugged. "She moved at the end of that freshman year. I don't recall where. But I remember she sent Harper a Facebook friend request and started following her on Insta." Grinning, she added, "Harper blocked her both places."

Dax kissed Ivy. "I like hearing stories about you and your family."

"That was more about Harper than me."

He gave her a look of mock horror. "How could you forget your major role leading to The Kiss? The critical note passer to both parties. You're undervaluing your contribution, Ivy."

She laughed, kissing him again. "I hadn't thought about The Kiss in years. I guess Braden needs to hear that story, too. He'd get a kick out of it. Fortunately, Harper is not a hothead anymore. She was quick to judge Danny, based solely upon what Tandy told her. Harper and I talked about it at length after it happened. Years later, she told me that was the day she felt as if she started to mature."

Taking her hands in his, Dax said, "I know we have a lot to talk about. Including our future. I'm not formally asking you to marry me now, Ivy, but that day will come. For now, I simply need you to know that I plan for us to be together for a very long time. Like cemetery plots next to one another long time. Are you in this for the long haul?"

She sighed dramatically. "You tried to get rid of me once, Dax. I think you're stuck with me. Correction— we're stuck with each other."

"Then let's go back to my place and have mind-blowing make up sex. I think that's a requirement."

A slow smile spread across her beautiful face. "You're on, Dallas. And this time? I'm going to be the one to make you scream."

24

Ivy stood proudly beside Harper. The grand opening of the event center had been more than a party.

It was serving as Harper and Braden's wedding and reception.

Harper had shared with Ivy her and Braden's plans to turn the opening of the center into the first wedding in the space. Practical as ever, Harper said all their family and friends would already be in attendance. She didn't mind her wedding serving as the dry run for an actual paying customer's wedding. Braden had taken it all in stride, saying he would marry Harper on a beach, in a snowstorm, or right here in the heart of Lost Creek.

As her sister and one of her closest friends spoke their vows, she couldn't help but think of doing the same with Dax someday. She knew they had a future together, but she was in no rush to push him to the altar. Right now, she liked how their relationship progressed, learning more about one another and falling more deeply in love every day.

Judge Grady, retired from the bench but on tap to perform ceremonies for couples who used Weddings with Hart, pronounced Braden and Harper man and wife, leading to a round of cheers. Ivy watched them walk up the aisle and then joined her father, who had served as Braden's best man.

As they walked together, Dad said, "You'll be next, Ivy. You know how much we like Dax."

Dax had become a fixture in her life, which meant he was growing close to those she loved. Dax had already been friends with Braden, and Ivy had begun inviting Dax to come to dinner so Harper could also get to know him. The two couples had gone dancing at the roadhouse together, with Ivy being the one to teach Braden how to two-step. Dax also began coming to the weekly dinners with Emerson and Finley, and she knew the two teachers enjoyed his company. Dax had invited her parents to Java Junction to hear him perform. When he had played *Forever's Embrace*, it had brought her mom to tears.

The new tasting room and gift shop had also opened, with Ivy thrilled by the amount of space available. She'd hired workers for the gift shop and ordered the merchandise to fill it. The patio areas were open, and people were starting to come to the winery with friends, sitting indoors, on the patio, or taking advantage of the picnic tables scattered about. Harper still wanted to have musical acts play on the weekends and had asked Dax to evaluate the local talent and pass along his recommendations.

Most likely, they wouldn't start the musical events until spring, but a curated list of musicians was now available, including Dax's band, which had settled on Lone Star Rebels as their name.

Dad led her to Mom, who hugged Ivy. "Oh, you and Harper both look so beautiful up there." She dabbed her eyes with a handkerchief. "I can't believe Harper surprised us and married Braden tonight." Mom paused. "But you knew, didn't you?"

Ivy admitted she had, and her mother laughed. "I think it was a marvelous idea. And just think—now that the event center is open, you and Dax can be married here."

"Don't push, Cecily," her dad warned. "They'll decide when they're ready in their own time."

Harper had the party guests move to the other side of the event center, where Shy and Shelly Blackwood would be in charge of catering the dinner. Harper had thought teaming with Blackwood BBQ would be the perfect choice for most brides to make. After all, the Hill Country oozed barbeque and wine, not to mention craft beers.

She took a seat and watched to make certain Dax, who was DJ-ing tonight, received his own plate. Harper had gotten with Dax about the selections she wanted used at the wedding, along with the soft music playing in the background now while guests dined. She'd also given Dax a list of songs to be played for the dancing once dinner concluded. Ivy only wished she could steal a dance with him, but she knew he was working tonight.

That didn't mean she couldn't talk to him, though. When it came time for the cakes to be cut, Ivy made her way to Dax so they could watch those festivities together. Emerson, who had agreed to be Harper's cake vendor, had made both the wedding and groom's cakes.

"You'll have to go steal a slice of both," Dax said, gazing at her with such love in his eyes, Ivy almost fainted from happiness.

"I'll be right back," she told him, weaving through the crowd and taking a slice of each cake.

She returned to Dax, and they shared, having a hard time deciding which one they liked best.

"Emerson is really talented," he said. "She's made some great desserts for our dinners, but these cakes—well, they take the cake," he quipped.

Harper signaled Dax, and he said, "Time to get back to work." He gave Ivy a quick kiss and then as Harper and Braden took to the dance floor, Dax announced the song they would dance to, their first as husband and wife. As Ivy had expected, it was a golden oldie, *Just the Way You Are*. She remembered their grandparents dancing to that tune and how much her grandfather had admired Billy Joel.

She did dance a few times, once with Braden and again with her dad. She even took a spin with Shy Blackwood, who was thoroughly enjoying himself on the dance floor now that the catering portion of the wedding had been completed.

Ivy slipped away to the restroom and felt her cell buzz in her purse. She had turned off the ringer for tonight's event and wondered who might be calling her on a Saturday night. Unknown Caller lit up the screen, and she almost let it go to voicemail before changing her mind.

"Hello?"

"Ivy Hart, please," said a crisp voice with a British accent, causing her heart to speed up. "This is Clive Crutchfield."

"This is Ivy," she managed to say, immediately recognizing Crutchfield's name.

Crutchfield owned a gallery in New York, one of the most exclusive in the country, as well as others in London, Rome, and Berlin. She had dealt with his assistant once several years ago when Crutchfield had purchased a painting from her Houston gallery for a client.

"Ah, Miss Hart. Thank you for taking my call on a Saturday evening. I'm in San Francisco, about to step on a plane to Hong Kong, but I had to speak to you before I did so. You see, a friend of yours showed me pictures of a few of your paintings. They are simply outstanding. If they look half as good as they photograph, I believe you will have quite the career."

Arlo had texted Ivy and Paloma yesterday, telling them his gallery had a big name in the art world coming in. He had to have been the one who showed Crutchfield her art.

"Thank you, Mr. Crutchfield."

"Clive, please. I'm only thirty-five. Anytime I hear Mr. Crutchfield, I look around, seeing if my father has entered the room."

She laughed. "All right, Clive."

"As I mentioned, I haven't the time now to speak at length, but I would like to meet with you and see your paintings in person. Your friend Arlo tells me that you have captured the essence of the Hill Country of Texas in them. I can see your love for the land. Such variety! It's quite remarkable."

Trembling, Ivy stepped outside, allowing the cool of the mid-October night to calm her. "When would you be able to meet in person, Clive?"

"I'll be in Hong Kong and Tokyo for at least the next week. Arlo suggested I fly into Houston or San Antonio. Then, I would need to rent a car to find you in your quaint little town."

"San Antonio is a much smaller airport than Houston Intercontinental," she shared. "I would say fly to Houston or Dallas, whichever fit more conveniently into your schedule, and then take a short domestic flight to San Antonio. Lost Creek, where I live, is about forty-five minutes from there." Gathering her courage, she added, "I would be happy to pick you up in San Antonio and make arrangements for you to stay in Lost Creek if you provide me the details."

"Ah, the name sounds charming, just as your paintings are. Very well, Ivy Hart. I shall be in touch with you regarding my travel plans. I have a feeling we are going to have a close working relationship. I plan to make certain your name is on the lips of every art dealer in the U.S.— and beyond."

A thrill shot through her. "Thank you, Clive. I took a hiatus from painting, but I currently have eighteen completed canvases and will most likely have finished another by the time we meet."

"I look forward to viewing your art, Ivy. Have a pleasant evening."

Crutchfield ended the connection, and she had to refrain from shouting for joy. Ivy had put off finding representation after her experience with Jameson Polk. Even though Polk had passed along two names of fellow gallery directors, she had not followed up, choosing instead to continue painting and expand her collection before taking the plunge and looking for representation. Now, Clive Crutchfield had come to her, all thanks to Arlo.

She called him now, and he answered on the first ring.

"Did Clive call you? Isn't he amazing?" Arlo said, not bothering to say hello.

"You really went out on a limb for me, Arlo," Ivy told him. "It was a big risk to approach someone of his stature. He's been the boy genius of the art world forever, and he's still only in his mid-thirties."

"I was happy to show him your paintings, *mio caro amico*. I think I took him aback, approaching him so boldly, but I quickly handed him my phone. He was mesmerized by what he saw, Ivy. He said he did not know places like that on earth existed."

"He wants to come here. To Lost Creek, so he can see my work in person," she marveled, the realization of Crutchfield's upcoming visit finally hitting her.

"He will adore you and your art," Arlo assured her. "When is he visiting? I just dropped him at the airport not half an hour ago."

"At least a week," she said. "He's going to Hong Kong

and Tokyo and will let me know when he's coming to Texas. I suggested he fly into Dallas or Houston and then take another flight to San Antonio. I told him I'll pick him up."

They chatted a few more minutes, and then Ivy returned to the reception. Things were beginning to wind down, so she went to make sure guests formed two lines outside as she and Dax passed out the bags of biodegradable confetti, one of several options Harper had for wedding exit ideas. The confetti went to one side of the line. To the other, they handed out bells on a stick, which had ribbons tied to it, telling everyone to shake their sticks the minute they sighted Harper and Braden.

The happy couple appeared, their hands linked, raising them in triumph as they walked down the sidewalk to rousing cheers. As Harper reached Ivy, she stopped and kissed Ivy's cheek.

"I love you, Sis," Harper said, embracing Ivy. "And be sure to supervise the cleanup crew. The first time, they might need bossing around a bit. I promised Braden you'd handle that."

"Will do," she said, laughing. "Go enjoy your wedding night with your husband."

After Harper and Braden passed, Dax slipped an arm about Ivy's waist. "Does she ever stop thinking about work?"

"Only when Braden's kissing her," Ivy said smartly. "All Hart women put work on hold when they're being kissed."

"Then I better get one in before you go manage shutting down the place for the night."

Dax gave her a long, slow kiss, which made Ivy's head spin. Every time this man touched her, it felt like heaven.

An hour later, the celebration had long ended. Guests had departed. Harper's cleanup crew was almost done. The Blackwoods' catering trucks had left hours ago. Dax had placed his DJ equipment in his truck. Ivy watched as the last of the floor was cleaned.

"I think it's a wrap, everybody," she said. "Thank you for making this first event so special."

"Follow me back to my place," Dax whispered in her ear.

Less than half an hour later, Ivy was naked in Dax's bed, enjoying hot sex and dirty talk.

Much later, she lay nestled in his arms, telling him about Clive Crutchfield's call out of the blue, thanks to Arlo putting her work in front of the art expert.

"This is fantastic, Ivy," Dax enthused. "My gut tells me your big break is right around the corner."

"That would be nice, but if it doesn't happen, I'm still happy with what I've been painting. I know Deke can always sell as many paintings as I can give him."

"Wait to hear what this Brit has to say before you do anything."

"I know. I'm still painting away, assembling what I feel is the best of my work to date."

"Speaking of dates," Dax said. He reached for his phone, calling up his calendar. "I think it's about time we picked a date of our own, Ivy Hart." He paused, love shining in those chocolate brown eyes. "I love you. I want to marry you. I want to have a family with you."

He opened the nightstand's drawer, pulling out a black velvet box. The blood rushed to her ears.

"Will you marry me, Ivy?"

"Yes, yes, yes!" she said, taking his face in her hands and kissing him again and again. Then she said, "Let me see my ring."

Dax gave her the box, and she opened it—only to find it empty. Frowning, she looked at him, puzzled.

"I didn't really know what you'd want," he admitted. "Especially with all the painting you do. This box is from a jeweler in San Antonio. He said to bring you in whenever we're ready to pick out rings."

Ivy climbed into Dax's lap, wrapping her arms and legs around him, kissing him with everything she had. She had found her life's purpose, both in her art and working for her family's winery.

And Ivy had found the only man she ever wanted to love.

"Let's go tomorrow, Dax, and pick out a ring for both of us." She paused. "Thanksgiving has always been my favorite holiday. How about the Saturday after Thanksgiving for a wedding?'

His smile melted her heart. "You're on, Professor. We have a lot to be thankful for. Because we'll always have each other."

EPILOGUE

SEPTEMBER—NEW YORK CITY

"This has been a wonderful second honeymoon," Ivy declared as she and Dax strolled through Central Park. "I'm glad we've been able to see New York for the first time together."

They had gone to San Francisco for a week last November after their wedding, taking in the sights and even dining with Arlo one evening. It had been a perfect trip, but this one was proving to be even better.

They had been in the city five days, playing tourist, before her art exhibition opened at Clive Crutchfield's Soho gallery. Going out to Liberty and Ellis Islands. Visiting the 9/11 Museum. Walking the length of both the High Line and the Brooklyn Bridge. Even seeing a Broadway show. Their favorite place, by far, was Central Park. This was the third time they had walked through it. Ivy couldn't wait to paint different aspects of it, from The Mall and Literary Walk to Belvedere Castle.

"We need to come back sometime when the leaves are changing," Dax suggested. "I'll bet it's gorgeous then." He smiled at her. "But not as gorgeous as you, Professor."

Her husband of ten months kissed her, and Ivy felt cherished, basking in the warmth of the September sun and his love.

They continued strolling, heading back to The Plaza, where they were staying, at Clive's expense. Her parents had flown in last night for her art exhibition. Harper, who was seven months pregnant, had decided to sit this one out, and was home in Lost Creek, busy as ever with Weddings with Hart.

The Plaza came into sight, and they entered the Fifth Avenue hotel's lavish lobby, stopping at the desk to see if they had any messages. The clerk indicated a beautiful arrangement of roses sitting on the counter.

"These just arrived for you, Mrs. Tennyson. I was about to have someone bring them up to your suite."

Ivy thanked her and pulled the card from the arrangement. Opening it, she smiled as she read the message from Harper.

Wish I could be there to see you conquer NY. We're so proud of you, Ivy.
Love, Harper & Braden

Tucking the card into her purse, they went to the elevator, Dax bringing the flowers. Once inside their suite, she gazed up at her husband. Dax slipped an arm about her waist. His other hand went to her belly, his palm warm against the small bulge.

"Are you ready to give your parents the good news?" he asked.

She nodded. "I thought we could tell them at tea. Tonight will be too hectic."

They had decided to wait for six months after they married before they began trying for children. Ivy was almost at the twelve-week mark. The only other people at this point who knew about the baby were Harper and Braden. The two sisters were happy they would be first-time moms together, with Harper's little boy due in mid-November and Ivy's baby in mid-March.

Changing out of their casual clothes, they put on something more appropriate for taking tea in The Palm Court and returned downstairs, where her parents had already been seated.

"Isn't this the most marvelous place?" her mom asked.

Soon, they were sipping hot tea. Though Ivy would have preferred sampling the Lavender Oolong or Sencha Superior, she chose the caffeine-free Rooibos du Hamam, easily picking up the notes of berries and green dates.

They spent an enjoyable hour at tea. Ivy couldn't decide what her favorite had been. Musing aloud, she said, "I loved the cranberry orange and truffle scones and the meringue tarts, but that Jivara chocolate cake was also divine."

Dax laughed. "I've already texted Emerson a picture of that and sent her the cake's description. Chocolate sponge. Crunchy hazelnut pralines. Milk chocolate ganache with milk chocolate Chantilly. I told her by the time we get back to Lost Creek, I want her to have created her own version of it for us to taste."

Once tea was almost over, Dax slipped his hand around hers, squeezing it encouragingly. Their gazes met, and then she looked to her parents.

"We've got some news to share with you," she began, immediately seeing tears spring to her mother's eyes.

"Oh, sweetheart," Cecily said. "You're pregnant."

"We are," she confirmed. "The baby is due next spring. We'll have a sonogram to determine the gender next month, but my gut tells me it's going to be a girl."

"Congratulations, you two," her dad said, beaming with pride. "I can't believe we're going to be grandparents twice over."

"It will be wonderful for you and Harper to have your babies so close in age," Mom told her. "A new generation to be raised in Lost Creek."

Her dad generously paid for tea, and they told her parents they would see them at Crutchfield's gallery in a few hours. Dax took her back to their room and made slow, sweet love to her.

As they cuddled together in the afterglow, he kissed her belly, saying, "You are a very lucky baby because you're already so loved." He glanced to her. "You told your parents you think it's a girl."

"It just came to me. This feeling. Something I can't really explain." Ivy paused. "I know we haven't talked about names yet, but if it is a girl? I'd like to call her Kristina. With a K. That was my mom's name."

He kissed her belly again. "I think that's a terrific idea."

They showered, with Ivy changing into a midnight blue sheath cocktail dress. Clive was sending a car for them, and they went downstairs, finding it already waiting for them. The gallery owner had been incredibly supportive of Ivy, not rushing her as she felt Jameson Polk had. She'd continued painting at a steady pace, Face-Timing with Clive, wherever he was in the world, after she completed each painting. He had personally flown to Texas in order to look over the paintings she believed should appear in her show, selecting what he termed the best of the best, personally wrapping and seeing them crated for transport to Manhattan.

She and Dax arrived in Soho, being greeted by Clive's personal assistant. This was the first time Ivy would be seeing how her paintings had been staged. Clive had told her to trust him, and she did completely. Now, she walked the entire gallery, amazed at the placement of each painting and the lighting which showed each one to its full advantage.

Once she had made a complete turn about the gallery, Clive came to her, kissing her on both cheeks.

"What do you think, Ivy? Have I done your art justice?"

"I'm over the moon, Clive. It's as if I just walked through a wonderland of art. I can't believe everything on display is one of my creations."

"Your exhibition runs the gambit of all four seasons, which creates a lovely mood. They show off the Hill Country at its best."

When they had met the first time and Clive had

viewed her work, he had conceived the idea of showing the Hill Country at various times of year. With that theme in mind, Ivy had painted different seasons, along with different times of day. She was thrilled with the outcome and had high hopes for this show.

"You'll meet many important people this evening," Clive continued. "None more important than Winston Bartholomew." Pulling his phone from his pocket, he scrolled a minute and then handed his cell to her. "Read this. It's an article which will appear in the Sunday *New York Times* arts section."

Ivy read Bartholomew's critique of her work, excitement building within her. By the time she finished the article, tears stun her eyes at the renowned critic's review.

Whipping out a handkerchief, Clive passed it to her. "No crying at your exhibition," he said lightly, looking pleased. "Winston is measured in his praise. He practically gushed over your work, though. You are going to be quite the success, Ivy."

Her fingers found Dax's, threading through them. He squeezed hers in return.

"We should have brunch tomorrow morning to discuss tonight's success and the next steps in your career," Clive proclaimed.

"Why do I feel as if you've already booked reservations?" she asked, laughing.

He reeled off a name she was unfamiliar with but knew it would be world class. "Can you be there at ten-thirty tomorrow morning?"

"We'll be there," Dax assured Crutchfield.

Invited guests began flowing into the gallery, filling it within minutes. She took one of the canapés from a passing waiter and then thought better of it, handing it to Dax to eat.

"Getting queasy again?" he asked.

"I'll be back in a moment," she promised.

Where most women suffered from morning sickness, Ivy's came on about eight o'clock each evening. The only thing which settled her stomach was peanut butter. Usually, Dax went into the kitchen to make her half a sandwich. Tonight, she adjourned to the ladies' room and opened a pair of peanut butter crackers, something she carried in her purse these days in case of emergencies. Harper had been sick every morning during her first trimester, but her stomach had calmed, and she had blossomed during the second trimester, finding waves of energy during these months. Ivy hoped she, too, would hit a sweet spot now that her second tri was almost upon her.

She ate two of the peanut butter crackers and sipped a sparkling water she'd snagged from a passing waiter. The combination did the trick, and her nausea passed.

Returning to Dax, she assured him she was fine now and enjoyed the rest of the evening immensely. Clive introduced her to art critics, numerous artists he represented, clients of his, and various movers and shakers in Manhattan.

Finally, she came face-to-face with Winston Bartholomew, saying, "Clive let me read your critique which will appear this weekend."

The art critic thoughtfully stroked his salt-and-pepper

goatee. "I have never been one for heaping praise on regional art. Your work is different, however, Miss Hart. It possesses a beauty in the starkness of some of your landscapes, with an undercurrent of violence as nature molded those cliffs and valleys. Then you bring a calm in your sunrises and sunsets, as well as your views of the water. The mesas rise majestically. The wildflowers call out playfully. A painting should evoke strong emotions. Yours certainly resonant with me. In fact, your work has convinced me that I must come to Texas and see your Hill Country in person. I've visited both Dallas and Houston but never the heart of Texas."

"We would be happy to have you come and stay with us, Mr. Bartholomew," glad she could offer him their hospitality, thanks to the large home they had purchased in the spring. "I can drive you around and show you some of the very spots I've painted."

He smiled broadly. "I may take you up on your offer, Miss Hart."

It seemed a bit odd for Ivy to hear herself addressed that way, but Dax had insisted she keep her maiden name and sign it to her paintings. He told her that she could be Mrs. Tennyson around Lost Creek, but when it came to the art world, Ivy Hart simply had a ring to it like no other.

She found herself growing suddenly weary, having been on her feet the last two hours.

Dax was by her side immediately. "Are you all right?"

"I'm plain tuckered out," she said, her Texan shining through. "Let's slip away."

Catching Clive's eye, Ivy nodded to him. He excused himself and came toward them.

"Leaving?"

"Yes. I'm tired. I think the past several days of non-stop activities has finally caught up to me."

"Growing babies will do that to you."

She blushed furiously. "You knew?"

Clive smiled. "I suspected. You have a glow about you which I've seen my sister wearing three times now."

Patting her belly, Ivy said, "A glow—and a growing bump."

"This is the perfect career for a working mother," he assured her. "I will never rush you. I may nudge a bit, but you will not feel pressured by me to produce, produce, produce."

His words only verified that she had done the right thing in separating from Jameson Polk and signing with Clive.

He added, "By the time we do a London show for you, you'll have to bring the little one along. It's never too soon to introduce a child to proper tea and biscuits."

Dax escorted her to their waiting car. Ivy snuggled against her husband, relishing his warmth and feeling such tremendous love for him as the bright lights of New York surrounded them. The driver told them he would return at a quarter past ten in the morning to take them to brunch, and they told him goodnight.

In their hotel room, she went to stand next to the floor to ceiling window, gazing out at the vibrant city and park below them. Dax came and slipped his arms about her waist, nuzzling her neck.

"You've conquered Texas—and now New York," he said. "What's next?"

"Motherhood," she responded, turning and slipping her arms around his neck. "I can't wait for us to become parents."

Smiling at her, Dax said, "We've got a wonderful life ahead of us, Ivy. But until our little one arrives, let's enjoy these special moments between us."

His kiss let Ivy know that no matter wherever they were in the world, they would always be home.

Because they had one another.

PREVIEW: SCRIPT OF LOVE

Read on for a preview of Script of Love, book 3 in the
Lost Creek, Texas Hill Country series.

PROLOGUE

BROOKLYN—DECEMBER

Holden Scott turned the final corner, walking briskly up his quiet Brooklyn street, headed toward the brownstone he'd rented for the past five years. Usually, he had his cell phone in hand, dictating into it as he walked each morning. He had read a few years ago that movement sparked creativity and had taken to talking into his phone on his walks. Holden dictated story ideas. Character sketches. Even entire scenes. He faithfully transcribed everything once he arrived home, no longer struggling to recall a plot point or witty line of dialogue. The habit had made him a much more efficient, productive writer.

No. Author. Anyone could be a writer, but an author was someone who saw his work published. Thankfully, he'd had success out of the gate, one of the fortunate few who did.

He had come out of the renown Iowa Writers' Workshop with a completed novel, immediately pitching it to several New York agents recommended to him by Dr. Ingram, one of his favorite professors in the program. Evan McGill had quickly signed Holden and gotten him a high, six-figure deal for that novel. *Capitol Crimes* had been an instant bestseller, and Evan had then sold the book's rights to a major Hollywood studio, where up-and-coming director Wolf Ramirez turned it into a block-buster hit.

Holden had wanted to do something completely different his second time. Where his first novel had been a thriller with a ticking time bomb plot, the second was a murder mystery set in a quiet Texas town close to Austin. *Hill Country Homicide* had released to excellent reviews and had sold briskly over the last year. Evan was now fielding offers from studios to also turn it into a movie.

He jogged up the stairs to the brownstone, inserting his key in the lock. "I'm home," he called, secretly hoping no one would answer.

Locking the door behind him, he went to the kitchen, chugging a bottle of water he'd left on the counter so it wouldn't be so cold going down.

Madison wasn't home, for which he was grateful. Things were no longer working between them, at least, romantically. They had met at the Iowa Writers' Work-shop, a two-year residency program, and become fast friends from day one, sharing their writing with one another and offering critiques. When the workshop ended and they'd graduated with their Master of Fine Arts degrees, their relationship was just heating up. Since

Madison was from Scarsdale, she told Holden they should move to New York together. She had been the one to find the brownstone for them to rent, and they had moved in with high hopes for both their careers and their relationship.

Unfortunately, Madison had yet to sell anything. Although he used to read every word she wrote, he'd seen nothing from her in over a year now. On the other hand, she gave him excellent notes, some of which he implemented into his manuscripts. He had told her she would make a fine editor and encouraged her to pursue the editorial end of the literary business. Her temper had flared, and she had told him she was a creative, not a hack who edited others' work.

That had been the moment he sensed the shift between them.

From then on, she'd kept her work to herself, disappearing for hours each day with her laptop. She told him she went to different places to write. Coffeehouses. Benches in Central Park. The public library. Holden had no idea if she really spent her time writing, especially because he'd seen train tickets in the trash to places beyond the city and the clothes on her side of the closet continued to increase.

They had started out splitting everything equally, him drawing from the advance he'd received on his novel, while she had freely accepted money from her wealthy family. Eventually, he had taken over paying the rent and all the bills, not wanting to accept any money from her parents since he disagreed violently with their politics and lifestyle. The three days they'd recently spent with her family in Scarsdale over Christmas had cemented the fact that he never wanted to be a part of the Parmalee family.

He knew Madison wanted to get married from the numerous hints she had been dropping recently, but Holden hadn't been ready to put a ring on it, especially since he felt them drifting apart. At this point, he felt nothing romantic toward her. She had become no more than a roommate that he was subsidizing.

Today needed to be the day to end things with her. It wasn't fair to keep the status quo any longer when he knew they didn't have a future together. They would both get a fresh start. Their breakup might even help spur Madison's writing.

Leaving her the brownstone would be his best move. Their lease ended at the beginning of March. She could either renew the lease on her own or find another place to live. Or a job. She had resisted his encouragement to find at least part-time work.

Holden showered and toweled off, wrapping the towel around his waist as he shaved. He had just finished brushing his teeth when his cell rang. Glancing down, he was pleasantly surprised to see Wolf Ramirez calling to FaceTime. The director was only in his mid-thirties and had a stellar reputation in Hollywood, both as a kind man and a professional who delivered strong films. They'd become friends during the filming of *Capitol Crimes* and spoke occasionally.

Picking up his phone, he tapped it. "Hey, Wolf. What's going on with you?"

"Quite a bit since we last spoke, my friend. I'm striking out on my own. I've formed my own production company, Holden."

He went to the den, taking a seat. "That's fantastic, Wolf. Will Ana be a part of running things?"

His friend smiled. "You know my wife is the real brains in our family. With her accounting background, she'll definitely keep the books—and keep my budget requests in line. Ana is also very organized, so she'll share co-producer credits with me on all productions. She'll handle everything from scouting locations to helping with casting to finding the right food trucks. And my brother Rey is a lawyer. He's already set up the company for us and will serve as its general counsel."

"I couldn't be happier for you, Wolf. You won't have to worry about the big boys coming to you in the future. Instead, you can go after the projects which truly interest you."

"Funny you should mention that," Wolf said, a gleam in his eyes. "I haven't seen in the trades where *Hill Country Homicide* has been optioned yet. I'd like to step in and bid on it and make it the first film from WEBA Productions. I've lived in the Hill Country my entire life. I know these people, Holden. I can make this film sing.

"I know you've been well compensated in the past, but after the success of *Capitol Crimes* and the strong sales with book two, Evan has set the bar pretty high as far as bidding goes.

"That's why I'm calling you first and not your agent. No, I can't afford to buy the rights to your novel at the price a large studio could fork over. What I can guarantee, however, is giving you percentage points from the profits."

Holden whistled. "That's an intriguing offer. Especially because the movie version of *Capitol Crimes* did so well."

"I can't promise my film of *Hill Country Homicide* would generate the kind of profit our first effort together did. It's a completely different story. A totally different audience. But to sweeten the pot? I have an idea that I hope you'll go for." Wolf paused. "I want you to write the script for it, Holden."

The director's words took him aback.

"I've never had any experience with screenplays," he blurted out. "The only thing I know about them is that one page of script equals one minute of film. *Homicide* is about three hundred and fifty pages long. I don't know if I'm up to the challenge of trimming it down to a hundred pages or less."

"One thing you are is a master of description, my friend. You set a scene incredibly well. Your readers can see it crystal-clear in their minds. You also describe your characters at length. Visually, a film allows an audience member to see that scene and character, taking it all in within seconds. That alone would help you cut down on pages. You came on set before. You know how things work."

He shook his head. "Seeing how they work and actually *doing* that work? I'm not sure, Wolf. It's way out of my wheelhouse."

They fell silent, and he knew his friend was giving him

a chance to mull over the offer. Holden made an instant decision, one which he hoped he wouldn't regret.

"I've just finished my third novel. Given the last of it to Madison to read. That means I'm between projects. What if we worked on the screenplay together?" he offered.

The director nodded enthusiastically. "You know the characters and story better than anyone. You could take the first pass at it. I could read over and make my tweaks. Yes, that would work." He hesitated. "I don't want this kind of thing happening long distance, though. Yes, it's easy to email back and forth, but I like what we did with our first project."

Wolf referred to the three days they'd spent together, talking about Holden's story and characters, allowing the director to soak up everything firsthand from the author before shooting anything.

"Would you consider coming to Texas? Your murder mystery happens in a small town here. We could talk things over, and then you could write the first draft. You're welcome to stay at the ranch. Ana and the kids would like that."

"I could come for a few days and talk things to death with you, Wolf, but then I'd need to have my own place. I'm better when I have no one around. No distractions."

"Will you bring Madison with you?" the director asked.

"Ironically, you've called on the day I've decided to end things with her. We've been in a rut for a long time. If I clear out of the brownstone and come to Texas, I think it would help it be a clean break."

"I'm sorry things did not work out." Wolf didn't look

sorry at all. "At least you figured that out before you married her. Divorce can be messy, my friend. Especially if children are involved."

Knowing the chance to leave and stay at Meadow Creek Ranch made Holden say, "I'll call Evan now and tell him that I want to sell the rights to you for the price you name. Make it fair, Wolf. I'll also tell him that I'll be writing the screenplay."

"You'll receive a salary for that, as well as what I can give you, point-wise." Wolf smiled. "I look forward to working with you, my friend. Maybe our partnership will yield several films to come."

"Wait to hear from Evan," Holden said. "But from my end? It's a go. I'll let you know when I'm heading to the ranch."

He went and dressed, hanging his towel neatly, ignoring the one Madison had left on the floor. It was only one of a hundred little things she did which bothered him. He knew a part of their problem had been that she came from money, and he hadn't. The Parmalees had maids to pick up towels off the floor and launder them, while his family had barely scraped by. If he hadn't won a scholarship to college, he would most likely be laying bricks or driving a truck now instead of being an author.

Going to his desk, he sat, calling Evan.

"I was just about to call you, Holden," his agent said when he answered. "It's been a good day to represent you. I have four different offers to bring you regarding *Homicide*. Two are preferable, but I always like to let you hear all the players vying for you work and make an informed decision."

"Save your breath, Evan. I've already promised the book to Wolf Ramirez."

"What studio is Wolf attached to? No one pitched him as the director in our negotiations."

"He's striking out on his own and is starting up his own production company. Wolf wants *Hill Country Homicide* to be the first film he directs for it."

"I like Wolf, Holden. You know that. I know the two of you have become friends, but you've got to think with your head and not your heart. He won't have the kind of financial backing that a major studio does."

"I don't care. He's promised me a healthy percentage of the profits if I'll sell the rights to him at a lower price."

Evan was quiet a moment, and Holden could almost hear the agent run the numbers in his head. He knew this was a big ask. Not only would he take a big cut, but Evan would also lose money if they sold the screen rights to Wolf.

"*Homicide* is selling extremely well. I don't think it'll do the box office numbers of *Capitol Crimes*, though. You have to take that into consideration. Points or no points."

"Wolf has also offered me the opportunity to write the screenplay, Evan. I want to do this. Wolf gets me. I know this cutting a deal with him eats away at your percentage, but it's what I want."

"We've already made good money together. I see that continuing in the future. If you were my only client, I might be pissed, but I have other lines out there. Would I have wished to sell it to a big studio and claim a huge payday? Of course. In the long run, though, I want a happy client so that I have a happy life. If writing this screenplay challenges and inspires you, then I'm all for it. I'm definitely into the idea of sharing points. Because we'll be dealing with a fledgling company, I have way more leverage in the negotiations."

"Wolf's brother Reynaldo Ramirez is his attorney. Rey will be hammering out the contracts with you. I suggest you call Wolf and get the ball rolling."

"I'll do that now. I suppose he'll want you down in Texas since he's based there. After you write the screenplay, he's certain to film in Texas, as well, since the book is set there." Evan paused. "How will that go over with Madison? Have you run this by her yet?"

"Madison doesn't figure into my life anymore. We're done. I'm going to tell her today."

"Good luck with that," Evan said. "That is one woman who doesn't like to hear the word no."

Madison had wanted Evan to also represent her, but he had refused to do so, saying he didn't want any conflict of interest, with Holden being whom he'd originally signed. She had begged, wheedled, cajoled, and finally screamed at the agent, demanding he sign her, which had embarrassed and angered Holden. Evan had remained firm, however. Madison had found representation, but she had since gone through three different agents and had no one repping her interests at the moment.

He spent the rest of the day scouring the Internet, reading everything he could about writing a screenplay.

There was no time to enroll in classes. He'd have to learn on the fly.

Taking out his leather-bound copy of the screenplay for *Capitol Crimes* which Wolf had gifted to him, Holden read the first twenty pages of it and compared it to his novel, seeing how his work had been condensed. He would have to really give things some thought. Perhaps use a few composite characters. Already, though, ideas were swirling in his head, and the thought of authoring the screenplay for his novel excited him.

About four, he heard the front door open and knew Madison was home. He went to greet her, seeing her place her messenger bag on the kitchen counter.

"How was your day?" he asked, his gut churning with the news he was about to give her. "Any good pages written today?"

"I really think I'm on to something, Holden," she said brightly. "I've gone through a long dry spell lately, but I got a really interesting idea today and ran with it. I wrote twenty pages. Twenty!"

A great day for Madison was usually five pages, so he nodded enthusiastically. "That's wonderful."

"Did you start anything new yet?" she asked, opening the fridge and removing a sparkling water. She popped the top and took a big swig before setting the can on the counter.

He swallowed. "I've told Evan to sell the film rights of *Hill Country Homicide* to Wolf Ramirez."

She looked at him quizzically. "To Wolf?" Then a

knowing looking crossed her features. "He's started his own production company, hasn't he?"

"He has. We're eager to work together again."

Frowning, she said, "He won't be able to pay you nearly what you deserve. I've been reading the trades, and I know what Evan can get for the rights. No, Holden. Call both of them back. Cancel the deal."

He couldn't believe what she was saying. Looking steadily at her, he told her, "It's my novel, Madison. My decision. I want to work with Wolf. In fact, I'm going to write the screenplay for the film."

Astonishment filled her face. "Are you serious? You have zero experience with writing a script. If you want to torpedo your own reputation and his, that's the fastest way to do so."

Her words let him know he was doing the right thing by splitting with her. Where once, Madison had been supportive, now she was demanding and spiteful. "You don't believe I can do it?"

She looked at him in exasperation. "What I'm saying is you're a fool if you walk away from the kind of money Evan can get you for this book. Stick with what you do best, Holden. Writing novels is your forte."

Her words assured him that he was making the right decision. "It's my book. My choice. And I'll be going to Texas." Holden paused. "It's not working between us, Madison. It hasn't for a while now. With me being in Texas to write the screenplay and staying there during filming, this is the right time for us to end things."

Red blotches of anger stained her cheeks. "You don't

get to decide that. We're getting married, Holden. You're going to keep writing books. You'll make enough for us to leave this dump and move to a nice high rise in Manhattan. We'll—"

"There's no *we* anymore, Madison. Listen to what I'm saying. We're not happy."

"We are," she insisted.

"*I'm* not happy," he said with brutal honesty, trying to get through to her. "We had some good years, but it's over now."

Out of nowhere, she slapped him, so hard that he saw stars.

"You mean I'm not some bestselling novelist. You're embarrassed by me."

"No," he said firmly. "I think you're talented. I hope you'll get a break. And I wouldn't care if you were a trash collector or a plastic surgeon. I'm not breaking up with you because you aren't published, Madison." He hesitated but knew he had to cut all ties. "I simply don't love you anymore."

Holden wasn't sure if he ever had. They'd had writing in common. She had seemed so sophisticated and exciting when they'd first met, but he'd grown bored with the airs she put on. Actually, he'd grown tired of living in New York. The call of home sounded loudly within him. He'd thought leaving Texas was the best thing he'd ever done. Now, he could see it was the place which would always be home.

She huffed, anger sparking in her eyes. "You are nothing but trailer park trash, Holden Scott. You might have made good money from a couple of books, but you'll never fit in with people who have good breeding."

"I agree," he told her. "Your parents have made it perfectly clear that you could do better than me. Go find your kind of people to be with, Madison."

"Get out!" she screamed at him.

"Gladly. Give me ten minutes."

Holden went to pack, filling two suitcases and his backpack. Madison hovered at the doorway to the bedroom, glaring at him as he did so. The brownstone had come furnished, so all he really needed were his clothes and his laptop, along with a few books.

Facing her, he said, "The rent is paid through the end of February. You can renew the lease or move. It's up to you."

He pushed past her as she shouted profanities at him the entire way. When he reached the door, he removed the key from his pocket and tossed it on the table. Without another word, Holden walked through the door, ready to start a new chapter in his life.

Get your copy of Script of Love!

ALSO BY ALEXA ASTON

Hollywood Flirt

Hollywood Player

Hollywood Double

Hollywood Enigma

LAWMEN OF THE WEST

Runaway Hearts

Blind Faith

Love and the Lawman

Ballad Beauty

SAGEBRUSH BRIDES

A Game of Chance

Written in the Cards

Outlaw Muse

KNIGHTS OF REDEMPTION

A Bit of Heaven on Earth

A Knight for Kallen

SUDDENLY A DUKE

Portrait of the Duke

Music for the Duke

Polishing the Duke

Designs on the Duke

Fashioning the Duke

Love Blooms with the Duke

Training the Duke

Investigating the Duke

SECOND SONS OF LONDON

Educated by the Earl

Debating with the Duke

Empowered by the Earl

Made for the Marquess

Dubious about the Duke

Valued by the Viscount

Meant for the Marquess

DUKES DONE WRONG

Discouraging the Duke

Deflecting the Duke

Disrupting the Duke

Delighting the Duke

Destiny with a Duke

DUKES OF DISTINCTION

Duke of Renown

Duke of Charm

Duke of Disrepute

Duke of Arrogance

Duke of Honor

SOLDIERS AND SOULMATES

To Heal an Earl

To Tame a Rogue

To Trust a Duke

To Save a Love

To Win a Widow

THE ST. CLAIRS

Devoted to the Duke

Midnight with the Marquess

Embracing the Earl

Defending the Duke

Suddenly a St. Clair

STANDALONE ROMANTIC THRILLERS

Leave Yesterday Behind

Illusions of Death

ABOUT THE AUTHOR

USA Today and Amazon Top 100 bestselling author Alexa Aston lives with her husband in a Dallas suburb, where she eats her fair share of dark chocolate and plots out stories while she walks every morning. She enjoys travel, sports, and binge-watching—and never misses an episode of *Survivor*.

Alexa brings her characters to life in steamy historicals, contemporary romances, and romantic suspense novels that resonate with passion, intensity, and heart.

KEEP UP WITH ALEXA
Visit her website
Newsletter Sign-Up

MORE WAYS TO CONNECT WITH ALEXA